I0748494

MAGIC AIN'T A GAME

MAGIC AIN'T A GAME

REG RAWLINS, PSYCHIC INVESTIGATOR #11

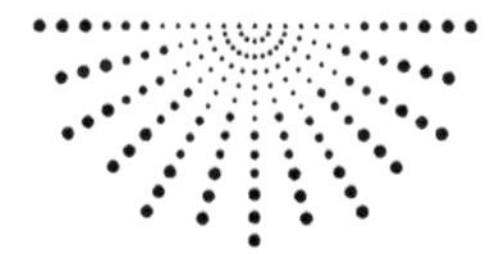

P.D. WORKMAN

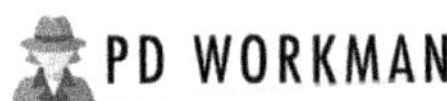

ISBN: 9781774680971 (IS Hardcover)
ISBN: 9781774680964 (IS Paperback)
ISBN: 9781774680988 (IS Large Print)
ISBN: 9781774684979 (KDP Paperback 2 ed)
ISBN: 9781774683163 (Lulu Paperback)
ISBN: 9781774680940 (Kindle)
ISBN: 9781774680957 (ePub)

ALSO BY P.D. WORKMAN

FIND MORE BOOKS AT PDWORKMAN.COM

MYSTERY/SUSPENSE:

Reg Rawlins, Psychic Detective

Paranormal Mystery & Adventure

What the Cat Knew

A Psychic with Catitude

A Catastrophic Theft

Night of Nine Tails

The Immortal's Key

Yule's Sinister Spell

Fairy Blade Unmade

Web of Nightmares

A Whisker's Breadth

Skunk Man Swamp

Magic Ain't A Game

Without Foresight

Careful of Thy Wishes

Time to Your Elf

Undiscovered Tomb

Missing Powers

Thrice Spared

Cloaked Campaign

Sleepwalker's Sanctuary

Cat Tales in the Swamp (Short Story)

Tainted Truffle Treachery

A Fowl Play on Christmas Day (Christmas crossover story)

Lunar Lies

X Marks the Past

Spellbound Statues

Fur and Fury

Enchanted Mirror Maze

The Hidden Hoard of Drakuntsee (Coming Soon)

Breaking Unboundaries (Coming Soon)

Kenzie Kirsch Medical Thrillers

Unlawful Harvest

Doctored Death

Dosed to Death

Gentle Angel

Rushin' Death

Posed for Death

Death of a Corpse

Endowed with Death

Shattered to Death

Captured in Death

Currying Death

Healed to Death

Death's Charm

Discharged to Death (Coming Soon)

Following Death (Coming Soon)

AND MORE AT PDWORKMAN.COM

To good friends and family
who have been there

CHAPTER ONE

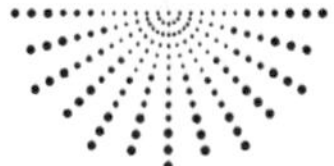

"You should print up some flyers or brochures for the Spring Games," Sarah told Reg, as she bustled around tidying up. The older, gray-haired woman opened the planner on Reg's kitchen island to review her appointments.

"I don't have anything to do with the Spring Games," Reg said, frowning and rubbing her sticky eyes. "Why would I print flyers for it?"

"It's a good time to get those tourist dollars! People come from all over to watch the Games, and they love to get in on the action and get a psychic reading or some other taste of the unseen world."

"Oh." Reg nodded. She tripped over Starlight, her tuxedo cat, on her way to the coffee machine. Even though it wasn't early by Sarah's standards, it was still before noon and Reg wasn't quite ready to take on her day. She had never seen the Spring Games. Damon had described them as a sort of magical Olympics. Witches and warlocks from around the world gathered to participate in friendly competition to pit their magical abilities against each other.

Reg herself was still just learning about the unseen world. She'd had various encounters with abilities and magical beings that she had always assumed were only the stuff of fairy tales. But apparently, the magical races were just as real as Reg's ability to read people. What she had always assumed was a talent for cold reading was, apparently, actual psychic ability. And then there were the ghosts. She had grown up being told that the voices she heard and people she saw were either the results of vivid imagination or mental illness. It had never occurred to them that she simply had sight that others did not. There wasn't anything wrong with her brain—or not that, anyway—it was just a paranormal ability that most of the world did not possess.

But she still had a lot to learn, and she was looking forward to the Spring Games not just for entertainment value, but to educate herself more in what was possible in the magical world.

"You really should take advantage of the opportunity," Sarah pressed. "It will be a good time to pick up some more clients outside of Black Sands as well as locals."

"But if they're not here, I'll only be able to meet with them once," Reg pointed out. The real bread and butter was in repeat clients. Those who came back again and again to learn more about their future or their past, or to communicate with lost loved ones.

"You can do phone contacts. Lots of psychics do phone readings."

"Oh. I guess I never thought about that."

"Sure, it's big business. You even see advertisements for them on late-night TV, running up against all of the dating app commercials."

"I always thought those were just scams. Another way to get money from lonely hearts." Not that Reg was averse to a good con. Scams of one kind or another had kept her off the street in her lean years before moving to Black Sands. "They always seemed sort of sleazy."

"That's why I didn't recommend going that way. But getting face-to-face contacts here during the Spring Games and then converting them to phone clients who you talk to once a month or even once a week, that's good business. And they've seen you face to face, so they are far more likely to keep in contact with you, rather than calling a hotline when they have a problem."

Reg watched the coffee dribble into her mug, eventually pulling the mug out a second or two too soon, impatient to get the mental boost she needed. Coffee dripped onto the counter. Starlight jumped up to the counter to watch the growing puddle.

Reg took a few sips of the hot coffee. "I'll do something up on my computer then," she agreed, "and then get it over to the printer to make some copies. What do I do, just… hand them out to anyone I see at the Spring Games?"

"Pretty much. Anyone you talk to or who is sitting close to you. Don't worry about offending; people are there to see magic. They love to get a little taste of psychic powers for themselves."

Sarah was Reg's landlady. She was the one who rented the cottage in her back yard to Reg at a price that she had been able to afford when she first came to Black Sands, penniless but for her haul at the last town she had stopped in to make some ghostly contacts and maybe to leave with a few pieces of jewelry that people didn't need anymore. Sarah was a witch and lived in the big house at the front of the property, and she had taken it upon herself to help Reg establish her business, keep the cupboards and fridge stocked, and do anything else around the cottage that she thought needed doing.

So far, she had never steered Reg wrong. If she said there was money to be made off of the tourists coming to see the Spring Games, then there was.

Sarah was the only other person who knew about the gems hidden in Reg's cottage. She knew Reg didn't need to grow her psychic services business. But she kept Reg's secret. Reg did not want it to become known that she had valuables secreted away.

"I haven't seen Damon over lately," Sarah commented. "Are the two of you… on the outs?"

Reg considered her response carefully. "We were never actually that close… he helped me in my trip to the dwarf mountain, I helped him in his trip to the Everglades… so we're even now. I don't think we'll be seeing a lot of each other in the near future. Besides, he's busy with security for the Spring Games, and I take it that's a pretty big responsibility."

"He will be busy with that," Sarah agreed, puffing out her cheeks and then blowing out the air in a whistle. "It's really too bad that you couldn't find that wizard for him. That would have been a big deal."

Reg nodded. "After fifty years, though, who could have expected to find him?" she said in a neutral tone.

"Ah, well, I know young folk and their magical quests. It doesn't really matter how impossible they are."

Sarah, though gray-haired, did not look anywhere near her age. She claimed centuries, though Reg wasn't sure if she believed it. Sometimes she wondered how much of the time the supposed witches and warlocks of Black Sands were just putting her on, seeing how much she would believe. She'd seen a lot of weird stuff, so she knew it wasn't all made up. But she couldn't help wondering if she were just as naive a mark as she had ever targeted herself. Regardless, anyone under sixty, or who looked under sixty, was definitely "young folk" to Sarah.

"I don't think you'll see Damon around here any time soon."

Sarah nodded. "Just as well. The two of you always were a little rocky."

Reg wanted to like Damon, she really did. He was handsome and funny and seemed like a nice guy. As Sarah said, they had gotten off to a rocky start, with Damon disregarding Reg's feelings. They had become closer during and after the road trip to the Blue Ridge Mountains. But Reg couldn't let go of how he lied to her, not just with words, but by putting visions into her head that were impossible to differentiate from actual experiences or psychic visions. She couldn't trust him or anything that happened when she was around him.

And there was the fact that as a diviner, he could tell whenever she lied, which, under normal circumstances, was pretty often for Reg.

It was pretty hard to have a successful relationship under those circumstances.

CHAPTER TWO

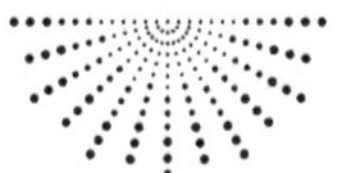

Reg thought that the new flyers for the Spring Games looked pretty good, if she did say so herself. She tapped the edges to the coffee table to square them up and set them down in a pile. She looked at Starlight, who was snoozing in one of the wicker chairs that caught the afternoon sunshine. Starlight opened his blue eye to look back at Reg.

"I think I've done pretty well today," Reg told him. "I got these all put together and printed so I'll be ready to hand them out at the Spring Games. I could have just sat around all day in my pajamas thinking it was too late to get them done, but I didn't."

Starlight closed his eye again and started to purr. His aura was cool colors, relaxed and unbothered by her chatter. He was good at reading her moods and was probably happy that she was calm and relaxed instead of worrying about any of the things that could go wrong.

And there were a lot of things that could go wrong. Reg wasn't in charge of the Spring Games, she didn't have any role to play in it, but it could still affect her. If one of the powerful beings that she had encountered recently decided to show up at the Games and disrupt things, it could have long-reaching effects. That wouldn't be her fault, of course. But she still felt a sense of dread in the pit of her stomach.

Because if one of the powerful beings that she had encountered *did* show up at the games and cause chaos, injuries, or death, she couldn't help feeling like she was a little bit responsible. It wasn't her job to go around banning or binding magical creatures, but if she had the ability and didn't, then that was sort of like a doctor walking away from a traffic accident, wasn't it?

But what if she only thought that she might have the ability to stop them but was afraid to put her powers to the test? Or if she were afraid that doing so might harm her, so she didn't get involved or didn't put all of her power into it? There were a lot of less powerful and more vulnerable victims out there. If she chose not to lay it all on the line, what did that say about her?

That she was wise?

Or that she was a coward?

The phone rang, jolting Reg out of her dark thoughts. She picked up her phone and looked at the screen. It was Officer Marta Jessup, a friend. Or as much of a friend as a police officer could be to a con man. Jessup was too honest to let Reg get away with much of anything, but did try to look the other way when she could. Reg didn't know if she were too naive about Reg's somewhat checkered past to believe that she would do anything really wrong, or if she knew too much about Reg's history and knew that sooner or later, she would. And she just didn't want to have to be the one to report it.

Jessup had already been disciplined for losing evidence in a case that she had involved Reg in. She probably shouldn't have asked for Reg's help in the first place, but she had, and Reg had been able to locate Jessup's missing person, but things had gone much further than that. Reg's involvement always seemed to go a bit beyond what anyone else was willing or able to do.

So their friendship was a fragile one. They tried to spend girl time together and not to get involved in each other's cases. Each looking the other way and pretending that there wasn't a conflict.

Reg swiped her phone. "Hey."

"Are you all set?" Jessup asked.

"Um… all set." Reg really wasn't sure what she was supposed to do to prepare for their night out. She hadn't exactly been given any instructions. "I thought... it was just a celebration. What am I supposed to do to get ready?"

"Oh, it is. Just a... not a party, exactly, but a... celebration or observance. Yes."

"Then what am I supposed to do? I thought we were just going to get together and... get some drinks, watch the floor show, whatever. I'm not exactly prepared for anything else."

"You don't have to prepare anything. Just show up. We'll show you what to do."

"Which will be what?"

"Nothing to worry about. You've gone to Easter parties before, haven't you?"

"Easter parties... no, not really. Maybe when I was a little kid, but I don't remember. Certainly nothing as a teenager or adult. What exactly happens at an Easter party? I don't suppose we'll be bobbing for hard-boiled eggs."

"No, but we might color some eggs. You've done that before, haven't you?"

Reg could remember a couple of disastrous attempts at dyeing eggs using a grocery store kids' kit. It looked perfectly simple but had always ended up in spilled dye, fights with foster siblings, and tears.

"Not... exactly what you would call successfully," she said with reluctance.

"Well, maybe there will be egg dyeing. There will be other stuff too. Maybe planting flower seeds or bulbs, prayers and chants, blessings over the upcoming season. Stuff like that."

"I'm really starting to wonder if this is for me. You know that I'm not into all of the spiritual stuff."

"You don't have to be. There will be food. Sarah is bringing some baking, and so is Letticia. I don't know who else. But that's always good. And there will be some kind of show for the kids to watch. Just come and hang out. You don't have to participate in anything that you're not interested in or comfortable with. Trust me, you know that my powers are pretty... dim, even when compared with the least powerful of witches. I'm not there to do anything, just to participate and have a good time. Celebrate the upcoming spring equinox together."

"I don't know. What about clothes? Should I dress up? I didn't even ask Sarah if there's some kind of dress code."

"It isn't a sky clad ceremony," Jessup said, her voice teasing, "so clothing is not optional."

"I know that!" Reg's face got hot, embarrassed even though there was no one there to see her. "I mean… is it like a ball? Or a garden party? Do I need to wear something pink and frilly? Or is it just casual? Are people going to be wearing blue jeans?"

"I don't suppose anyone will be wearing blue jeans, but there isn't any prescribed dress. People will be wearing things all over the spectrum, from dressy casual to formal garden party. What you wear normally, your gypsy skirts and headdress, is perfectly acceptable."

"Are you sure?"

"Yes, I'm sure."

There were times that Reg wished she had Damon's gift of divining. She would really like to know whether Jessup was being completely honest or was just trying to calm Reg down. She didn't want to be *handled*.

"What are you going to wear?"

"I don't know. Dress slacks. Some kind of blouse. I'm not a frilly person, so it's not going to be some kind of Easter froth. Just something… spring colored with nice lines."

"Okay." Reg felt a little better about that. As long as Jessup was telling the truth about what she was planning to wear and didn't show up for the party with thirteen crinolines layered under a Little Bo-Peep dress.

"And should I bring something? I didn't bake anything. I could boil some eggs for the egg dyeing or pick something up at the bakery."

"No, the food and activities are all handled. Just bring yourself."

"So that's tonight, and the actual equinox thing is during the opening ceremonies of the Games?"

"The opening ceremony of the Games is during the equinox," Jessup corrected.

"Yeah, whatever. That's when the equinox is."

"More or less, yes. Just a couple of days, and we will be experiencing the most *balanced* time of the year. A very important date on our calendar."

"Because day and night are the same length."

"That is one of the measurements we use. But other things come into balance during that time too. Light and dark, good and evil. A sense of peace and security."

"Seems sort of strange to have a competition in the middle of all of that. Doesn't it sort of contradict the whole 'peace and balance' thing?"

"There are those who believe so," Jessup admitted. "One thing that the police force will be doing is trying to keep any protests under control and make sure they don't interfere with the games or people's private ceremonies."

"There are protests?"

"There are protests in connection with any big event."

"They are protesting... what? Spring?"

Jessup laughed. "They're protesting the Spring Games being held over equinox, like you said. That it's supposed to be about balance and cooperation and peace, and the Spring Games are about competition and singling people out for awards. But I don't see why you can't do both. The games are fun. It isn't like they take over our lives. We enjoy watching them, seeing people show off what they can do; no one gets really hard-core competitive about it."

Reg wondered if that were true. She'd seen the real Olympics, and things got pretty competitive there—athlete against athlete and country against country.

"How are they run? The games? Do they split people up by country?"

"Countries are an artificial construct that doesn't follow magical traditions. The teams or competitors tend to be split more by kinship than by geographical location."

"So… fairies against fairies, or fairies against pixies?"

"There aren't a lot of different magical species participating. There will be some fairies, but I don't think I've ever seen the pixies take part. But more along the lines of… covens that follow certain traditions banding together and competing against covens that follow other traditions, or that trace their ancestry or heritage back to a particular witch or warlock or family."

"It's mostly witches and warlocks?"

"Yes."

"But no one we know? Sarah isn't in it?"

"I don't know who is or isn't in it, really. Not Sarah. Not as far as I know. She's not interested in competing, just in enjoying the celebrations."

Sarah was retired. Sort of. She still used magic, but she didn't seem to sell a particular service or kind of magical assistance. She helped Reg set wards that would keep Corvin and other dangerous practitioners away. She gave Reg tea or helped to treat her when she wasn't feeling well. Brought her soup and other food, knowing that Reg tended to just forget about meals and constantly graze on junk food.

"And making cookies."

"She makes good cookies."

"I know Letticia does. I've had hers before."

"Yes, she's a good baker."

"I can't believe she can do that in her little wood-burning oven. It must be really hard to keep it a constant temperature."

"A little bit of magic probably helps."

CHAPTER THREE

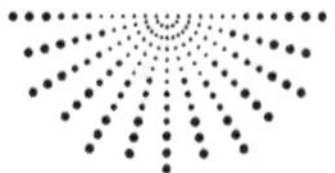

Despite Jessup's reassurances, Reg changed her outfit several times, trying to find something that would be just right. She'd never been at a spring equinox event before and had no idea what everyone else would be wearing. She considered going to the clothing shop by Marian's psychic storefront. She'd only been there once before. They were expensive, but she loved the dress she had gotten there. Maybe that was what she should wear.

She stripped off her latest outfit and tried on the dress with the lace-up bodice.

It looked great, but she didn't know if it were too formal or not formal enough. Reg sighed, looking at herself in the mirror. It wasn't like she had a lot of clothes. She had basically tried on everything in the closet at least once. But many of them could be worn in different combinations. Maybe there were a few more she should try until she was sure she had just the right ensemble.

When the knock sounded at her door, she still had not decided. She pulled the dress back on again and hurried to the door to let Jessup know she would only be a minute or two longer. It was down to the wire now. She needed to lace up and find some shoes or switch to the outfit she was going to go with.

Reg opened the door without checking the peephole first, which she knew better than to do. Luckily, it wasn't Corvin this time, or Wilson, or some dark creature who wanted to harm her. But she didn't recognize the man who stood at her threshold. She frowned, looking at him and trying to remember if she knew him from somewhere. He looked vaguely familiar; she should know him from somewhere, but it was just beyond her reach. Who was he? Someone she had seen at the grocery store? Maybe the bag boy or someone she usually did not look at carefully? She was pretty sure he hadn't been a client at any time. Who, then? Her circle in Black Sands was fairly small.

He was a slim man around her age, late twenties. Taller than Reg. White hair cropped short. His eyes were colorless. His gaze was disconcerting, as if he were looking down into her soul instead of just at her face. He knew her. Even if she didn't know him, he knew her from somewhere. He had to, for him to be able to look into her soul like that.

"Reg Rawlins?" he asked politely.

Reg gave a brief nod, looking him over, still trying to put a name to the face.

"Julian Sabat."

The name was familiar. But Reg hadn't heard it in a long time. She shook her head, trying to remember.

"Julian… Sabat…"

"I am here in an official capacity." He reached a couple of fingers into the pocket of his crisp white shirt and held it up so that she could see it.

Julian Sabat
Magical Investigations
Endangered Species Division

Reg blinked at it. She reread it, making sure that she had it right. Reading wasn't her strong suit and she frequently confused long words. Magical Investigations. Endangered Species.

"Who are you again?" Reg asked, sure she had missed something.

"I'm here as part of an active investigation. Into some recent activities in the Everglades National Park."

"Oh. The Everglades."

What could he be investigating in the Everglades?

Just about everything had gone wrong in the Everglades. There was probably plenty to investigate. Who knew how many lines she had crossed in trying to find Wilson and to stay alive? She hadn't understood before she went just how dangerous it would be. Corvin was right; she had dashed into it headlong without knowing anything about what she was facing. Thinking that she would be able to just walk in and out without coming to any harm. Like going to the zoo or the playground.

What could happen?

Now she knew.

"Well, I don't know what this is about, but I'm getting ready to go out." Reg gestured to her dress. "Now is not a good time."

"We can set up a time to meet tomorrow," Sabat offered, a notebook and pencil appearing in his hand. Reg blinked, unsure whether it was sleight of hand or some kind of telekinesis or reveal spell. Or something else she had never heard of.

"I don't know my schedule tomorrow. Things are… pretty busy right now with it being the Spring Games. We have a lot to do."

"I'm sure we can find an hour somewhere to talk."

Reg hesitated. Her appointment book was on the island in the kitchen, but she didn't want to commit to anything. She wanted to know about who this Sabat was first. Was he legit? And if he were, did she have to answer his questions? If he decided she was guilty of something, could she be charged? Could she be bound or disciplined for something innocent that had happened while she was in the Everglades?

Sabat raised an eyebrow at Reg. "You don't remember me, do you?"

Reg shook her head, baffled. She hadn't met him in the Everglades; she was pretty sure about that. And if she hadn't met him there, then what could he know about what had happened there?

There was a small smile on Sabat's face. A secret, superior expression.

"I always thought you had powers."

CHAPTER FOUR

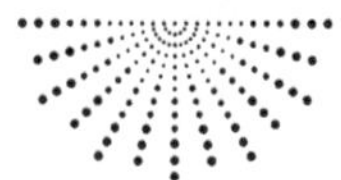

Reg stared at him. "You thought… who are you? You know me? Where do I know you from?"

He chuckled. Reg felt cold. She didn't know who he was, but she knew she didn't like that laugh. It sent waves of goosebumps all over her.

"Who are you?" she demanded again.

"You have to think way back. Way, way back."

Reg thought back to when she had first arrived in Black Sands. Had she seen him the first day there? On the street or in The Crystal Bowl, the restaurant she had ended up in? That was where she had first met Sarah. And several of the other residents of Black Sands. She didn't remember talking to anyone else outside, other than an old homeless man who had called her a witch. Could that have been Julian Sabat? Disguised somehow?

"Back farther than that," Sabat told her, as if he knew what she was thinking.

Back before she had arrived in Black Sands? Had she known him in her old life? Before she even knew that she had any powers? It fit with what he had said, that he had thought that she had powers when apparently Reg or others did not. But that would mean…

Where? Had she scammed him? Or had she done a reading for

him that had been unexpectedly accurate when he had been expecting her to con him? Maybe that was how he had known that she had powers. Somehow, she had inadvertently revealed herself to him at some point.

"Do you remember Mrs. Newburg?" Sabat asked.

Mrs. Newburg.

She had been one of Reg's foster mothers. It had been a long time. She hadn't even been a teenager then. How old? Eleven? Twelve?

And who had he been? He was close to her in age. So a child in the neighborhood or someone she went to school with? Or was he another foster child?

Then she finally placed him. Julian. She had probably not even known his last name. It was hard to keep track of foster children's last names when they were all different from the foster parents' and each other's.

She remembered a tall boy. A year or two older than she was. Blond. Someone who had tormented her.

Reg had often been targeted by the older foster kids, or even those her own age or younger than she was. Reg had never been one to take it, though. She had not been the shy, scared little girl that they expected her to be. She fought back and she gave as good as she got. At least, she did her best to.

"Julian."

He nodded at the tone of recognition in her voice, apparently satisfied that she had placed him. "It's been a long time."

"What are you doing here?"

"I already told you. I'm an investigator. I'm looking into some complaints in the Everglades. It sounds like you stirred things up pretty good on your recent excursion."

"No… we were just looking for a missing wizard. We didn't cause any trouble."

"That's what I will be determining."

Reg didn't like the sound of that. She hadn't liked Julian when she had lived with him back at Mrs. Newburg's house, and she was equally certain that she wasn't going to like him now.

"So you're… you're a practitioner."

He nodded. "Yes. Of course. I always was. You don't remember?"

"No."

He shook his head. "Non-practitioners. Always rewriting memories. Pretending that they didn't see what they cannot explain. I didn't think that you would because you were magical too. But maybe since you didn't know… you learned to deny it."

Reg nodded slowly. She had denied a lot of things about herself. It shouldn't be any surprise that she would suppress information about others' paranormal powers as well. They were taught in foster care to be normal. Not to let on that anything unusual was going on. They had been trained at secret-keeping both at home and in care. Taught not to speak about the things that they saw. To suppress them, pretend that they hadn't even happened. That was life in foster care. Keep your head down—your eyes on your own page. Keep out of everyone else's business.

"And you… you knew that you had powers back then?"

"Sure," Sabat agreed readily. "I came from a family of practitioners, so I knew from the time I was born. It was hard being shoehorned into non-magical homes… I think it might have been a bit traumatic for me. Having to pretend all of a sudden that I wasn't what I knew I was… to have to suppress my powers, not let anyone see them. But you… I always thought that you were like me."

Reg shook her head. "I don't remember you talking to me about it."

He considered her. He motioned into the cottage. "Maybe we could sit down for a few minutes. I can tell you what I remember…"

"No." Reg looked behind her, suddenly aware of the time. Jessup and the others were going to be there any time, and she needed to finish getting ready. "No, this is a bad time. I'm just getting ready to go out."

"I could help you to tie that up," he indicated the lace-up bodice.

"No. I can do it. You need to leave. I don't want you to be here when the others arrive."

"They're going to find out about my investigation anyway. There is no point in trying to hide it. This kind of thing is not kept quiet."

"I don't know what kind of thing you're talking about. But I need to get ready. So, we'll have to meet some other time." Reg bit her lip, realizing that she had just told him that she would meet with him when she had no intention of doing so. She didn't want anything to do with Julian Sabat, investigation or no investigation.

He gave a small, superior smile. He liked the way he could manipulate her. He enjoyed the power he had over her as some kind of magical law enforcement officer. She had seen that trait in ordinary cops in the past. Part of the reason that they gravitated toward law enforcement was that they liked the power and prestige it brought them. They wanted to be in control.

"You need to leave now," Reg told him firmly. She started to close the door.

He pressed his toe against the bottom to keep it from closing. "Take this," he ordered, reaching toward her with the business card in his hand.

Reg shook her head. She wasn't taking anything of his. She wouldn't have anything of his in her house. She had learned enough about magic in the months since she had arrived in Black Sands to know that there were ways to sneak past the magical wards that Sarah had helped her to set against strangers and those who might wish her harm. It was possible that if she had something of his, he would be able to enter her house to retrieve it. Or maybe there was a spell of some kind associated with the card, something that would give him power over her or the ability to transport himself to it.

"You'll need to call me to set up an interview for a more convenient time. And I assume you'll want to know my phone number so that you recognize it if I call you. I'm sure you would rather that I called you first rather than just showed up on your doorstep."

Reg shook her head. "I don't think… I'm not interested in talking to you. Am I being charged with something?"

"Magical investigations are not the same as the ones in the conventional world. You are required to talk to someone. There is no 'right to remain silent.'" He rolled his eyes. "Non-practitioners come up with such ridiculous notions. Why would you build such a thing into your justice system? Someone really goofed up on that one, and then no one has bothered to fix it."

"I don't have to talk to you," Reg asserted.

"Yes, you do." He held her gaze steadily. If he were lying or trying to mislead her, he was very good at what he did.

"I don't even know that you're really who you say you are," Reg asserted. "Any joker off the street could come knocking on my door claiming to be magical law enforcement. Or someone from my past. There's no proof."

He fluttered the card in front of her. "It's right here in black and white."

"Anyone can have business cards printed. Or even print them on their own printer at home. Having a business card that says something like that doesn't mean anything. It's not real identification."

"I'll prove who I am when we meet to discuss the charges."

Reg couldn't suppress the goosebumps and shudder that accompanied his words. She tried to keep her body under control, but wasn't able to shake the feeling of coldness and dread that worked its way into her stomach and into her bones.

She focused instead on getting rid of him. He didn't have any control over her. He couldn't exercise whatever powers he had over her in her own house. She had wards and protections. Just to be sure, she wrapped a protective barrier around herself. She gave the door a shove, dislodging his toe.

"Goodbye." She pushed it shut. Julian didn't try to talk to her through the door. He did stand there for a minute longer, silent, and Reg looked through the peephole, trying to figure out what he was doing and why he was still there. He pressed his hand against the door as if he was dizzy and steadying himself. She wondered if her protection spell had affected him somehow. Then he finally turned and walked away.

CHAPTER FIVE

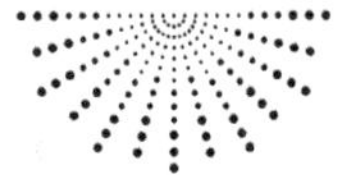

Luckily, Jessup was a little late getting there to pick Reg up. Reg had time to have a steadying drink, lace up her bodice, and add a few accessories to her outfit. Starlight stalked around the cottage, sniffing the windows and doors, turning to glare at Reg every now and then.

Reg shrugged at him. "I didn't ask Julian Sabat to come here," she pointed out. "I got rid of him as soon as I could. Sorry if you don't like him. I don't either."

Starlight gave her another look, but not so accusing this time. He continued his tour of inspection.

There was a knock at Reg's door, and this time she checked through the peephole, even though she was pretty sure that it would be Jessup. She could hear voices and figured that Sarah must have joined Jessup. She hadn't been sure earlier whether she would go out with Reg and Jessup but had apparently made up her mind.

Reg saw Jessup through the peephole, and another shape behind her. She opened the door, hearing Jessup laughing over some joke.

It wasn't Jessup and Sarah, but Jessup and Francesca. Francesca, a white Haitian transplant, had entered Reg's life when Francesca had lost her cat, Nicole. They had ended up fighting an immortal, a powerful being known as the Witch Doctor. It had taken all of them to eventually overcome him in battle, and one of the results was that Francesca became responsible for nine more black cats that she and Reg had needed to find homes for. Reg loved Francesca's lilting Creole accent and was glad that she had decided to join them as well.

"Oh, this is going to be a fun night," Reg said, smiling. She displayed her outfit to them. "What do you think? Will this do?"

"Sure," Jessup agreed, "I told you anything would be fine. All of the stuff you usually wear is dressy enough."

"I just wanted to be sure that—" Reg cut herself off, looking at Francesca.

Francesca was staring at Reg's door, all humor gone from her face.

"What is it?" Jessup asked.

"What is this?" Francesca demanded. It sounded like 'What ees thees?'

Reg looked at Francesca and looked at the door.

"What is what?" Jessup asked, her head tilted to the side. She obviously couldn't see anything out of the ordinary.

"That mark," Francesca said.

Reg turned her head to look more closely at the door. There was an initial carved into it. Not quite. It wasn't an initial, but a rune, like the ones she had seen when she had visited the dwarfs. And it wasn't carved into the door. She wasn't sure what it had been made with, but it glowed around the edges. Somebody must have taken the time to pick up glowing paint from Michael's.

"I don't know where that came from. Some vandal? Is it a gang sign?" Reg looked at Jessup for her analysis. It wasn't like any gang tag that Reg had ever seen, but that didn't mean it wasn't. Gangs adopted all different kinds of symbols.

"What are you talking about?" Jessup moved closer to the door, her face just inches from the mark.

"You can't see that?"

Jessup shook her head and stepped back again. "Can you?"

Reg nodded. "But I don't know how it got there. The only person who has been here…" She trailed off, deciding that she really didn't want to talk about Sabat and the news he had brought.

"This is an official seal," Francesca said, her nose wrinkling as she studied it. "Who left it?"

Reg didn't answer.

"What does it look like?" Jessup asked.

Francesca traced the lines with her fingertip for Jessup. The policewoman thought about it for a minute.

"Hmm. That looks sort of like the seal for Magical Investigations."

Both women looked at Reg, expecting further explanation. Reg shrugged, spreading her arms wide.

"If we stand around here looking at the door all night, we're never going to get to the party. Let's go!"

Francesca and Jessup looked at each other, then agreed. They led the way back to Jessup's car.

"Is Sarah going to come?" Reg asked, looking at the big house as they walked around it. She could sense that Sarah was still at home.

"I think she'll probably show up later," Jessup said. "She didn't want a ride, but I don't see her passing it up. She's wanted to go to all of the celebrations lately."

"Ever since she was revived, she's been… acting like a twenty-year-old," Reg said, shaking her head and rolling her eyes. "I don't know where she gets all of the energy. It's not even just the physical effort I'm talking about. With all of her new friends and dates and every event on the community calendar, I don't even know how she keeps them all straight."

"It is not natural," Francesca agreed.

A fact that they all knew. Her emerald amulet slowed Sarah's aging, and a spell had reversed many of the years she had already put on. Reg knew that Sarah was an old woman, far older than she looked, but it was pretty hard to wrap her mind around the fact when she was gallivanting all over town.

Gallivanting. Reg felt sixty herself.

"What else do you think is going to happen at this equinox celebration?" Reg asked once they were on their way.

"Don't think that I'm going to forget that seal on your door," Jessup said in a flat, even tone.

"I don't want to talk about that. Don't wreck the evening by insisting on discussing problems. I want to enjoy myself."

Francesca nodded. "There will be plenty of time to worry later," she agreed. "Ostara is a time for peace and balance, not a time to worry about life's troubles. Everybody has troubles. But not for Ostara."

"Ostara," Reg repeated. "That's like Easter? Is that where the word Easter comes from? I know it's like Christmas; the Christians adopted a bunch of pagan traditions…"

"Actually, many of the Easter traditions come from Jewish Pesach, not paganism," Francesca advised. "Hard-boiled eggs, for instance, are traditional for Pesach."

"Oh." Reg nodded and looked out her window. She didn't want to delve deeply into the traditions and where they had all originated. If she wanted a lecture, she could call Corvin and ask him about it. She was sure that he could put her to sleep if she were having insomnia when he got into professorial mode.

Over the phone, anyway. If he were there in person, there were too many other distractions.

CHAPTER SIX

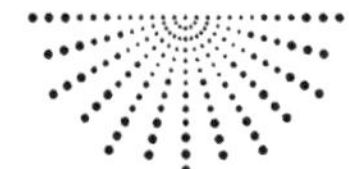

Reg looked around at the hundreds of people crowding the community center hall and yard. It was a good thing that Florida had such pleasant weather. If they'd had such a celebration outdoors in the north, where she had grown up, nobody would have been able to stay outside without freezing their fingers and toes. But the nice weather in Black Sands allowed them to spread out and to accommodate far more people.

She recognized many of the faces, people she knew from around the neighborhood, even if she didn't know them all by name. And there were people she didn't recognize as well. Mothers with young children, out-of-town guests who were identifiable by their clothing, a number of warlocks in robes that she didn't think she had met before. She wondered if they were from Corvin's coven or another. Maybe local, maybe from halfway around the world, there to enjoy the Spring Games.

Reg saw Letticia putting out cookies in the kitchen service window and headed toward her. She remembered the last time she'd had one of Letticia's chocolate chip cookies. They were worth going out of her way for. And she was starting to get used to Letticia. She wasn't just an old crone, the witch who led Sarah's coven. She looked severe and definitely didn't mind sharing her opinions with anyone who asked, but Reg had learned that she had a softer, more human side too. She had helped Reg and had shown compassion and sympathy for Reg and for Sarah when she had been dying. It had been a challenging time, and Letticia had tried to make it easier for her, not harder, and had been an unexpected ally during Corvin's tribunal hearing.

Letticia saw Reg coming and nodded at her. "Miss Rawlins."

"You don't need to call me that. Call me Reg," Reg insisted, her face burning. Letticia was much older and more senior than Reg was; it was embarrassing to be treated like an equal or superior. Reg was barely an initiate in the magical world.

"Have a blessed Ostara," Letticia invoked, reaching out with her tray of cookies so that Reg could reach past the others in the throng to grab one.

"Are these ones your cookies?" Reg asked, grabbing one.

"Some of them." Letticia nodded. "That one is."

Reg bit into it. It tasted like it had just come out of the oven. It was the perfect taste and texture. Reg looked past Letticia to the oven in the kitchen, trying to see whether she was cooking them right there.

"This is fabulous. Thank you."

Letticia nodded. "How are you doing?" she inquired, as Reg made her way over to the wall, where she was closer to Letticia, in order to talk to her and away from the pressing, noisy crowds.

"I'm good."

"You've been through quite a bit during the last few months. You're well? And your cat?"

"Yes, we're both fine. Fully recovered, I think. There don't seem to be any long-lasting effects."

"Excellent. And how did things go in the Everglades?"

"Oh." Reg looked around. It wasn't really the kind of thing she was prepared to discuss in public. "Well… we all survived. So that's a plus. Things didn't go quite the way we had hoped."

"The Everglades is a very ancient place. It is a long time since I have been deep into the park." Letticia's home was on the fringes of the Everglades. Reg didn't know if it were actually within park boundaries or not. "There are things… best left undisturbed."

Reg nodded slowly. "Yeah. I guess so."

"But, young people have to try everything once," Letticia said dryly. "That's what you young folks say, isn't it? 'I'll try anything once.' Not really the best motto to live by."

"Yeah. I don't… I don't say that."

Reg looked around, needing a distraction from the topic of conversation. As Francesca had said, it was a time to celebrate and enjoy themselves, not a time to worry about all of the rules and consequences.

Or something like that.

"Will you be going to the Spring Games?" she asked Letticia.

"Yes, of course. I think you will find that most of the practitioners around here will go. It's only natural to want to see what other people are doing. Figure out they can tweak their own practices, improve their powers. Everyone always wants to stretch and to reach new heights."

"Sarah said there are protesters."

Letticia looked more sour than usual at this. "There are protesters for everything. It doesn't *mean* anything. There will always be detractors. To everything."

Reg nodded. "I guess so. I'm glad you're going to be there."

Letticia smiled thinly. "Why is that?"

"Uh…" Reg cast around for an answer, trying to put it into words. "Just that… I want there to be people I know there. I want to know that it's okay to go watch them; I'm not breaking any rules by attending. It's just new… I guess I want some reassurance."

"And I'm sure your girlfriends have already told you everything you need to know," Letticia dismissed. She looked across the room and Reg saw she was focusing on Jessup and Francesca.

"Yes, they're always very helpful," Reg acknowledged. "But Officer Jessup is… she doesn't have much in the way of powers and Francesca isn't from around here, so her traditions might be different."

"Good points." Letticia nodded. "But Marta was raised in a practicing home. She knows her way around the magical laws and traditions surrounding Black Sands."

Reg reached across a platter of cookies to get herself a drink of punch. The chocolate chip cookies were so sweet, she needed something to cut all of the sugar.

"How does that happen? Someone like Marta," Reg substituted in Jessup's first name. They were friends, but Reg had a hard time calling her by her first name. "Where her family were practitioners but she ends up without any powers? Or with only very weak powers. Is it just… genetics? Like some kids end up with brown hair and some of them with blond hair? Or is it choice? Or because she didn't practice every day like learning an instrument?"

"You only need to look at your own life to answer most of those questions," Letticia pointed out. "Did you practice your spells regularly?"

Reg laughed.

"No. I didn't even know that I had any… special abilities. I tried to not do things that would attract people's attention. When kids spend more time talking to the air than to the people in their family or at school… they think there's something wrong with you. You get visits with a therapist or get smacked around until you start behaving. I didn't even know what was the matter with me. Why I was so different."

"So, no one needed to teach you how to do what you do."

"No. But I keep finding out other things that I can do, other abilities I have or things I need to be careful of. If I had grown up with others who were… like me… then I would know more about that kind of stuff, right?"

Although, from what Reg had learned about her possible parentage, either one of them might have chosen to kill her instead of nurturing her as was expected in most human homes. It was to Reg's advantage that she had grown up in foster care, even if she hadn't known anything about her abilities because of it. She wouldn't have survived if she hadn't been removed from her mother's care.

"Even those raised in practicing homes still find that there are things they don't know about themselves. That is why we have a lifetime to keep learning and events like the Games to expand our horizons."

Reg nodded and sipped some more of the punch. It was too sweet to completely cut the sugar of the cookie. Milk would have been better. And she suspected that the punch—at least the cup she had taken—was not child safe. But it was giving Reg a pleasant buzz. Making her more relaxed. She could forget about what's-his-name and just have a nice equinox celebration like Jessup had promised.

"Davyn is helping me with my firecasting," she told Letticia. "I have to do practice exercises for that."

Letticia nodded. "Because you are not strong enough?" she asked with a dry smile. She knew that was not the case. Reg had been lighting fires without even knowing she was the one responsible for it. And when she had used her fire in the Dwarf kingdom to help to unmake Calliopia's blade, she had been so strong she had been worried about blowing up the entire mountain.

"No…" Reg laughed and looked down at her punch. "Because… I don't know how to control it really well."

"And that is another thing that we learn from our families. Not everyone has the same strengths and talents, and sometimes innate talent can be more dangerous than not having any magical power at all. It needs to be refined and controlled. You can definitely practice your talents and build up levels of spell craft. But sometimes what is important is to be able to tamp those powers down when they are not appropriate."

"Well… growing up in non-practicing families definitely helped me with that. I suppressed a lot of things."

Her mind turned back to Julian. He had guessed she had powers. With everything that her foster parents and social workers and therapists had done to try to make Reg act more normal, he had still seen something in her. She was curious about what it was and whether other people had known it at the time.

CHAPTER SEVEN

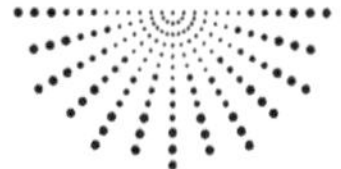

"Time to stop being a wallflower," Jessup told Reg, drawing her out of her corner. Reg had eaten several cookies and she wasn't sure how many cups of punch she had drunk. She'd smiled and talked to some of the community members that she knew, but she knew that Jessup was right, and she was just wasting her time standing by the wall eating cookies. It was a celebration. She was supposed to be joyous. She was supposed to be doing things.

"Okay," she agreed. "Just as long as you don't expect me to do the thing where they stand an egg on its end."

"That's just a myth," Jessup scoffed. "You can do that any time of year as long as you are patient enough. How about some egg decorating?"

"I can do that," Reg agreed. "I'm really good with the stickers. Not so good at the dye."

"We'll show you some tricks. You'll be decorating like a pro in no time."

Reg allowed Jessup to lead her to a room that was a little quieter. There were several different stations around the room with different kinds of dyes or decorations. Reg picked up an egg at the nearest one. But it was much lighter than she expected and flew out of her hand. She tried to grab it out of the air and ended up crushing it in her hand. She looked down at the bits of eggshell in dismay and looked at Jessup.

"I thought… this one was empty!"

Jessup started to laugh. Not polite little giggles, but a loud, hearty laugh that went on and on. Reg held her hands up to her face as if she could hide the fire she felt there.

"Hey…" she protested.

"It's blown," Jessup told her, between chuckles.

"Blown?" Reg dropped the eggshells of the exploded egg into a nearby garbage can and brushed off her palms.

"For kids, we usually do hard-boiled eggs, and that's probably what you were expecting, right?"

Reg nodded. "Yeah. Right."

"But when you're more experienced or want to try some of these other techniques, then a lot of times we use blown eggs. Hollow shells."

"But how do you get chickens to lay hollow eggs? And how do you know which ones are hollow and which ones are… eggy?"

Jessup wiped at her eyes, still giggling a little in between answering Reg.

"The chickens don't lay hollow eggs. They wouldn't be able to. They'd get crushed in the… egg canal." She picked up one of the eggs from the basket Reg had taken one from. She held it out for Reg to see. "You see the hole?"

"Yes."

"They drain or blow the egg out of the hole."

"But wouldn't that be really hard? How do you do that?" Reg had a hard enough time peeling eggs for an egg salad sandwich. She couldn't imagine trying to blow one out.

"Raw eggs," Jessup said. "It's not hard. I mean, you can still mess it up and end up breaking it, but once you've had a little practice, it isn't that bad. Why don't you grab one? Carefully this time. We'll take a look around and see how you would like to make yours."

Reg picked up a hollow egg from the basket. The witch behind the table smiled at her, hundreds of wrinkles and lines shifting and getting deeper, yet making her look lighter and younger. The egg had practically no weight at all. Reg followed Jessup gingerly, feeling like she was going to bump into someone and crush the second egg before she got a chance to do anything with it.

Jessup showed her several methods of decorating her egg, and Reg felt like a little kid again. She hadn't celebrated Easter or done any handicrafts for years. She watched some of the other ladies around her as they worked on their eggs, taking great care and attention. They didn't seem embarrassed to be doing it. There were even a couple of warlocks who tried their hands at some of the different dyeing methods. Reg tried not to stare at them, but couldn't help herself.

"Regina!"

Reg turned to see Francesca approaching her, slipping gracefully between the crowds to reach her. "How are you enjoying our Ostara so far?"

Reg smiled and shrugged. "It's kind of fun," she admitted. She had expected something more mystical and less third-grade, but she was having a good time dyeing eggs, so she couldn't complain. She was still feeling pretty good from the effects of the punch.

"This is for you," Francesca offered, reaching out to place a circlet of small white flowers on Reg's head. "There. You are beautiful!"

Reg reached up to touch it and wondered how it went with her red hair and headscarf. She didn't exactly have flowing locks of ebony that would show off the pretty flowers.

"Uh, thank you."

Francesca cocked her head this way and that, admiring them. "They are perfect."

"Okay." Reg tried not to fiddle with them. If she just left them alone, they would stay in place and not look like they'd been pecked by birds all day. But she had a hard time not feeling them and trying to pat them back into place. They would be ragged by the end of the night. If she didn't throw them out.

Francesca bent over to talk to Jessup, who was painstakingly painting a flower on an egg. "You must come over to the terrariums next. You must plant some seeds. It can't be spring without new seeds!"

"Okay, we will," Jessup agreed.

"Will you decorate an altar?" Francesca questioned, looking from Jessup to Reg.

Reg slid her gaze over to Jessup. She didn't want to offend, but Jessup had told her that she didn't have to participate in any rites that she wasn't comfortable with.

"Reg isn't really into the spiritual practices," Jessup said. "Keep it to earthborn stuff."

Francesca shrugged and wandered away. Reg nodded to Jessup. "Thanks."

"No problem. You don't need to do anything just because someone suggests it. We're all about people celebrating in their own way. As long as it doesn't hurt anyone else, go ahead and do what's right for you."

"I don't want to offend anyone."

"You won't. It isn't like going to church, where everyone is expected to do the same things. Everyone finds their own way to mark the occasion. And if you don't like something, you adapt. Try something different. Next year, you can try something else again. Just find out what resonates with you."

Reg had lived with several foster families who had tried to force their versions of religion on her, even when it was against child services' strict regulations. Her view of religious and spiritual practices was therefore somewhat disenchanted.

"I don't know. It's all pretty new to me."

"No one is pushing. We are only offering."

"Okay."

"You don't even have to wear the crown if you don't want to."

Reg patted at it again. "I'll wear it for a while. Until it starts to drive me crazy."

"Fair enough."

When Reg grew bored of the egg decorating and Jessup was happy with her creations, they went on to find the terrariums that Francesca had suggested. Reg studied the shy-looking woman at the table who was clearly in charge and showing others how to put together their terrariums. She had a red, pointed hat and her wrinkled cheeks were rosy. Reg took a swift glance under the table and saw that the woman was sitting on a high stool, her short legs not even close to reaching the ground.

She directed her thoughts at the woman. *Are you… gnomen?*

The woman's eyes widened in surprise. She gave Reg a toothy smile, nodding.

Yes, gnomen, she agreed, her voice in Reg's head rather than audible. Reg had discovered from Forst, Sarah's gardener, that gnomes generally spoke to each other telepathically in what they called their "inside words" and found it very difficult to speak aloud to humans.

The gnome woman motioned for Reg to take the chair closest to her and started assembling the materials she needed for her terrarium. Jessup followed suit, sitting the next chair over and mirroring what the woman collected.

The gnome looked shyly at Reg's flowered circlet. *Beautiful fleabane.*

Fleabane? That's not a very pleasant name!

Fleabane can be powerful. Good physic. And very pretty.

Reg patted at it, hoping she wasn't smushing it down too badly. *Thank you. My name is Reg.*

Zinnia.

That's a beautiful name.

Jessup looked over at Reg. "Are you talking? Am I interrupting?"

"Interrupt away," Reg said. "This is Zinnia. Zinnia, this is Marta Jessup."

Zinnia bowed her head in acknowledgment. She handed Reg and Jessup each a plastic cup and indicated the small pebbles.

Put pebbles in? Reg asked.

Just over the bottom. For draining.

Reg followed Zinnia's instructions and Jessup copied her. Zinnia let them pick out the seed or bulb they wanted to plant and then helped them mix the right soil for that particular plant, plant it at the correct depth, and give it the amount of water it "wanted."

Reg and Jessup then enclosed the miniature garden with a plastic dome over the top, and Zinnia gave them instruction sheets on when to transfer the seedling from the terrarium to their gardens.

Reg sat with her eyes just a couple of inches from the terrarium, imagining the seed awakening and growing up into a tiny, perfect plant. And then she could give it to Forst and he would plant it in Sarah's garden.

Forst is mine cousin, Zinnia said shyly, looking up through her lowered lashes at Reg.

Is he? He is a wonderful gardener. And I met his brother, Fir, too.

Zinnia blinked rapidly. *Fir has no woman.*

Oh. I… didn't know that. What about you, do you have a man?

Many years ago. He died very young for gnomen.

I'm sorry. Do gnomes… remarry?

She shook her head slightly. *Rarely.* Another look at Reg through her lashes. *But sometimes.*

Reg smiled, thinking of Fir and Zinnia holding hands sitting under a tree. Zinnia's cheeks grew a duskier red, but she gave Reg a small smile.

CHAPTER EIGHT

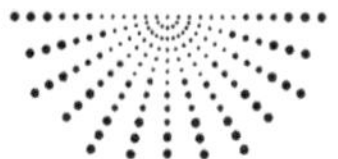

Music started blasting in the main hall as Jessup and Reg labeled their creations and set them aside for later.

"Time to dance," Jessup announced.

Reg wasn't sure whether there would be some kind of ceremonial or ritual dancing, or whether it was just going to be a ball. She followed Jessup reluctantly. She was curious, but she wasn't going to be doing any dancing herself if she were just going to end up looking like a fool. Or if it were some complicated traditional dance or spiritual ritual.

Others who had been working on crafts were also headed to the hall to watch or participate in the dancing. Reg at least didn't stand out too much. There were plenty of colorful costumes, many more formal than Reg's, and many more casual. She seemed to fall right in the middle of the pack, which drew little attention. Sometimes it was good to stand out, but Reg didn't want to be anyone's focus when it was something she was so new to.

The warlock who was emceeing the dance cut the music and called for everyone's attention. It was a few seconds before everyone quieted enough for him to continue. Reg looked around as he chattered, announcing the dance and that it was celebrating the vernal equinox, which everyone already knew, and on and on. There had not been many warlocks working on the crafts, so Reg was glad to see more of them in the hall. If they were having a dance, it would be best if the men were not in short supply. Although Reg supposed she could dance with other witches too. But that always felt just a little bit awkward. Like everyone was watching and making judgments.

The dance was to kick off with a traditional piece, and the emcee called on several couples by name to begin. The music began, a slow instrumental piece, and the couples that swept out onto the floor began a graceful dance with carefully choreographed steps.

"After this, they'll do regular stuff," Jessup whispered.

"Just one special dance?"

"There are more outside," Jessup made a small gesture toward the doors. "Like he said, some smaller group dances, performed outside under the moon."

"Oh. Right." Apparently, if Reg had been listening, she would have known that. "Sorry, there's just so much to take in."

Jessup nodded.

After five minutes, Reg was more than ready for the traditional dance to end. The sounds of the instruments were getting on her nerves. The repetitive patterns of the steps, with the dancers drawing in towards each other and then out again in geometric exactitude were too much for her. She made her way around the hall to the refreshments table to snag another cookie and a couple more glasses of punch. After ten minutes, the dance sounded like it was wrapping up. Eventually, they stopped, bowed to each other, paused for the audience's applause, and left the dance floor. Reg's applause was more for the fact that it was finally over than the dancers' skill and patience in executing the dance. It felt more like they were executing the audience.

The band started playing something more bouncy and popular. Reg looked around. She wanted to move her feet and work off some restless energy, but while she recognized a few of the men who were watching, she didn't know them well enough to approach them.

She felt a sudden rush of heat and pressed her fingertips to her cheek. What was that? A hot flash? The beginning of a fever? Or just too many people crammed into the small hall? Maybe she'd had too much to drink.

"Regina," a pleasant voice murmured behind her, and Reg immediately knew what it was. Not a hot flash. Corvin.

She turned to look at him. She knew him well enough now to recognize that his robe was not his everyday wear, but something special, made of a different material. It had a high collar rather than a hood, and underneath he was wearing formal wear. Not tails, but something fine with a red sash.

"You look nice," Reg blurted, then pretended to herself that her cheeks were not getting hotter still.

He looked down at her, his eyes drinking in her laced bodice and circlet of white flowers. "And you are looking very festive yourself." He extended a hand to her. "Shall we dance?"

Reg remembered the last time they had danced. It had been an amazing experience, the two of them anticipating each other's moves and perfectly in sync. But it had led to Corvin being able to overpower her with his charms. He had nearly succeeded in stealing her powers, and would have been able to if it hadn't been for the intervention of the fairies.

She didn't take his hand.

"I don't think so." She resisted the warmth and the smell of roses that he exuded, starting to build up invisible protections around her.

"I promise I wouldn't do anything," he told her huskily.

"You already are. And I know what your promises are worth." He'd promised the last time, too. And he was still being shunned by his coven for what he had done.

"You are strong enough to resist," he pointed out, switching to flattery. "We can enjoy ourselves without fear of… something untoward happening."

"Something untoward. Like you deciding to drain all of my powers." He had spoken as if it were something beyond his control. Something that might just *happen* all by itself.

"You know how difficult it is trying to resist instinctual behavior. Can you blame me for what comes naturally to me? Without an external source of power, I would…"

Reg frowned, waiting for him to finish. But it didn't appear he was going to. "You would what? I don't think you've ever said what would happen if you weren't able to find a source of powers to consume. Would you stop being able to charm anyone? Stop being able to perform any magic? Would you die? Exactly what would happen?"

He looked offended, as if she had said something rude. And maybe that wasn't something that you were supposed to ask a warlock with Corvin's "affliction." But she thought that as his favored target, she deserved to know the answer.

"Warlocks such as I will eventually die if they are not able to consume the powers they require," he said slowly. He was so careful with his words that Reg knew he was lying or misleading her somehow. Maybe what he said was technically true, but he was trying to cover something up. The fact that he only needed an external source of power once a year? That he would die within the normal lifespan of a human being? She had never seen him so desperate that she had feared for his survival.

He had forced her to feel his hunger, which was also against the rules, as it turned out. So she knew how desperately hungry he could get if he could not feed on someone else's powers. Or from some power-imbued object. But she didn't know how often he was really that hungry or if it were something he could distract himself from.

"I'm not dancing with you," she reaffirmed.

He scowled. "One dance, Regina. I'm not asking for the whole night."

Reg shook her head again.

Another warlock came over. Reg recognized him as one of the bartenders at the Crystal Bowl. Not someone she knew well, but they knew each other to say hello to.

"Reg. How about a dance?"

Reg obligingly reached out her hand to him, and he led her onto the dance floor. Even looking away from Corvin, she could feel his rage at being snubbed so obviously. Other people may have seen. It was humiliating. Reg focused on Bill. She kept her eyes on his face and tried to anticipate his movements and to enjoy the dance. It was hard not to be distracted by Corvin when she could feel his feelings so clearly. They had shared each other's thoughts too many times for her to just shut him out. She had to listen to his angry growlings about how she had embarrassed him in front of everyone. And how she was being a hussy throwing herself at another man on the dance floor.

Bill raised his brows at her. Reg tried again to focus on him and on dancing naturally to the song. But her movements felt awkward and she knew she wasn't moving in sync with him.

"Sorry," she apologized. "I'm just not in the groove yet."

"No worries. Relax and enjoy yourself."

Reg nodded her agreement.

She was relieved when the song ended, and she moved toward the side of the hall again. But another warlock stepped in front of her. Davyn. Her mentor and the leader of Corvin's coven.

"Could I tempt you into another dance?" he offered.

Reg looked around for Corvin. She could still feel him close by. It was probably a good thing if she stayed with Davyn for a bit. Part of his job was to keep Corvin in line and make sure that he followed the coven's rules.

"Yes, sure," she agreed, and they found a space on the dance floor. Reg knew she was dancing even worse with him. His eyes flicked around the room and back to her.

"I'm not going to let anything happen to you. What's going on?"

"Oh, just Corvin being Corvin. He wanted to dance, I said no, so he's going to have his little temper tantrum over it."

"He's a powerful warlock. His little temper tantrum could be a pretty big thing."

"Yeah, except that would embarrass him in front of everyone, and he's already embarrassed by being turned down. If he explodes and has a big meltdown in front of the whole equinox celebration, it isn't exactly going to look good."

Davyn nodded. "I'm glad he cares about what other people think. The way he acts sometimes… I do wonder."

"Well, I can tell you he does. Even if he pretends that it doesn't make any difference to him."

"Then you should be safe tonight. Try to just enjoy yourself. Have you had a good time here so far?"

Reg nodded. "It feels sort of like a kids' party. You know, crafts and cookies and punch, and a dance… but it's been fun. And I know it's all symbolic. It just seems… a little juvenile."

"You can perceive and enjoy it on whatever level you are at. It can be childish and simplistic, or it can be complex and laden with meaning. It all depends on you."

"Jessup says I'm… earthbound. I guess that means I'm not into the religious stuff."

He nodded. "That's fine. That's where you are. That's where many of us are most comfortable. No one expects you to suddenly start chanting or participating in rituals you haven't been properly introduced to."

Reg glanced around once more for Corvin but couldn't see him. His anger level seemed to be subsiding. She didn't know whether he were still watching her and just knew that she wouldn't get romantically involved with her mentor, or whether he had gone off to participate in some other activity that took his attention away from the anger and humiliation. She tried to relax her shoulders and to move more smoothly in time with the music.

"How about you? Have you been enjoying the celebration?"

Davyn smiled. "Equinox is one of my favorite times of the year, one of my favorite celebrations. The renewal, increasing energy levels and growth around us, all of the focus on balance and new beginnings…"

Reg smiled. That sounded good to her too. She was glad that she had agreed to attend with Jessup, despite the scene with Corvin.

The dance ended, and Reg smiled her thanks. "I think I'll just go get another glass of punch—"

She was cut off when yet another warlock stepped in, reaching out to take her hand and pull her into the next dance. By the time she had a chance to focus on him, she was already in position and moving her feet. Then she saw who it was.

CHAPTER NINE

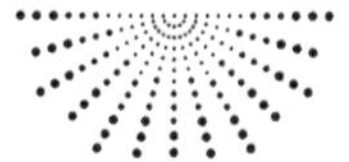

Julian.

Reg groaned aloud. "No…"

Julian smiled. He was handsome, his smile rakish, and he was stunning with his white hair and whip-thin physique. But it was like the smile of a swamp goblin.

And Reg would know.

"What are you doing here?"

"Everyone is welcome at the Ostara celebration."

"But you're not even from here. Shouldn't you… I don't know… be reporting back to the mother ship or something?"

He danced along to the music. He was good, his movements perfectly timed and executed. But he was too good. She didn't feel drawn into the dance. It was like she was standing apart from him, watching a performance.

"I am not an alien," he said, his face expressionless.

His blankness reminded her of the boy he had been when they had been in foster care together. Blank, with no affect. He hadn't yet learned to be charming, to react to people naturally. Instead, he was like Mr. Spock or Data on Star Trek. An outsider trying to learn about human emotion by observation, not because he actually felt it himself. She and the other children had known that he was different.

That there was something alien about him. They had probably teased him for it. Reg didn't remember seeing anything blatant, but she had been aware that there was something bad going on beneath the surface.

"I am an investigator," Julian told her. In case she hadn't read or had already forgotten his business card. "That's an elite position. There are not very many of us; we have to go through a rigorous training and vetting program. It's very prestigious." He drew himself up even taller, proud and straight, towering over her.

She could see that it meant something to him. He had actually accomplished something in his life, despite his less-than-favorable start. So many of the kids Reg had known in foster care ended up on the streets or in prison. Foster care wasn't a fast track to success.

There *were* success stories; kids who had been given the right opportunities or who had pulled themselves up out of the muck by sheer force of will. But many of them fell by the wayside, discarded and forgotten by society.

"Good for you," she said, soothing his ego. She didn't have a clue what he was investigating her for, but she assumed that he would be much better disposed toward her if she stroked him and got him on her side. "That must have been really hard. You must have really had to work at it."

Julian nodded. "Yes, exactly," he agreed eagerly. "It wasn't just handed to me. I had to fight for it. I had to make something out of myself."

"That's amazing. Me… well, most of the time, I've barely been able to keep body and soul together. I've done all right since I got here in Black Sands, but before that… Well, things were not going too well for me. I was lucky to find this place and to meet up with Sarah, my landlady. She's been a big help to me. Giving me a cottage at rock-bottom prices, helping me to get new clients. She's really been awesome."

"I looked into your background. What I could find. You managed to stay out of sight for long periods of time."

Reg shrugged. "I only started using my own name again recently. And a lot of the time… well, you run a cash business, you don't report to anyone. You use different names and you move on at the first hint of trouble."

Maybe something she should be considering now that Magical Investigations was after her. She couldn't understand why Julian was knocking at her door. What they thought she had done wrong.

"I figured something like that."

They danced for a few minutes in silence. The song was stretching out too long. Reg wanted it to be over so she could go get another drink. Maybe find Jessup and Francesca and go home. The party was bound to run all night, but that didn't mean Reg had to stay there the whole time. She could beg off sick. Or say that she was too upset about Corvin being there, stalking her again.

It wouldn't be a lie.

"Reg Rawlins," Julian said, looking down at her, in a tone that was halfway between hunger and admiration. It gave her the chills.

And not in a nice way.

"That's me," she said with a shrug. "No one special. Just… you know, making a bit of coin reading palms or tea leaves. Without Sarah's cottage, I never would have been able to afford to live here."

"The *great* Reg Rawlins."

It always made her uncomfortable when people used adjectives in front of her name. She didn't want to have to live up to a reputation or to somehow find a way to show that she had earned it. She didn't want to be *great* or *famous*. She just wanted to be Reg.

"I don't know who's been talking to you. I'm not anything special. Someone has been exaggerating."

"Have they. I think I've done a pretty good job of investigating your background. Some of the stories have been… difficult to believe. But they have been corroborated. And I remember you." He took her by the hand to bring her close to him and then to spin her out. "I remember the feeling I used to have around you. The… electricity."

And yet, her fingers and skin did not tingle when she touched him like they did when she touched Corvin. Between the two of them, there was always a buzz of electricity. Did that mean that Julian was less powerful? Or just that the two of them did not connect in the same way?

"Looking back, sometimes you see things that weren't actually there before," Reg cautioned. "You embellish. Add things. Insights. Things that… didn't actually happen that way."

"I don't do that. I have a very good memory. I don't need to embellish."

"Everybody does it."

Did a shadow of doubt cross his face? Reg thought she sensed a slight weakening. But it was so very small, she might have imagined it.

"What is all of this about?" Reg demanded. "I haven't done anything wrong. I've just been here, doing my thing, not harming anyone. That's what it's all about, isn't it? It's all good as long as you're not hurting anyone else?"

"Not exactly the poetic turn of phrase that I usually hear, but yes, that is a basic tenet of our faith." he gazed down at her. "Not that you are exactly a believer."

"I believe… in some things."

"What? In what you can see and touch with your own eyes and hands? There is so much more to the world than what you can see and touch."

"Other things too… some things you can write off as coincidence, but I have seen some things that… defy description."

"You've *seen* things."

"Yes… but I've also felt things. Heard things. I've been able to do things that… I shouldn't be able to do. I've had experiences that…" She trailed off.

"Defy description," he repeated.

"Yes. I guess. I don't know how else to put it. Things that, if we had seen when we were kids, back in foster care… we would never have believed."

"I would have been a lot harder to surprise than you. I grew up in a magical home, remember."

"For a few of the early years," Reg temporized. "You weren't raised by them."

"I was. I was only put into foster care for a few years at the end. I remembered my family, all of the things that we used to do. The powers that they had. That I had." His voice was angry as if she had accused him of lying. Or had tried to take his past away from him.

But that wasn't what Reg remembered. He had not been grown when they had been in Mrs. Newburg's home. He was only a couple of years older than Reg, and he had been in other homes before arriving there. He had a reputation as a child who had been put through a lot of different programs and families.

"I was in foster care since I was four or five," Reg told him. "I remember..."

He cocked his head, waiting to hear what she remembered from those early years. Reg thought of Norma Jean, her mother, the last couple of places they had lived. The grinding poverty, watching her mother shoot up with drugs, men in and out of her life over and over again.

"I didn't remember magic from back then," she said. "I guess I had... a guardian who tried to help me. But my mother... she was too far gone to use her powers back then."

Until Weston had taken Reg back in time, had changed things, had made it so that Norma Jean survived. That the Witch Doctor hadn't been able to kill her. But Reg had grown up without her anyway, moved from one foster home to another, pretending there was nothing different about her. Nothing at all.

"You liked being different?" she asked Julian. That was what she remembered. That he had been attention-seeking. He got in trouble and he did things that demanded lots of attention, that he had relished it when he was punished for his misdeeds, because at least then he knew that they had noticed him. That he was able to have an effect on the world around him.

"Yes. I'm proud to be different. I would never want to be the same as all of those milksops that we grew up with. No power. No talents. No gifts. I didn't want that. I never wanted to be like all of the other kids."

"Yeah."

CHAPTER TEN

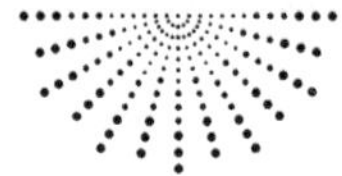

The song ended, and Reg took a couple of quick steps back to separate herself from Julian.

"I have to go. I'm tired."

He looked at her, knowing that it wasn't the truth. His white hair made him look like some kind of angel. But Reg didn't feel warm and safe around him. Far from it.

"I'm still going to need to set up an interview with you," Julian said, following her off of the dance floor. "There are questions which must be answered."

"I don't know what it is that you're investigating, but I haven't done anything wrong."

"Then you can answer my questions honestly and you won't be punished for anything. But if you have broken the laws of the magical community, we will take action."

"I haven't done anything wrong. I don't know all of your magical laws. I'm not part of that community. I'm just a psychic. I don't cast spells."

He took a step toward her and opened his mouth to argue. In a flash, Corvin was there in front of Reg, inserting himself between her and Julian.

"I think you've finished your dance," he told Julian sharply, baring his teeth in a smile. "It's someone else's turn now."

He took Reg by the arm, and she found herself pulled away, leaving Julian behind to fume once more over her refusal to talk to him. She faced Corvin on the dance floor, her face flaming hot, her own fury bubbling up this time over his presumption after she had made it very clear to him that she wouldn't dance with him.

"What was that?"

Corvin shrugged. "I became aware that you were dealing with a warlock you did not want anything to do with, and I devised a plan to get you out of the situation."

"I told you I don't want to dance."

"And since then, you have been dancing. Surely you can spend a couple of minutes with me, if only to protect yourself from an intrusive stranger."

Reg's feet moved of their own accord. She felt herself swept up by the beat of the music like she hadn't been for any of the other dances she had participated in that evening. Somehow, the music thrummed inside her as well as out. Her whole being moved with the rhythm and the winding melody, as if she knew the song.

"He's not a stranger."

"Oh, my mistake. He is unfamiliar to me. Where have you met him before?"

"He was… I knew him years ago. Before Black Sands."

"How mysterious. I thought you left your former life behind when you came here. I thought that you had certain reasons for not wanting your past life to catch up with you here."

"Yes. I do. And yet… here he is."

"And you would like him removed from your life?"

"It's not that easy."

Corvin scanned the crowd behind Reg. "He's already disappeared. I don't think you need to worry about him."

"He'll be back. He said he has to interview me."

"Has to? What is he? A reporter?"

"No. Something called Magical Investigations."

Corvin's brows went up. "Really?" He leaned closer to her. "Tell me what happened."

"Nothing happened. He showed up at the cottage, said he wants to talk. I told him I was going out. Then he shows up here, dances with me, and starts asking me questions again."

"About what?"

Reg looked around to make sure that no one was paying any attention to their conversation. "Something to do with the Everglades."

Corvin nodded slowly, rubbing the neatly trimmed whiskers on his chin. "Maybe you'd better fill me in on the stuff that happened while you were alone in the swamp. Or… not alone. We can go through it, figure out what it is that he wants to talk to you about, devise a plan. I'll back you up. I'm sure Damon will too."

"I didn't do anything wrong, so I don't need to explain myself. I don't have to lie."

His mouth twisted in a wry smile. "I'm sure you didn't. But sometimes, enforcers see things differently. The wrong shading, and something perfectly innocent can suddenly appear to be a gross misstep. Like our little incident," he reminded her. "A misunderstanding. A little slip-up, natural under the circumstances, and suddenly I am in the spotlight, under examination by the tribunal. Even though you never filed a complaint. It wasn't your idea. But when someone else makes a complaint, and they are determined to railroad you…"

Reg snorted at Corvin's characterization of his attack against her. *A misunderstanding? A slip-up?* He knew very well that wasn't the case, and so did she.

"I don't need your help," she snapped. "I don't need anyone's help. I'm not even going to talk to the guy. He can take a hike."

"You'll talk to him."

"I don't have to. What is he going to do? Force his way into my house? He can't. It's protected."

"They have far-reaching powers, these investigators. Maybe he can't get past your threshold. But even if he can't, he can track you down other places. How did he know to find you here tonight?"

"Where else would I be tonight? This is where everyone is. I said I had to go out, and it didn't take him long to figure out where. But that doesn't mean I have to tell him anything. I know my rights."

"You don't know your rights. Or the rights that you don't have. We are not talking about the laws of the land. These are ancient laws and they can be very complicated. Breaking them can have… lasting consequences."

"I didn't do anything wrong," Reg insisted.

"Perhaps not. But we should talk about it. Make sure before you say anything to him."

Reg shook her head stubbornly. If she needed help, she would seek it from someone other than Corvin. She'd dealt with him in her life enough already.

When the dance ended, Jessup was there to rescue her. And Jessup held something over Corvin, some kind of threat or promise. When she told him something, he listened to her, even if he scowled and didn't like it. Jessup put one arm around Reg's shoulder and smiled sweetly at Corvin. "I think you're done here tonight, Hunter."

"I have as much right as anyone to participate in Ostara."

"Not since you were shunned by your coven, you don't."

"I don't have to be here under the auspices of a coven. Everyone is welcome."

Jessup opened her mouth to argue.

"Everyone," Corvin insisted.

"Well, you've worn out your welcome. I think it's time for you to go home. And you know better than to show up at the Spring Games, don't you?"

Corvin swallowed, his face red with fury. He didn't argue with her on that point. Jessup steered Reg away from him, but kept an eye on Corvin until he headed for the door. Reg helped herself to another glass of punch.

"Why can't he go to the Spring Games?"

"His kind have been banned from the Spring Games for hundreds of years. Too dangerous to have a being like him where there is such a large gathering of practitioners."

Reg thought about that. So many people with powers gathered together in one place would be like a smorgasbord to Corvin. An all-you-can-eat buffet. It wouldn't be hard for him to separate one or two unwitting victims from the crowds of observers and to charm them into yielding their powers to him. And he would become stronger and more insistent with each one.

"Yeah, I guess I can see how that would be a problem," she admitted. Thinking back to how Corvin had fed on the Witch Doctor's artifacts and directly from him, Reg couldn't help wondering if they had made a mistake. They would not have had any hope of defeating the Witch Doctor without him. Yet those powers were all held by Corvin now. Even if he only understood how to exercise a fraction of them, it was still a vast reservoir of power residing in just one person. And she was coming to understand that was a bad thing, even if his intentions were good.

"I think… I'd like to go home now," she told Jessup. "Is that okay? I don't mean to take you away from all of this, but…"

Jessup nodded. "Sure. If you're getting tired…"

Reg didn't say that she was getting tired. But she was tired of having to fend off Julian and Corvin and didn't want to take the chance of having to face either one again.

"I'll just see if I can find Francesca," Jessup said. "I'll see whether she wants to go home now, or if she wants me to come back or can get a ride from someone else."

"Sarah is here." Reg looked around, trying to spot Sarah's gray head among the crowd, feeling her presence. "Francesca could get a ride from her. Or Letticia."

"I don't know that I would recommend riding with either one of them."

Reg smiled. She'd ridden with Sarah, and that was a pretty frightening experience. She suspected that Sarah didn't have a license. Who would give her one with the way that she drove? "Letticia isn't so bad. I haven't ridden along with her, but I followed her from her house back to town, and she didn't put any lives in danger."

"Maybe not when she's guiding someone else, but the way she tears around town in that convertible when she's on her own…"

Reg remembered Letticia behind the wheel the day of Corvin's tribunal, and she didn't have a hard time imagining her tearing around town. She might look old and grumpy, but she had a little bit of the reckless teen in her too. She didn't drive any old rust-bucket.

Jessup left Reg to find Francesca. Reg had another glass of punch and considered whether or not to have one more cookie. She had danced; that was exercise. Surely she had burned off the previous cookies, and it wouldn't hurt her to have another. Except that the punch was also sugary and full of calories. Reg knew the waistbands of her dresses were getting tight. She sighed and just sipped the punch, waiting for Jessup to return.

CHAPTER ELEVEN

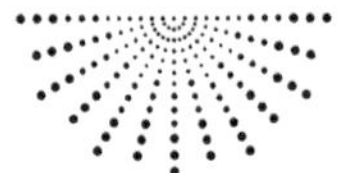

Reg had known that she wouldn't be able to get to sleep right away after the party. When she got home, she was wound up rather than sleepy. She didn't normally go to bed until the small hours of the morning, being a natural night owl and booking seances and other consultations for the midnight hours. So she was wide awake and knew she wouldn't be heading to bed for quite some time.

She looked at the mark on her door as she entered. It gave her a knot in the pit of her stomach. What was up with Julian showing up on her doorstep? Was it really what he said, that he was investigating something that had happened in the swamp and had just been randomly assigned to investigate someone he happened to know from childhood? Or had he sought out the assignment or made it up altogether? Maybe he had seen her name on something. Or maybe he had remembered her from childhood and sought her out.

But why?

Why would he be interested in someone he had just happened to know in one of his homes? Some foster kids were lucky and ended up staying with the same family until they aged out, almost like a bio kid. But then there were the ones like Reg and Julian who were trouble and hopped from one foster family to another throughout their growing up years. How long had they been with the Newburgs together? A few months? A year? She wasn't sure how long she had been there, but she was pretty sure it wasn't more than a year. Why would Julian seek her out just because of that?

Starlight greeted her when she let herself into the cottage, stretching and meowing conversationally. Reg scratched his ears and got him something to eat, then went into her bedroom and looked at the suitcase on the shelf of her closet.

She had been in Black Sands for a long time. Longer than she stayed in most places. If it was getting too hot, if Julian really did have something on her, then maybe she should disappear. She had the gems. She could go wherever she wanted. She hated to leave. It was the first place she'd actually felt like she had real friends and fit in with the community. But maybe she could find another magical community somewhere else. She wasn't going to Salem, but there had to be other places someone like her would be welcomed. She could visit the dwarfs and Nico. She could go back to Tennessee and drop in on Erin. Just for a few days. Things should have cooled down enough for her to pop in and out without the residents finding out.

Starlight made a little meow and rubbed against her legs. Reg bent down to pet him. "I'm not going to leave you behind," she promised. Sarah didn't like cats. Reg could leave him with Francesca, but she didn't want to leave him behind somewhere. She wanted to take him with her. That would complicate things a little bit, but she had money. She wouldn't be sleeping on the street this time.

Eventually, Reg moved away from the closet. She would think about it. She wasn't ready to run yet, but if it seemed like things were going to go bad with Julian Sabat, she would have a plan. She wasn't going to stick around while he brought charges against her. She would find out what he had, and then she would decide.

* * *

As morning approached, Reg was usually yawning and getting ready for sleep. But instead, she felt edgy and anxious. Her legs were restless and she couldn't sit or lie still. Pacing seemed to be the only thing she could do to keep herself calm. And she couldn't pace all day. She needed to sleep sooner or later.

The sun rose and the sky brightened. The sunrise was beautiful, of course. People were always gushing over sunrises. But Reg didn't feel good about it. It just made her feel more anxious and uncertain.

The cottage door opened behind her. Reg whirled around, her heart leaping to her throat. There was a loud bang like a firecracker going off, followed by a wave of concussive force. Reg's hands were up, ready to defend herself against the intruder, her mind going immediately to Julian Sabat. Had he somehow gotten past all of the wards? He had said that he would talk to her. How had he already forced his way in?

"Reg! Oh, dear. You startled me. I'm so sorry, I didn't expect you to be up."

Reg focused on Sarah, pressing her hand over her heart. Not Julian. Not someone who had broken in and was bent on attacking her. Sarah had a key, of course. And while there were laws that said landlords had to give notice before entering a tenant's premises, Sarah had never paid any attention to them, and Reg had grown used to Sarah letting herself in. Sarah helped keep her datebook up to date, stocked the fridge, fed Starlight some mornings if Reg wasn't up yet, and generally acted like she was Reg's mother or grandmother instead of her landlady.

She knocked if she thought Reg would be up, but of course she wasn't expecting Reg to be up at eight o'clock in the morning. When was the last time that had happened?

But what about the explosion? Why had Sarah done that? Just because Reg had startled her?

"I couldn't sleep," she said lamely.

"Too much excitement in the air?" Sarah guessed. "Things are always more stimulating around equinox, and with the Games getting started today..."

"I don't know what's wrong with me. I just can't seem to calm down."

"Maybe some tea," Sarah suggested, moving into the kitchen.

"What did you do to make that explosion?" Reg asked, a bit of a whine in her voice. She could understand Sarah entering without knocking, but not blowing things up.

"Oh, I didn't do that, dear." Sarah looked at her, eyes wide and innocent. "That was you."

"Me? I didn't do anything!"

Sarah raised her brows. "You are the firecaster," she reminded. "I could mix up a potion that would cause a small explosion, but I can't just conjure one out of the air."

"It wasn't me."

"I scared you. It's not your fault."

Reg frowned at her, trying to understand why she would make such a claim. "I can't do that."

"Just like you couldn't kindle the fires at Corvin's hearing? And things just kept… happening around you when you were upset?"

Reg remembered arguing then about how she wasn't the one starting fires, breaking glasses, or knocking things off of her shelves. It wasn't until later that she discovered her firecasting abilities, so maybe she had been the one who had started those, but all of the other stuff? She wasn't really buying into it.

Reg watched Sarah prepare the tea. "I never slept last night."

"No? Well, we can't have that, can we? Did you enjoy the celebrations last night?"

"Yes… mostly. It was a bit much, maybe. I came home early."

"I noticed that. I see you've had a visitor." Sarah nodded toward the door.

Reg looked at it. "What?"

"I saw the notice on your door. What has Magical Investigations got their tails in a knot about?"

"I don't know. I couldn't talk to the guy last night because I was going out. And then he showed up at the party and wouldn't leave me alone there. He says it is something about the Everglades."

"Oh, I wouldn't worry too much. These guys are very exacting. You step off of a trail or eat the fruit from a protected tree or something of that nature and they read you the riot act. Just act properly contrite and he'll go on his way again."

This lifted Reg's spirits. With all of Julian's ominous portent, she had assumed that it would be something serious. Magical Investigations sounded like something she would have to be worried about. That they might bind her for a hundred years or take away her ability to practice. Then where would she be? If Sarah wasn't worried about it, that made Reg feel a lot better.

"Really? So you don't think it is anything?"

"I'm sure it's just some minor misstep. They love to make people think that they are the all-knowing, ultimate power. That the buck stops with them. But really… it's just another bureaucracy. A bunch of little bean counters looking for something to complain about." She shrugged as she spooned tea leaves into a cup for Regina. "Like the IRS."

Reg wasn't about to admit how afraid she was of the IRS. For most of her life, she had run a cash business, taking whatever she could get and never paying a cent of taxes on it. There had been one or two jobs where she'd had to fill out forms and they had withheld her taxes, but other than that, she had done everything she could to avoid ever setting off the Internal Revenue Service's radar.

She shuddered. "Another organization I don't want anything to do with."

Sarah chuckled. "I run afoul of them every few years," she admitted. "But then I convince them that there is a bug in their system because I couldn't possibly be two hundred years old, and they try to fix it, and leave me alone again for a few more decades."

Reg shook her head. She could just see some poor little bureaucrat in a sweat-ringed white shirt trying to sort that one out.

The tea kettle began to whistle, and Sarah poured hot water into two cups. She motioned for Reg to sit on the couch. "Why don't you put your feet up for a few minutes. You don't have to go to sleep, just have a little break and see if a cup of tea will help you to calm down a bit."

Reg obeyed. She didn't feel as anxious and uptight with Sarah there to soothe her and tell her there was nothing to worry about. Sarah's pleasant, relaxed manner and ability to laugh off an IRS audit gave her a sense that everything would turn out all right.

After she sat on the couch lengthwise, stretching her feet out in front of her, Starlight jumped up at the end of the couch and started to knead the cushion, purring. Reg sipped the tea and tried to make her breathing slow and even. There wasn't anything to worry about. She had just gotten overexcited at the party. Having to deal with both Julian and Corvin had been unsettling. She knew she couldn't trust either one of them.

She wasn't sure what Sarah had put in the tea. She could detect valerian, and something floral with a sweet undertone. Erin would have been able to tell her with one sniff. She had an amazing sense of smell, especially accurate where teas and herbs were concerned. If people cared about ingredients half as much as about their fortunes, it could be Erin's side hustle. Just in case anything ever happened with the bakery.

"When is this investigator coming over, then?" Sarah asked.

"I don't know. I didn't set up a time. I just wanted him to go away."

"They're like vermin; they don't just go away. You have to smoke them out. But don't you worry, we'll take care of him. Investigating perfectly innocent people about the silliest things. Trying to trip them up. You don't have anything to worry about."

"I hope not." Reg thought again of her suitcase. She would run if she had to. But would she know when it was time? "If things look bad, though, will you tell me? If you think that… maybe they're not going to work out as well as you thought?"

Sarah studied Reg for a moment over the brim of her teacup. Then she nodded. "Of course."

"Thank you."

Reg didn't want to leave Black Sands. But if she had to…

"You are going to attend the Spring Games, aren't you?" Sarah asked. "You're going to the opening ceremonies?"

"Yes… I guess I might not ever get the chance to see them again, so I should take them in while I can."

"Oh, you may be surprised and see them more times than you expect. But it is worthwhile to have a look. Enjoy the competitions. Pick up a new trick or two." She winked at Reg.

"You're not competing?"

"Oh, no. I'm retired. Competing in the Games takes a lot of dedicated practice. And the right politics. I don't have the time for either. I'm quite happy where I am, with dominion over my own house. I don't need to prove my powers to anyone. I don't need to be the best at anything."

"Are they... more powerful than you?"

"I'm just your run-of-the-mill house witch. Nothing special."

Reg wasn't sure that was true. But if that was the story Sarah wanted to stick with, Reg wouldn't argue with her.

"More powerful than Corvin?"

Sarah's eyes flashed. "Where is Corvin Hunter these days? I certainly hope he is behaving himself. Corvin's powers vary, so I can't tell you how much more or less powerful he is than the competition. But he isn't going to get a chance to prove his prowess."

"I know. Jessup told me that he isn't allowed to be around the games."

"He shouldn't even be in town right now. I was not happy to see him at the celebration last night."

"He didn't do anything."

"It is too big of a temptation for him, being in Black Sands when the Games are being held. He really should not be here."

"Is there a rule? Does he have to leave?"

"No. It's just prudent. I would be very careful of him right now." Sarah eyed Reg. "I know you don't like to be told what to do and you fancy yourself friends with him, but heed my words. Stay away from him during equinox and the Games."

Reg swallowed. She took another sip of her tea, trying to nod nonchalantly. Of course she would stay away from Corvin during the games. Just like she always tried to stay away from him.

And failed.

There wasn't much she could do when he showed up on her doorstep or at an event she had been invited to. She didn't go out of her way to find him. He would show up without warning.

"I'm getting stronger though," she told Sarah. "I can usually resist him. Use a protective barrier or even reflect his own powers back at him."

Or just watch her if she got her feet in the ocean… but Reg hadn't told Sarah about that particular issue. She preferred to keep it quiet unless she were forced to divulge it. Sarah knew about Reg's mother being part siren, but didn't know about the abilities Reg had apparently inherited.

CHAPTER TWELVE

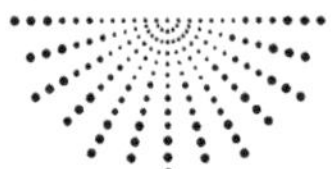

Reg felt so much better by the time Sarah left that she decided she would just flake out on the couch for a while. She was relaxed and reassured by Sarah and whatever she had put in the tea, and the cat purring comfortably at her feet. She didn't want to break the spell by going back to her room and trying to go to sleep. Instead, she just let herself drift, curled up comfortably on the usually-uncomfortable wicker couch.

She managed to get a few hours in before her body finally rebelled against both her position on the couch and the fact that she hadn't had anything substantial to eat. She shifted around uncomfortably until she couldn't stay on the couch anymore. Then with a sigh, she sat up and got to her feet. Starlight looked up, yawned, and stretched in place, his whole body quivering. Reg thought that it must be nice to be a cat. They always seemed to have such satisfying stretches.

"I guess if I'm going to these Games, I'd better get myself together," she told Starlight. She stretched her arms back and tried to release a kink in her neck. "You know, shower and clothes and something to eat."

His ears perked at the mention of food.

"Not yet, though. It's going to take a few minutes before I'm any good in the kitchen."

Starlight put his head back down, nestling it into his tail, forming a soft, cozy ball. Reg fought the urge to lie back down, maybe to pick him up and take him to the bedroom where she could resume her nap in comfort. But once she picked him up, he would probably start begging for dinner in earnest, and she wouldn't be able to go back to sleep anyway. She would just end up grumpier and more irritable, and she would not be good company at the opening ceremonies.

Reg shuffled to the bathroom to start with a hot shower. Then she would face the day.

* * *

Eventually, her blood was circulating, she had actually presentable clothes on, and her stomach was growling for sustenance. Reg had intended to be ready considerably earlier, so she just rifled through the fridge, looking for something she could eat cold. Sarah would be by to pick her up and she hadn't even had a mouthful of food. Even microwave reheating would take too long.

Starlight meowed and rubbed against her ankles, demanding that his bowl be filled as well, even though he already had enough crunchy kibble to last him the rest of the day and through the night.

"Hang on, just hang on. I need to get something to eat too. I haven't eaten all day."

He gave her a yowl that clearly meant that was her own fault, and her lack of planning and motivation should not affect when he got his food.

"There's a pork chop. You liked those the first time." Reg pulled out the cold piece of meat, ran a paper towel over it to remove the majority of the sauce, and pulled it into chunks, which she tossed into Starlight's bowl. Normally she would have cut or shredded it into smaller pieces, but he was a predator, wasn't he? He could undoubtedly manage to rip and chew his own meat.

She found a cold chicken drumstick that would have to do and ate it much too fast. She chased it with a drink, and then found a small yogurt cup in the fridge for dessert. No vegetables, but she had her other food groups covered. Mostly. And she hated vegetables.

Sarah gave a quick rap on the door and opened it to look in at Reg. "Are you all ready? I should have called ahead…"

"Yes, I'm ready." Reg tossed her leftover bits in the garbage, her spoon in the sink, and brushed her hands together as if they were dusty. "All set."

"Excellent."

Reg followed Sarah out to the front of the house, where she saw Sarah's black jeep parked on the street. Reg looked around in surprise. Usually, Sarah had a car service when she went out in the evening.

Sarah caught her look. "The drivers were all booked up today. The Games, I suppose. You don't mind me driving, do you?"

Reg tried to swallow a bray of nervous laughter. She had not prepared herself for Sarah's madcap driving style. "We could see if Officer Jessup is going. I'm pretty sure she planned to."

"Well, there's no need for her to drive out of her way to pick us up. We are perfectly fine getting there are our own. Aren't we?"

"Yes. Of course."

Reg didn't want to insult her. And she couldn't think of another solution. She assumed that cabs and Uber would have the same problem; they would already be booked up by the tourists. Sarah had a car available. She was capable of driving. They could get there in one piece.

"Reg, you don't mind, do you?"

"No. Let's… get on our way."

She climbed into the passenger seat, buckled her seatbelt, and pulled it tight across her body so she couldn't move. She held on to the door while at the same time trying to relax her body. They said that a person fared much better if she were completely relaxed during an accident. That was why drunks seemed to survive without a scratch while their victims did not.

Reg should have had several more drinks before leaving the house.

* * *

Reg was not a religious person, but she said enough prayers to make up for the rest of the year on the way to the stadium where the Spring

Games were being held. They screeched abruptly to a stop when they had to join the slow-moving line to get in. Reg tried to look around all of the cars to see why they were moving so slowly. Maybe they were being held up by a horse and carriage? Or someone arguing with one of the ticket vendors. But she couldn't see anything.

Eventually, when they made it to the front of the line, Reg saw the protesters.

All kinds of people, young and old and hailing from various magical races, shouted and carried signs, blocking the cars entering the event or gesturing at them to go home. Reg was not going to be bullied, and it didn't appear that anyone else around her was planning to turn around and go home. Sarah kept the car moving forward at a very slow pace, and Reg looked over the signs.

Magic isn't a game

Cooperation, not competition

Balance and peace

Equality over equinox

Even though Jessup had said that there would be protesters, Reg hadn't expected quite so many. Or for them to be calling for peaceful cooperation at the tops of their voices.

"Just ignore them," Sarah advised. "There are always a few nutcases."

"You don't agree with them? About how equinox is supposed to be about cooperation and balance?"

"Of course it is. But that doesn't mean we can't showcase our talent. There's no need to go overboard. Some people are very… rigid. There's no reason we can't play games during equinox. We're not talking about the Colosseum."

What exactly did that mean? Reg shrugged as if she understood, and watched out the window as they inched forward, making their way through the crowd of angry protesters.

Eventually, they were able to park and a security guard saw them safely in through the stadium doors. Reg looked around for Damon, knowing that he was in charge of security for the event, but she didn't see him. He was probably off in another building giving instructions and watching a dozen camera feeds for any sign of trouble. She predicted she wouldn't see him for the entirety of the Spring Games.

Reg and Sarah found their seats and made themselves comfortable. As comfortable as one could be in chairs which were apparently not meant to cradle the human body in any way. Maybe they were designed to keep students awake during lectures. Reg couldn't think of any other reason they would be so hard and uncomfortable.

Because it had taken them so long to get in, they didn't have to wait long for the opening ceremonies. Reg looked around at the people in the crowd, trying to spot witches and warlocks she recognized and pick out the tourists or guess what countries various people were from. Or identify what magical races various beings belonged to. She could definitely see fairies and pixies in the crowd. Gnomes near the front, and she thought even some dwarfs, though Sarah had previously said that they would not get so close to the ocean. There were others she wondered about. Was the ill-dressed, slender woman a few rows in front of her fully human, or did her lack of fashion sense give her away as an immortal? Was the large man with the full beard sticking to the shadows just a hipster, or was he part Bigfoot? There were many races Reg hadn't yet been introduced to and wouldn't recognize on sight.

"Ladies and gentlemen!" came the announcer's voice, gratingly loud, overpowering all of the individual conversations going on around the hall. In swooping, dramatic tones, he described the magical games and welcomed everyone. Reg tuned him out when he segued into instructions about waiting until intermissions to get out of their seats for restrooms or snacks. She continued her people-watching.

"Enjoying yourself?"

Reg's head snapped around to see the man who had just spoken in her ear.

Julian, of course.

Anger welled up in her immediately. Memories her body had of his tormenting her, even though she couldn't consciously recall what had happened. Whenever she heard his voice or saw his face, she was ready to fight. Or to run. She was furious that he would show up at the Spring Games to harass her again. Why couldn't she just enjoy herself? Why did he have to keep showing up and wrecking everything?

Julian jerked back as if she had hit him. "Calm down there," he warned.

"Just leave me alone!"

Sarah turned to see who Reg was talking to. She raised one penciled eyebrow. "Young man. In case you didn't notice, the Games have begun. It is very rude to be starting a conversation now. Take your seat. Or I will call security to have you forcibly removed."

Julian snickered at her. "Thanks, Grandma. I'm here in an official capacity. You can't have me thrown out."

"You are not authorized to start an investigation here. We are at a public event, for goodness sake. Go back and read your manual."

"I am authorized to interrogate a suspect wherever I want to."

"No," Sarah said flatly. "You are not. Do I need to call your superior and talk to him?"

Julian drew back a step, scowling. "I don't know who you think you are, but this is a very serious matter. If you interfere with my investigation, things will not go well for you."

"I was acquainted with Magical Investigations when your predecessors were still speaking Latin. When you were still messing your diapers, I was well-known to the head of MI. So, you can get off of your high horse and leave Reg to enjoy the Spring Games, or I will start making calls. If you want to have your license pulled, you just keep it up."

Julian's mouth twisted. Reg was sure he was going to call Sarah more names and challenge her, but then he finally nodded jerkily. "If that's the way you would like to play this, then that's just fine. I will add charges of assault against the famous Reg Rawlins," he nodded toward Reg, "And of hindering an investigation against you...?" He realized he didn't know Sarah's name and looked questioning.

"Sarah Bishop," Sarah said serenely. "You go right ahead, young man. You go right ahead."

With another angry look, Julian walked away from them.

Reg breathed out slowly, watching him until she could no longer see him. "Good grief. What's wrong with that guy?"

"You showed great restraint in not lighting him on fire," Sarah complimented.

Reg snorted. "It was pretty tempting." She breathed in and out again, trying to convince her body it was okay to unclench and relax. "But now that I know something about how to control my fire and my abilities are known, I would probably get in a lot more trouble for it, wouldn't I?"

Sarah nodded her agreement. She listened to the announcer and pointed out several people on the podium to Reg, both officials and competitors.

"Do you really know people in Magical Investigations, over his head?"

Sarah nodded. "Of course. It's a small world, smaller when you are talking about the magical community. And I've been around for a lot of years. I don't know what family your young man hails from, but I probably know his parents or grandparents as well. Sometimes a call to a parent can be even more effective than one to a boss."

"He was in foster care. I don't know if he has any family."

"Ah." Sarah looked sideways at her. "That's interesting. Does he know who his parents are?"

"I guess so. He said that he grew up in a magical home. He could remember them from before he went into foster care. I was too young to remember much of anything, but he didn't go into care until he was older. I don't know what happened, whether his parents died or he was apprehended."

"They must know something of his family history for him to get into Magical Investigations."

A few people around them were glaring and shushing them. Reg fell silent, not wanting to get kicked out. Not after all of the preparation and risking life and limb in Sarah's jeep to get there. She turned her attention back to the field and listened to the speeches about the importance of the games and their long history going all the way back to ancient times. She came away with the impression that the

Olympics were just some non-magical spin-off from the Spring Games, a less-prestigious competition for those who didn't have any powers.

But she was distracted, thinking about Julian and how sooner or later, she was going to have to face him and answer his questions.

CHAPTER THIRTEEN

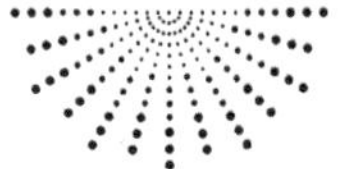

The contestants started to enter the stadium. They entered in small groups, with the announcer calling out what coven or tradition they hailed from. Some of the teams were larger or garnered louder cheers from the audience, a couple of them bringing the audience to their feet with loud clapping and cheers. Reg didn't know any of the different factions and was completely in the dark about whether she should be cheering for one team over another. Mostly she watched Sarah and followed her lead.

They wore cloaks or capes of varying styles, most of the men in hoods and women in traditional peaked witch hats. Reg watched closely for any of the witches or warlocks that she knew, but it didn't seem that any locals were present. She supposed that, like Olympic athletes, the witches and wizards probably spent long hours training and didn't socialize in the same circles as Reg.

Eventually, all the teams had been introduced. "Let the Games begin!" the announcer called out, to thunderous applause, all the spectators again jumping to their feet to clap, holler, stomp their feet, and blow air horns. The noise was tremendous. Reg covered her ears to muffle the sound, smiling and rolling her eyes at Sarah. Sarah clapped and let out a couple of whoops of encouragement.

Eventually, the noise died down as everyone returned to their seats. The air crackled with energy.

"We will begin with the traditional stade."

Reg looked at Sarah for an explanation. She'd never heard of a stade before.

"One of the oldest games," Sara contributed, but didn't explain.

Reg watched, transferring her attention between the field and the big screens in turn. Competitors from various teams shed their cloaks to reveal Spandex athletic wear and took their places at one end of the straight running track. It was a sprint, then. Reg was a little disappointed. She had been expecting something more... magical.

An official called cues in Greek or Latin, some form of "ready, set, go!" At the third call, the competitors shot out of the blocks and, in a pace or two, vanished.

Reg gasped, startled. Only one runner remained, a powerful-looking witch, moving down the track alone. But in a split second, a cheer went up from the crowd and Reg saw the other competitors cross the finish line, bunched close together.

"What happened?" Reg demanded. She blinked and shook her head, trying to come up with an explanation.

Sarah chuckled. "A magical stade is not a foot race. It is a leap through space." At Reg's dropped jaw, she explained further. "Teleportation, as the scientists would call it. There are several things that make it very challenging."

"Besides... teleporting themselves?"

Sarah's eyes were on the one competitor who had ended up sprinting down the entire track instead of disappearing and reappearing as the others had.

"Besides teleporting," she agreed. "They do not have the benefit of quiet meditation and focus to prepare themselves for the leap. They must be able to leap on command, running out of the blocks. If they disappear from the blocks, they are disqualified, they must run at least a couple of paces before leaping. Teleporting from a run is very difficult, even for those who are talented. These are world-class leapers." Sarah nodded to the competitors. "Most practitioners with the gift of teleportation cannot manage it. They also must leap into position before the finish line, in their own lane, and cross the line at a sprint. All of these things are to make it even more challenging. The contestants are the cream of the crop, the very elite."

Reg nodded, impressed. It didn't just sound challenging, it sounded downright impossible, even if she were to accept that people could just teleport themselves at will.

"There will be additional heats throughout the games," Sarah explained. "Opening day is a taste of everything that is to come. A demonstration of each challenge."

"So was this not a real competition, just... an exhibition game?"

"Oh, no. This counts. But not all the leapers will compete today."

Reg watched the witch who had not been able to leap as she was received by her team. She hung her head in shame. They slapped her on the back and didn't make any sign to the cameras that they were disappointed in her or blamed her for her failure. That would come later, Reg supposed. In the change room or back at their accommodations in the evening. Then the witch would be dressed down for her performance.

"The pentathlon!" The announcer boomed over the speakers.

That was track and field, Reg knew. Five different sports like long jump and discus, that ancient Greek Frisbee thing.

What sort of magical *spin* would they put on the discus?

There were fewer competitors for this one than there were for the stade, which Reg thought made sense. They had to be good at five different things instead of just one.

The pentathlon also began with a teleportation leap. All the competitors performed perfectly, no one failing to leap, and all of them were bunched very closely before the finish line. Reg watched the replay on the big screen several times, listening to the spectators around her arguing over who had crossed the finish line first. The judges studied the video on their equipment and eventually declared the winner to be the Merlin team. There were cheers from around the stadium. Reg heard a couple of boos, but they were quickly drowned out by the applause, and ushers made their way to the culprits, leaning down to speak to them, faces grave. Apparently, booing was *not* tolerated at the Spring Games.

They proceeded to the long jump. It looked like what Reg had seen in track and field before. A straight track leading to a long sand pit. Jumpers sprinted down the track, then jumped as far as they could across the sand pit. How would the magical version be different? It didn't make much sense that the jumpers would start sprinting, teleport to the end of the track, and then jump into the pit without any momentum. They wouldn't be able to jump as far as a non-magical jumper, and they claimed that the Magical Games were better than the Olympic competition.

Reg didn't ask Sarah to tell her what was going to happen ahead of time. She wanted it to be a surprise.

The first jumper got into position. Reg watched her sprint all the way down the track and then jump before the sand pit, just like in the normal long jump. But then... instead of a quick jump and landing in the sand, the jumper remained in the air, impossibly suspended on nothing, all the way past the end of the pit, where she landed gracefully with a little finishing move. There was an *oooh* of appreciation from the audience and a rush of applause.

"That was picture perfect," Sarah murmured to Reg. "Ten out of ten."

None of the following jumpers were able to pull off the jump with quite the same grace as Tera le Fey, the first jumper. Most of them were much more like the conventional long jump, managing to hover only a fraction of a second before landing in the sand. The distances were longer than those managed by long jumpers at the Olympic games, but only by a few feet. The points definitely went to le Fey on that one.

CHAPTER FOURTEEN

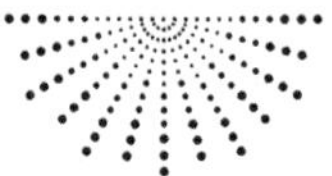

"The next events in the Olympic pentathlon are discus and javelin," Sarah told Reg. "They underwent quite an adaptation from the magical 'defend' and 'attack.'"

"Defend and attack?" Reg's heart beat a little faster at this, even though she obviously wasn't the one who was going to have to attack or defend. She thought about the fights that the ancient Romans had. Contestants fighting each other or facing off against wild animals. She hoped that magical attack and defend were not the magical equivalent of blood sports.

"You'll see. It's very gripping."

Reg could see up on the big screen that contestants' names were being drawn to match opponents at random. These contestants were not in Spandex like the leapers and jumpers, but in heavy cloaks and gear. They looked like gladiators. Tough and battle-hardened.

The first pair stepped into a wide, marked field and faced each other across the expanse. One was assigned as defender and the other as attacker. Reg leaned forward in her seat, drawn into the competition despite herself. It was just a game, after all. There surely wouldn't be any real violence.

The defender held his arm away from his body and out to the side slightly, as if he were holding a discus. He crouched slightly and rotated back and forth, wary, watching for the attack. The attacker drew back his arm, then ran forward, and with an overhead motion that did look remarkably like a javelin throw, he hurled a bolt of lightning at the defender. The defender whirled and blocked it, so that it bounced away harmlessly. A murmur of approval was raised by the audience.

"How do they do that?" Reg asked, sitting right at the edge of her seat. She stared at the screen for a couple of replays of the action, then looked down at the field. The two contestants had not stopped, but still moved slowly, in and out and side to side as the attacker looked for weaknesses in the defense. He threw another lightning bolt, and it was again met with the defender's shield spell.

"It is an energy spell," Sarah explained. "It is very dramatic, isn't it?"

"Could it really hurt him? Or is it just for show? It's just a sport, right?"

"People can get injured in many sports," Sarah pointed out. "Have you ever watched a football or hockey game? Or boxing?"

"Well... yes. But that's not the same as attacking someone with a lightning bolt. It looks like it could be..."

"There have been fatalities," Sarah admitted. "The witches and warlocks who do this train very hard and are very good at what they do. But there have been accidents in past competitions."

Reg gasped and jumped when the attacker hurled another lightning bolt. It was a close call; she could see it catch the edge of the warlock's cloak just before he managed to use his small shield to bat it away. He rubbed his arm briefly and returned to his defense stance.

"How long does it go? Is it timed? When does it end?"

"They don't usually last very long. If the attacker fails on three attacks, or the defender is hit three times, the match is over."

"Was that a hit?"

Sarah nodded. "Yes. So it is two successful defenses to one successful attack."

"Then what? Then they switch?"

"They will be matched up to someone else in the opposite position for their next conflict. They will not play each other again unless they are the final two successful contestants."

"Has that ever happened?"

"A couple of times."

There was a flash of light so bright that it made Reg close her eyes. A shout went up from the audience. She managed to pry her eyes open to watch the replay on the big screen. The attacker had sent a brilliant lightning bolt that looked fast even on the slow-motion replay. But somehow, the defender had still managed to whirl around in time to combat it. Three failed attacks. The match was over.

"A very powerful attack," Sarah said, shaking her head. "It's quite the achievement to have been able to defend it successfully."

Reg looked at the screen as the defender's name was announced and displayed on the screen. The name was a scramble of letters, triangles, and other symbols. She blinked, hoping that her brain would be able to turn the symbols into letters she could read, but they did not shift.

"Is that all of the Pentathlon sports?"

"One more. Wrestling."

"Wrestling?" Reg thought first of the dramatic fights and colorful costumes of professional wrestling she'd seen on TV. It wouldn't be like that, she was sure. Maybe like Sumo wrestling? She thought that was closer to what the ancient Greeks had done, except the Greeks had not been so fat.

"You will see."

The announcer recited the formal rules in rapid sing-song like an auctioneer, too fast for Reg to process. He repeated them again in a second language, then called the names of the first two contestants.

Two witches this time. They were both lean and athletic looking. When the cameras zoomed in to their faces, Reg could see that they were older. Not twenty- or thirty-year-olds, but closer to Sarah's age. Or apparent age, since who knew how old she really was? Their faces showed lines of experience. Not soft-cheeked like Sarah, but hardened, embattled faces.

But wrestlers? They did not look as though they had the power to wrestle. Especially if the other contestants were not all the same age.

The two women approached each other. They reached out their hands and pressed each palm against their opponent's palm. Reg thought it was some sort of greeting, but they did not lower their hands again. They stood facing each other, eye to eye, nose to nose, hand to hand. Reg waited for the action to begin.

At first, it wasn't obvious what was happening. The audience was silent, staring at the screens. Reg thought that everyone was waiting, as she was. She turned to Sarah to ask her what the holdup was, why they didn't begin, but Sarah shook her head and shushed her. Reg returned her eyes to the screen.

The witch's faces were tense, their eyes unwavering. Reg thought about the staring contests she'd had with foster siblings or school friends, and stifled a giggle. They were *not* having an Olympic staring contest. Reg would have been awesome at that. She could always make her friends blink first.

Instead of watching the screens, she closed her eyes and extended out her other senses. Then she could feel the struggle between the two witches. It was not a staring contest, but a battle of wills, some kind of psychic wrestle. She kept her eyes closed, able to sense more that way than through the camera lens.

Waves of electricity seemed to flow from the center of the stadium outward. Reg's heart thumped harder each time one went over her. The battle was becoming more intense. Reg felt hot. A constriction in her chest.

"Reg, watch," Sarah whispered.

Reg was irritated by the interruption. She shook her head, but Sarah poked her and Reg opened her eyes.

The two witches were hovering several feet in the air, light emanating from the point at which their hands touched. Their "wrestling" had grown powerful enough that Reg had no trouble sensing it with her eyes open.

There was a loud report like a gunshot and one of the witches slumped over. Their hands separated and the defeated witch fell to the ground in a heap. Reg leaned forward in her seat, her heart pounding wildly.

"Is she okay? What happened?"

"She lost," Sarah offered. She was sitting back, looking relaxed, and had a big smile on her face. "I knew Wanda would win that match. I knew it!"

"You know her?"

Of course Sarah knew her. After how long Sarah had lived on the earth, she probably knew all the foremost witches and warlocks. Wanda, the victor, raised one fist above her head in triumph as she slowly drifted back to the ground. The witch who had fallen lay still for a few more moments, then rolled over and pounded her fist into the turf, lamenting her loss. Reg was relieved to see Wanda reach down and help the other witch to her feet.

"She's okay?"

"Yes, she'll be fine."

"What about..." Reg tried to put her concerns into words. "Umm... her mind. What if there is... damage?"

"Witches don't get to this level without a lot of practice and training. They learn how to protect their minds, like putting on one of those padded suits for self-defense training."

"But what if something happens? An accident, like you said with the defend and attack?"

"We are far more concerned with the protection of our minds than of our bodies. It's always possible... you can't eliminate all the risks. But it has been a very long time since there has been a wrestling injury in the Magical Games."

Reg nodded. The two witches walked off the field to tremendous cheers and applause. Reg watched the other groups of athletes on the field to see what would happen next.

"What else is there?"

"Oh, there are a number of events that have been added since the Games first began. Shot put. Weightlifting. Wand attack. They'll do a few more things tonight, and then really get into it tomorrow."

Reg watched a group of witches in matching uniforms make their way down one side of the field, waving at members of the audience.

They were each carrying a broom. Reg's eyes widened and her mouth fell open. She looked at Sarah.

"Are they going to... fly?"

Sarah followed Reg's eyes and laughed. "No, no, Reg. That's the curling team."

CHAPTER FIFTEEN

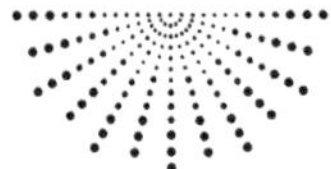

Reg would not have believed any of what she saw if it had been on TV or in some other venue. But she could see the sparkling auras of the performers and could feel the power as they demonstrated their gifts.

She could barely sit still. The combination of the hard, uncomfortable chairs and the incredible restlessness and anxiety that she had felt earlier in the day made it almost impossible to stay in her seat. She was sure everyone around her must be wondering why she was squirming like a six-year-old who hadn't been dismissed from class but badly needed to go to the bathroom. She could feel Sarah trying to soothe her, but there wasn't really anything the older witch could do to help her.

Then at the end, there were fireworks. Real fireworks that called to Reg to come and play. She jumped to her feet but wasn't that obvious because a lot of other people stood to watch as well, almost the entire audience eventually ending up on their feet, applauding for the fire dancing across the sky.

Sarah put a hand on Reg's arm, trying to quell Reg's instinct to join in on the fun. She grabbed an unopened water bottle and thrust it into Reg's hand. "Here. Have a drink. Try to stay cool."

Reg cracked open the bottle and took a long drag, trying to

quench the fire inside of her. She debated kindling just a small fire to try to bleed off some of the energy welling up inside of her. Sarah's hand was still on her arm to keep her calm.

"Maybe we should go back to the car."

Reg really wanted to stay and watch the fire playing across the sky. But she nodded, agreeing that it was probably the only way they would be able to get away from the Spring Games without mishap. Sarah led the way, guiding Reg up the stairs to the concourse exit. A large security guard moved to block their way.

"Please stay in your seats until the show is over."

"She's a firecaster," Sarah snapped. "Do you really want the whole place to go up in flames?"

Reg was too distracted by the fireworks to see the man's face clearly. But he changed his tune and escorted Sarah and Reg out.

"You would think they would at least publish a warning," Sarah snapped. "I realize that firecasters are very rare, but you are bound to get a few in a crowd this size. If you have spectators whose powers are not well-controlled…"

"Can I get you a water, ma'am?" the guard asked, giving only a brief nod in response to Sarah's complaint.

"I had one," Reg said vaguely.

"Get another one," Sarah snapped.

The security guard went to a first-aid station and returned with a couple of bottles of water.

"Drink up," Sarah ordered.

"I'm not thirsty."

"Keep drinking. You'll feel better."

Reg could hear the *oohs* and *ahs* of the crowd in the stadium and looked back toward the doors, feeling the draw of the fire.

"Drink," Sarah ordered.

Reg obediently brought the first bottle up to her lips and sipped at it. She was already feeling waterlogged. But Sarah was right, and it did reduce the draw of the fireworks a little more.

"They shouldn't be on much longer," the guard said apologetically.

There was an inquiry over his shoulder-mounted radio. The guard pushed the button in and answered with a 10-code. Reg wondered if they actually had a radio code for "trying to keep a firecaster from burning the facility down." Maybe it was just a code for giving medical assistance.

Reg did her best to get down the bottle of water and Sarah cracked the next one open.

"I feel like I'm going for an ultrasound," Reg protested. "Do I really have to drink any more? I'm going to burst."

Sarah just looked at her. Reg obediently took another sip.

Another guard came down the concourse toward them to check on the first. Reg didn't recognize him immediately. Usually, he was wearing a robe or cape, but he was dressed as a security guard with a white shirt, dark slacks, ballistic vest, duty belt, and a radio at his shoulder like the guard assisting them.

"Damon."

"Reg. Hey, what's wrong? Are you okay?"

Reg shrugged. "It was the fireworks. They're a bit much for me."

He looked at her for a moment before her meaning sank in. "Oh… I didn't think about it being a problem for you. You're doing so well with Davyn. He says that you've got good control. The only time you had any trouble was at the mountain."

Sarah shook her head at Damon. "You know she's a novice firecaster, and it didn't occur to you that you should warn her about the fireworks?"

"It didn't even cross my mind." Damon sighed and shrugged dramatically. "I'll add it to the control sheet. They haven't kept good security records from one year to the next, so I don't know what problems they have run into in previous years unless there was a huge debacle that made it to the media. Predatory species mixed with prey. Power drinkers. Catering issues. We brainstormed and made long lists of things we thought could be problems, but…" He gave an abashed shrug. "I never thought of fireworks triggering any issues."

"I'm sure Reg is not the only person that they bothered. You also have people who have PTSD, small children, companion animals or familiars, or skinwalkers who might be startled by them. You should at least announce ahead of time and include in the program that there are going to be fireworks."

"I'll put it on the control sheet," Damon repeated. "So, they'll have it for future events. And I'll make sure they add a notice for the closing ceremonies." He looked at Reg. "They'll have fireworks there too."

"Okay." Maybe Reg would skip the closing ceremonies. Or at least leave before the fireworks started.

They stood looking at each other awkwardly. There wasn't really anything else to say. Reg was determined not to show any interest in Damon. She sensed he was still angry with her for the way the Jeffrey Wilson case had worked out. But that hadn't been all her fault. He had made a lot of stupid mistakes himself and he had been fully onboard with Reg's approach. It hadn't turned out the way either one of them had expected.

"Can we go to the car now?" Reg prompted Sarah. "I'd like to get out of here before the crowds. Otherwise, it's going to take forever to get home, and I'm not going to be able to make it."

Sarah smiled. "Of course, dear."

CHAPTER SIXTEEN

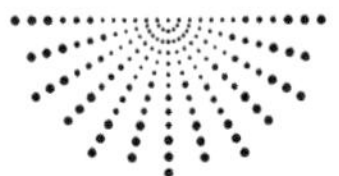

Sarah insisted on escorting Reg all the way to her cottage, and Reg knew better than to argue with her about it. Once Sarah decided to help Reg, there was little to dissuade her. As Reg hurried over the threshold, she tossed her purse to the side and made a dash directly for the bathroom. Luckily, she made it, but just barely. Her bladder was stretched painfully and it was several minutes before she could get up and rejoin Sarah.

Sarah nodded and smiled at her expectantly.

"Tea?" she suggested.

"No way," Reg protested. "I'm not drinking anything else all night."

"Well, it worked, didn't it?"

"Yes. It worked. I can't even think of using my fire right now."

Sarah prepared a cup of tea for herself. She was obviously still keeping an eye on Reg. And since it was Sarah's property that Reg would burn down if she lost control of her powers, Reg supposed she couldn't blame Sarah for that.

"Do you want to tell me about what happened in the Everglades that MI wants to interview you about?" Sarah queried. "I could help you to get your story straight."

It was almost exactly the same offer as Corvin had made. Reg wondered if all they really wanted was to hear what Reg was in trouble for. Or did they think it would help her to rehearse some sanitized version of her trip to the Everglades?

"I can't think about that right now. I don't know whether I'm too tired or too wound up." She glanced toward the bathroom. "Or just too distracted. But I really can't focus on it right now and it would take too long to explain everything that happened."

"Things did not go as you had hoped," Sarah probed.

"No. They didn't go the way that I hoped. Or the way Damon hoped. You probably noticed…"

"He did seem a little cooler today than usual," Sarah admitted.

"Well, he doesn't like the way things worked out and he blames me. I didn't like how he lied to me and got me involved in the whole thing, so I'm not happy with him. Put both together, and… I don't think you're going to be seeing the two of us spending much time together in the future."

"That's too bad. But there are plenty of other prospects in Black Sands or farther afield. There's no reason you have to stick to one suitor."

Reg laughed, which made Sarah's cheeks turn pink. They both knew Sarah was not known for sticking to one suitor. And many of the men that she spent time with looked considerably younger than Sarah did. Of course, if Sarah was as old as she said, they were centuries younger. But Reg suspected there probably weren't a lot of hundreds-of-years-old warlocks in Black Sands to choose from, so she couldn't really blame Sarah for picking from who was available.

"I'm not sure I'm even looking for… companionship at the moment," she told Sarah. "I'd like to… get my head on straight and figure out my powers and where they came from and how to control them…"

She thought in particular about the things she hadn't told Sarah. That she hadn't told anyone yet, because it was just too much. Being a psychic was hard enough. She didn't want all of the baggage and responsibilities that came with anything more than that.

Reg wished she could just go back to when she was reading palms and people were happy to have her pretend to contact long-lost loved ones for them. Things had been so much simpler.

"Corvin and Damon are not the only prospects, and they are not even a good representation of the warlocks you'll find in the community here. There are so many more options, Reg. You shouldn't limit yourself. Get to know more people. Have some fun."

Reg shrugged. "Right now, I feel like all I want to do is stay home. There are so many people in town for the Games..." Reg closed her eyes, trying to push away the sensation of so many consciousnesses intruding on her thoughts. She rubbed her temples. "So many thoughts and voices."

"You should work on blocking them out," Sarah advised. "There's no reason you have to be in contact with everybody in town."

"You think? I am trying, you know! But they're not quiet. It's not that easy."

"I imagine a lot of the people visiting town, especially if they are here to perform, are probably very strong and loud."

"Yeah. It's not easy to ignore." Reg paced across the room. "I don't know how I'm going to sleep tonight. I'm all hyped up after the opening ceremonies, and with all of these people disrupting things."

"Do you want me to make you something to help you sleep?"

"No." Most of Sarah's potions were vile, and Reg didn't want to try any new experiments. "No, thanks. Maybe I'll try a sleeping pill tonight."

"If you prefer."

"I'll be just fine. I'm sure. You don't need to stay with me."

Sarah sipped her tea and nodded.

"I just have to..." Reg motioned to the bathroom and again retreated. It was going to be a while before she had flushed out all of the water that Sarah had forced her to drink. It was a good thing she hadn't ended up with water intoxication, having to drink so much in such a short period of time. Reg still thought it would have been better to just light a small fire and let it burn off like a safety valve. That would have been a lot more satisfying.

She finished and returned to the kitchen, where Sarah stood drinking her tea and checking through the appointment book.

"You haven't had very many readings lately. I thought you would be able to get more with all of the people in town."

"Well, I've been busy. I haven't had a chance to contact a lot of tourists. And I've had that investigator on my case, harassing me to meet with him."

"I'm sure you'll have no trouble with that young pup. Just put him in his place. If you can't handle him, let me know, and I'll see what I can do. I'll have him pulled from the case before you can blink. He was very disrespectful toward me today." Sarah's cheeks took on more color, thinking back to the way that Julian had talked to her.

"I'll talk to him. That's all he wants, right? Once I answer his questions, he'll leave me alone."

"More than likely," Sarah agreed. Which was a little less definitive than the answer Reg hoped for.

CHAPTER SEVENTEEN

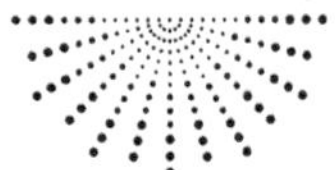

Reg took a sleeping pill to help her to get to sleep once it was past midnight. Several, in fact. She didn't know what time Julian Sabat would be pounding at her door the next day, but she suspected he would not want to wait until Reg had taken her beauty sleep. The man was a bloodhound. Reg just wanted to be rid of him and not to have to remember things from when she was in foster care. That life was behind her. She was her own person, strong and independent, and she wasn't going to let a few lousy childhood experiences get in her way.

She slept. It was a restless, nightmare-ridden sleep, and she still had to get up several times to the bathroom even though she was sure she had processed all of the extra water long before that. She'd had three bottles of water, but she was sure she had peed at least six.

Several times when she finally reached a deep sleep state, Starlight woke her up, pawing her face and meowing loudly. It wasn't something he normally did. Maybe he was irked by all of the extra souls in Black Sands during the Spring Games too. He was very sensitive psychically.

It was no wonder Reg was still tired and groggy when she got up in the morning. She wanted to go back to sleep but had been woken up so many times she knew that was not going to happen. After a couple of cups of coffee, she would be okay.

Reg waited for the coffee to brew and glanced over the datebook to make sure she was aware of any upcoming appointments. She saw the little terrarium she had made with Zinnia at the equinox celebration. Some tiny green leaves were poking up above the surface of the soil already. She remembered the seed-planting activities she had done in kindergarten or the early years of elementary school. Beans, usually. Something that would send up shoots within a couple of days and grow very quickly to get the kids interested in their projects. They never actually got to the stage where the plants would produce beans themselves. Which didn't hurt Reg's feelings too badly because she didn't particularly like beans. But she had been excited by those projects and seeing the first green leaves that indicated the magic of growth taking place. Reg picked up the terrarium and studied the little plant inside. As she watched, it seemed to get bigger. Just a trick of the eyes, Reg was sure. Plants didn't grow that fast, not even in Black Sands.

She put it back down. Starlight howled at her.

"Oh, brother. You can't tell me you're that hungry," Reg objected. "I just fed you."

He reached out his paw and clawed at her leg.

"Hey! You don't do that. Be nice."

He blinked both his green eye and his blue simultaneously, which was unusual for him. Reg glared at him, trying to match his disapproving gaze, but she had to look away. She wasn't sure what *he* was grumpy about. He wasn't the one who'd had two bad nights plus dealing with three bothersome warlocks while trying to ignore the thoughts and voices of several thousand witches and warlocks coming to Black Sands to watch the Spring Games. All he had to do was find a nice sunbeam to stretch out in, and that was the extent of his difficulties. Maybe in the next life, Reg would be a cat. She wasn't sure she actually believed in reincarnation, no matter what Harrison had said about Starlight's previous life.

There was a sharp knock on the door. This time, Reg knew to

expect Julian. Sarah would knock softly to give Reg a warning if she were up and not wake her if she were still sleeping.

Reg went to the door and peered out the peephole. She was correct; it was the uninvited, irritating warlock who had at one time been her older brother.

Reg swung the door open. "What do you want?"

"You know what I want. We have matters to discuss."

"You can't come in here."

He looked as though he had been expecting that response. He gave a brief nod. "Then you tell me where you want to meet. Somewhere quiet where we can discuss matters."

"You don't have some kind of branch office here?" Reg asked snidely.

"Black Sands is hardly big enough to warrant our notice," Julian sneered, giving as good as he got. "Why would we have a branch office here?"

"It's the town with the highest concentration of magical practitioners in the country. Why wouldn't you have an office here?"

He shrugged. "Do you have somewhere you wish to meet?"

"How about The Crystal Bowl?"

"A bar?" He wrinkled his nose.

"A restaurant and bar. And they have private meeting rooms. I know because I've used one of them before."

"Fine," Julian nodded. "Let's go, then."

"When do you want to meet?"

"Now."

Reg resisted. "I have things to do. We can meet later in the day…"

"You have delayed for long enough. We really must attend to this matter. Grab your purse, and let's go."

Reg looked down at herself to protest that she wasn't yet dressed for the day. But either she had slept in her clothes or she had already gotten dressed and didn't remember it. She looked behind her for some other excuse or distraction. Starlight. Her suitcase. Maybe she should reconsider her previous position. Set up a mid-afternoon meeting with Julian, then pack her bag and disappear. She could get a good start and he wouldn't know where she had gone. She wouldn't know where she was going, so it would be impossible for him to guess.

"Let's go," Julian repeated in a firm voice.

And why not? Why not just get it over with instead of avoiding Julian at every turn? The man was obviously a persistent investigator. He wasn't going to give in just because she dodged his calls for a few days.

"Okay." She picked up her purse. She again wondered if she should throw a few extra things in it. The gems that were hidden in her bedroom. Another set of ID so she could start somewhere fresh with a new name and be harder to track. Just a couple of necessities.

Starlight yowled mournfully and Reg gave up on that idea. He was her responsibility and she wasn't just going to leave him for Sarah or Francesca to deal with. He had picked Reg as his owner. It was the first time anyone had picked Reg.

"I'll be back," she told Starlight firmly. She didn't put anything else in her purse. She just picked it up and stepped out the door to join Julian.

"We can take my car," Julian suggested, walking toward the street in front of the big house.

"I'm not going in your car. I'll take my own vehicle."

"Wasting non-renewable energy sources," Julian observed, "not the best way to save the planet from further harm."

She just stared at him. She had never claimed to be living green or eco-friendly. Julian shrugged and continued to his car, which was a little two-seater that probably ran on batteries. Reg rolled her eyes at this and got into her own junker.

They didn't have to drive far to get to the Crystal Bowl. Reg wasn't sure what the procedure was for reserving one of the private meeting rooms in the back, so she approached the bartender polishing glasses to ask for one.

"It's early," he said. "I don't think anyone has anything booked. Wait here and I'll get right back to you."

Reg waited, avoiding looking at Julian, pretending that she was perfectly comfortable meeting with him. He just had a few questions about what had happened in the Everglades. Why should she be worried about that?

She didn't have anything to hide.

She had gone looking for the lost wizard, had helped Damon to find him, and they had taken him back to Black Sands. Under his own power and by his own choice. It wasn't like they had kidnapped him.

And if they had done something horrible like step on the last flower of a particular species, then it was an accident and not something they could have helped. She hadn't done anything intentionally harmful to anyone.

The bartender returned and nodded. "Yeah, you're good. Come this way."

Reg and Julian followed. He led them into a back hallway and unlocked a door for them.

It wasn't like a private room at Corvin's exclusive club. It was more like a stock room. Just bare walls and floor with a few chairs and a table. Something quick and dirty for when people needed to spread out papers or have a private place to carry on a discussion. Reg thought back to the last time she had been there. The night that she had been reunited with Harrison. That had definitely been an interesting time.

But this time, it was just to answer the questions of a bureaucrat. He needed to fill in some paperwork to do with their trip, and then it would be done.

Julian could go home and Reg would never have to worry about running into him again.

CHAPTER EIGHTEEN

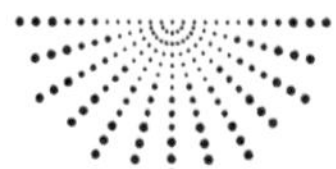

They looked at each other. The room was very quiet, every movement they made echoing. Reg pulled a chair away from the table with a loud grating noise and sat down.

Julian seemed to consider whether it was better for him to be standing, in an apparent position of power over Reg, or to be sitting down with her, offering camaraderie and ostensible equality between them. He eventually decided on sitting. He placed a folder he must have had in his car onto the table with dramatic flair. It was a textured black cover, very official-looking. He opened it and examined the first couple of pages contained within it.

"You are Regina Rawlins?" he said formally.

Regina rolled her eyes. "You know I am."

"For the record."

"Yeah. For the record, I am Regina Rawlins."

"Good. First question down." He gave her a thin smile, but his humor fell flat. "Your residence is in Black Sands?"

"Yes."

"How long have you lived here?"

"I… don't know. A while."

"A while?"

"A few months."

"And before that?" he raised his blond brows. "We don't seem to have a very good record of your previous residences."

"Here and there. Why do you need to know?"

"What was your permanent residence prior to moving to Black Sands?"

Reg considered, staring over his shoulder. "I didn't really have one," She shrugged. "I moved around."

He studied her for a minute and then moved on. "You are friends with one Damon Knight."

"*Friends* is a bit of a stretch."

"Oh?"

"We were… we know each other. But we're not friends. We never were."

"You haven't been… dating him?"

"Is this part of your investigation?"

"We need to establish what kind of relationship the two of you had before embarking on a trip to the Everglades together."

"Well then… we knew each other. He asked me to come along to help him."

"Help him in what way?"

"To find someone he was looking for."

"And how were you expected to do that?"

"He wanted me to use my psychic powers to find Wilson."

"Is that how you make a living?"

"No. I can find things. Sometimes. Or people. But you can't make much of a living from stuff like that. Unless you're finding really valuable objects."

"Like Mr. Wilson."

"Well… yes. If I had a few gigs finding things for a reward of a quarter of a million dollars, then yeah, I'd be able to make a living at it."

"A quarter of a million?"

"The reward money was five hundred thousand, and we were to split it fifty-fifty."

"That's remarkably generous."

"I was the one who would be doing the actual finding."

Julian nodded. He made a few notes in a yellow legal pad. Reg squinted at his words, but they were cursive, which she was useless at, and upside down, so there was no chance she could make it out.

"So that was your contract with Knight. You would use your powers to locate the missing person and he would share the pot with you half and half."

"Yeah."

"Any other provisions?"

"No, I don't think so. It was pretty simple."

"But you didn't actually earn the money."

"The reward wasn't paid out," Reg admitted in a grumble.

"Because you didn't find him."

"Because he wouldn't go back to the Spring Games. That was part of the requirement for the reward to be issued. He had to register for the Games. And he never did."

"Why not?"

"Long story."

He considered this, then decided to move on. Maybe he planned to circle back later after he'd seen what else he could get out of her.

"You traveled with Mr. Knight?"

"Yes."

"And was there anyone else in your company?"

"Uh… Corvin Hunter. He came along, but he wasn't really… he wasn't really part of it, though. He was just tagging along."

"Who was going to pay him?"

"No one. He was just interested in going to the Everglades at the same time as we did."

"He didn't go the same places you and Damon did?"

"Well… he stayed with us, yeah."

"But Knight wasn't paying him?"

"No… Corvin said he could help out. He could get us a good guide." Reg rolled her eyes at this.

"But he didn't?" Julian inquired.

"He found a guide."

Julian waited for more. Reg didn't feel the need to tell him anything else about their guide or how bad a choice he had ended up being. It wasn't that the guide was inexperienced or inept. It was worse than that.

"Are your Mr. Knight and Mr. Hunter good friends? Colleagues...? Lovers...?"

Reg snickered. "No. They don't like each other very much."

"Then why would Hunter attach himself to your company?"

"Because Corvin is used to getting pretty much whatever he wants."

"And he wanted to go to the Everglades."

"Yeah."

"Why?"

"He's a professor. He studies all kinds of stuff." Reg made a gesture to wave this off. "Different magical species. Even plants and animals. He talked quite a bit with Tybalt about them."

Julian wrote more notes in his legal pad. "Hunter was quite familiar with endangered species?"

"I don't know. He talked about a lot of stuff I didn't know anything about. And about... corvids...?"

"Birds?"

"No... that's not the right word. Rare animals that they can't prove exist."

"Cryptids."

"Right." Reg snapped her fingers. "That was it."

Julian wrote this down too. "Hunter is familiar with cryptids?"

"He knows about them. He loves to tell you all of the weird and unusual stuff he knows about zombies or pixies or whatever other creatures. He knows all of this mythology from all over the world. Likes to show off."

"Zombies?" Julian lifted his brows in disbelief.

"Draugrs. Apparently, they show up in all kinds of mythologies all over the world. I don't see how it makes any difference whether you call them zombies or draugrs. If all the different countries call it something different, what difference does it make whether you call them by their American name or Viking name?"

"I see." There was a frown line between Julian's brows. "What occasion did you have to be discussing draugar with him?"

Reg shrugged. She was cautious. Corvin and the others had not told her that she should *not* discuss the draugrs with anyone else. But she didn't want to cause herself or the others any problems if their actions came to the attention of the authorities. Reg had no idea whether they had been acting outside of magical laws. At the time, she had assumed that there were not any laws governing their actions. They certainly hadn't gone to the authorities for permission to do anything or called in magical SWAT to deal with the Witch Doctor and his draugar minions.

Sarah said that the cardinal law for magical practitioners was not to do harm to others. And they hadn't done any harm to the Witch Doctor. Not exactly. They had protected the people of Black Sands. They had saved a lot of lives by defeating the Witch Doctor.

"I don't remember. It was just a pet topic."

"I will definitely want to talk to this Corvin Hunter."

Reg had assumed that he would be talking to all three of them anyway. If he was investigating something that had happened in the Everglades, then he would need to speak to all three of them, wouldn't he? Because they had been together the whole time.

Well, almost the whole time.

Not quite.

She shifted uncomfortably. What was he asking about that only she was involved with? Julian eyed her, looking smugly pleased at her discomfort. This was what he liked. To be in a position of power. For people to be frightened of him. Sarah taking him down a peg had left him angry and impotent, and he was reasserting his position over Reg.

"Tell me about your trip. When did you arrive? What did you do when you got there?"

Reg took him through the initial steps of their trip and meeting up with Corvin, who had sped ahead of Damon and Reg. He took them to the boat, where they met their guide, Tybalt.

"What did you think of him?" Julian asked.

"I don't know… I thought at first that he was… pale for someone who spent all day in the sun. But other than that… nothing special. He seemed like he knew what he was doing."

"What did you do next?"

Reg was hesitant to divulge their actions in any detail. She still didn't know what crime he thought she had committed and didn't want to admit to something just because she didn't understand the magical laws surrounding it. Besides, it had been a quest. Weren't there different rules for a quest? An unspoken agreement that you didn't describe the details to anyone else? Wasn't she allowed to have trade secrets around her psychic powers?

She kept it as general as she could, watching Julian's face and aura for tells. For what it was that interested him the most. What was he looking for?

"When did your opinion of Tybalt change?" Julian asked.

"It didn't change. I didn't know him, so I didn't really have an opinion. I was just… developing one, I guess."

"You thought he was a competent guide. That was all."

"Yes. I was trying to figure out if he was a practitioner or not. What we could say around him and what we should keep under wraps."

"And your conclusion was?"

"He didn't seem to be surprised at the fact that I thought I had psychic powers. I figured he was open even if he wasn't a practitioner himself."

"You were okay with discussing your plans in front of him."

"Sort of. We didn't discuss anything detailed in front of him. Just the general stuff. And no names. We never asked him… if he'd seen Wilson."

"Do you think you should have?"

"No. I just mean… we didn't see him that way. As a witness. Just as a guide to take us from one part of the park to another."

"And did that change?"

"Not until… later…" Reg thought about how she was going to tell him about the later events. How much should she tell him and what did she need to keep quiet?

"You were satisfied with his services?"

"Sure."

"And what were your feelings about him personally? Didn't you like him?"

Had she given that away in her voice or manner?

"No, he was fine. It's just that… I wasn't feeling very well, and… well, he smelled bad. It made me feel sicker."

He wrote something down. Reg watched his pen move. He was writing down that Tybalt smelled bad?

"I just wasn't feeling well," she repeated.

"It was Hunter who hired him?"

"Yes."

"What did he tell you about Tybalt?"

"That he had… good references. People had recommended him."

"But you were more concerned about his smell."

"You asked me. I was trying to give you some details. That's something I noticed about him. And I didn't want to be around him because of it."

CHAPTER NINETEEN

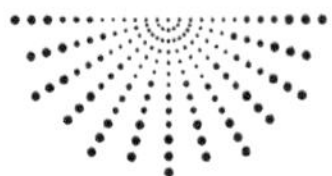

Reg couldn't figure out what Julian was writing down. Why would it make any difference whether she liked Tybalt or not? Or that he smelled bad? It wasn't exactly a confession to having done something heinous in the Everglades.

She had assumed that it was either something to do with Wilson and what had happened when they got him back to Black Sands or something like having stepped on a rare butterfly or trampled a plant worth millions of dollars. She tried to make sense of his questions and predict where he was going.

Julian looked up from his writing and smirked. "Still trying to figure it out?" he teased.

"I just want to know how much longer this is going to take. I don't know how anything I have to say could be of any interest to you."

"You might be surprised."

She hated the smirk. She hated the way that her heart sped up every time he looked at her. And not because she was attracted to him. Just the opposite. She was repelled and wanted to get away from him. She wanted him to take his papers and his smug expression and snide, needling words, and to go away. And never come back.

Reg took a few deep breaths. It wasn't like she was in danger. So far, all he had done was to ask her routine, easy-to-answer questions. It wasn't like when she had been in that room before, the Witch Doctor closing in on her. That had been one of the most terrifying experiences of her life.

But it was also when she had met or been reintroduced to Harrison. And that had been a bright point. She still wasn't sure what she thought of Harrison, but she had an affection for him. He might not always do what she wanted him to—in fact, she wasn't sure he had ever done exactly what she wanted—but he was her godfather, of a sort, and he had protected her when she was most vulnerable. And not only once. Despite his failings and quirks, she couldn't help her warm feelings toward him.

"I like you too," Harrison said, sitting on the edge of the table she and Julian were seated at. Reg and Julian both jumped back, startled by his sudden appearance. Reg should have known better than to think too deeply about him and his protections. She might as well have called his name.

"Who are *you*?" Julian squawked, standing up so fast that his chair clattered to the floor.

"This is Harrison," Reg said calmly, leaning back, overemphasizing how relaxed she was about having Harrison suddenly appear out of thin air.

"Harrison. And who or what are you?" the magical investigator demanded, his voice cracking, giving away his high emotion even though he was doing a good job at smoothing over his facial expression. He was still extremely pale and it was obvious he didn't know how to handle this sudden intrusion.

Then his face grew rigid. He looked at Reg, then back at Harrison. He swallowed hard, his Adam's apple bobbing down and up again. Reg gathered by his reaction that he knew Harrison. She supposed that if there were few immortals left in the world, they might be on some sort of magical endangered species list that Julian referred to regularly.

"I am who and what I am," Harrison said logically, never quite able to catch the nuances of human communications. "Harrison." He cocked his head to the side slightly, studying Julian. He leaned forward, looking even more closely, as if he were putting Julian under a microscope. “You… I have seen before.”

At the annual endangered creatures Christmas party, maybe?

Julian licked his lips.

“No. I would remember you.”

Harrison was hard to forget. His long, lanky body and limbs, his just-slightly-off sense of fashion, currently sporting a red beret and a blue, thick wool coat. And white trousers with black pinstripes. It might have worked for someone else, but the overall effect on Harrison was of a demented French man.

“No. I know you,” Harrison repeated. He rolled his eyes toward the ceiling as if trying to remember when he might have seen Julian before. Dramatic, playing it up. He had probably remembered all of the details as soon as he saw Julian, but he liked to dramatize. “You…” he pointed at Julian, “and you…” he pointed at Reg. “You two were… married?”

Reg was aghast. “Married? No! I’ve never been married. And I certainly would never marry someone like *him*.”

“No? Some other relationship, then.” He shook his head slightly. “Brother?” he asked finally.

“Yes. Sort of. He was a foster brother for a while.” She could understand why Harrison wouldn’t understand the difference between a natural brother and a foster brother. Immortals probably didn’t have an equivalent relationship to compare it to. Even the parent and child relationships seemed to be a little bit screwed up when you started talking about Olympian gods.

“Yes.” Harrison gazed at Julian. “You… were a problem.”

Julian took a step back. As if being one step farther away from Harrison would make any difference. Harrison could transport them all to a different place or time at will. He had the power to do whatever he wanted to.

“I don’t know what you’re talking about. You’re mistaking me for someone else.”

Harrison looked at Reg, raising his eyebrows. “He was, wasn’t he? He used to do things to upset you. Damage you.”

Reg didn’t want to think about it. She had put her former life behind her. She didn't want to be reminded of anything that might have "damaged" her. She looked away.

"I don't know. He wasn't very nice. It's like that sometimes in foster care. Even in natural families. Siblings don't always get along."

Harrison slid off the table and walked around Julian. Julian was tall, but Harrison was taller. He looked down at Julian, who clearly did not like being confronted by someone he had to look up to and was more powerful than he was.

"I told you to leave Reg alone," Harrison said slowly. "Did I not?"

Julian pressed his lips together. He darted a look at Reg. "I have a job to do here. I'm not doing anything to hurt her."

"He's been good so far," Reg confirmed. "I mean, he's been a jerk, but he hasn't done anything to… damage me."

Reg's stomach growled. Maybe a conditioned reaction to Harrison being there. Food was one of the things in the mortal world that interested Harrison. He was always eating around her. Harrison gestured to the small table, and it was suddenly covered with various dishes Reg might be interested in, from chocolate mousse to pizza to some kind of meat in a shape Reg did not recognize and probably did not want to ask about. She picked up a roll and spread some jam on it. Something easy for her stomach, since she didn't usually eat much in the morning. Julian looked at the laden table, then back at Harrison.

"You are… an immortal?" he asked, finally putting all of the clues together.

Harrison shrugged in a way that meant that ought to have been obvious. Julian drew closer to Harrison, fascinated, forgetting his fear of moments before. "An immortal. I've never seen one before. This is very rare. Very exciting."

"Well, you've obviously seen one before, if you met Harrison in the past."

"Well… I didn't know what he was then. I just thought… he was a wizard."

He had known that a magical being protected Reg. Maybe that was the reason he suspected her of having powers herself. It would be a pretty obvious conclusion.

Julian studied Harrison closely. But Reg knew there was nothing particularly odd about how Harrison looked, other than his style of dress. He looked completely human. There were no giveaways that Reg could see that he was another race. But Julian was trained. Maybe he could see something Reg could not.

Maybe he would have known what Tybalt was and not have been taken in by him as Reg had been.

CHAPTER TWENTY

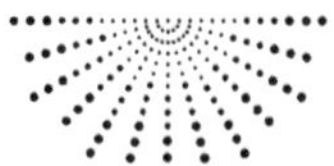

"How did you do that?" Julian asked, pointing at the table. "By all of the laws of physics, creating matter would require a great deal of energy. The law of conservation… this defies explanation. How could you do that without any apparent effort?"

Harrison blinked at him. "Humans are convinced that everything is impossible," he said blandly.

"Well… it kind of is. Where did all of that food come from? Did you transport it from somewhere else? Did you rearrange the atoms already in the room? What is your energy source?"

Harrison looked at Reg, rolling his eyes. "Do you want me to demonstrate making a whole human disappear?"

Reg laughed. "Where would you send him?"

"Where would I send him? Nowhere. I just told you, I will make him disappear."

"But you would have to move him somewhere else, right?"

"I would move him… nowhere."

Julian held up his hands, his face turning red as he choked and tried to find the words to protest. Reg looked at him. Her problem could be gone just like that. He would disappear and she wouldn't have to worry about any more questions or what else he might have in mind.

But there would be others. If one Magical Investigator disappeared, she could only imagine how many of them would descend upon her looking for him. And what kind of charges would she face for being complicit in making him disappear? Or they might think that she had killed him. It would be far worse than the current investigation.

"No... we probably shouldn't do that," she told Harrison gently, hoping he wouldn't be too disappointed. "Let him do what he came for, and then he'll go away on his own."

"I told him to leave you alone once before. He is not obedient."

"It was a long time ago. He probably forgot. And he hasn't hurt me."

Harrison considered this.

"I haven't," Julian choked out in a voice that didn't even pretend not to be scared. "I haven't done anything to hurt her... since that day."

So he *did* remember.

"Humans and their memories," Harrison said, shaking his head, not picking up on the fact that Julian did, in fact, remember. "They are like head cheese."

"Swiss cheese," Reg corrected.

Harrison raised his brows at her. "More like head cheese," he maintained.

"Umm... okay. But I'm fine." She put her hand on his arm to reassure him. "I didn't mean to call for help; I was just remembering when you came here before."

"When you were fighting Destine."

"Yes." Reg glanced aside at Julian, trying to warn Harrison not to say too much.

"Nachos," Harrison mused. He dug into a platter of nachos on the table, strings of gooey cheese dripping down his chin.

Reg waited to see if he would go. He picked at a few more things on the table. Julian didn't seem to be in any great hurry to shoo him out. Harrison was a find for Julian, a new creature to be observed and cataloged.

Eventually, Harrison looked around and, finding nothing to occupy his interest any longer, he vanished.

Julian hurried toward the door, waving his arms in front of him like Harrison might have just become invisible and Julian could catch him before he got out the door. But he didn't encounter anyone in his pathway. The door didn't open. Julian felt the door for some kind of hole or portal, muttering to himself.

"Fascinating," he said, shaking his head and marveling at the experience. "Really, truly fascinating."

"That's Uncle Harrison," Reg said, shrugging.

"*Uncle* Harrison?" Julian gaped at her. "You are part immortal?"

"Oh… he's not a blood relation." As far as Reg knew. "He's just… like my godfather. Someone who helps me out, protects me sometimes." She deliberately didn't reveal that Weston, who she believed to be her father, was also an immortal.

Julian gazed at the table full of food. Sometimes Harrison vanished the food that he apparated, but sometimes he left it behind. Reg was still hungry so, like a daddy bird, he had apparently provided for his fledgling and then flown away.

She picked up a muffin. Blueberry. She had really liked the blueberry muffins that Erin had made when Reg had visited her in Bald Eagle Falls. Big, plump, juicy blueberries in them, not those hard little nuggets of pseudo-blueberry that bakers sometimes tried to pass off as the real thing. The muffin was still warm. Reg didn't know if, as Julian said, Harrison had brought the food there from somewhere else, as he did when Reg had told him about Uncle Mike's ribs, or whether he had conjured them out of nothing, but they wouldn't stay warm forever. She broke the muffin open and dropped a large pat of butter into the steaming muffin.

"If you're hungry, help yourself," Reg told Julian. "I'm not going to eat it all."

He considered the bounty from different angles as if he might find that it was just an illusion or stage prop. "Do you think it's safe?"

Reg stopped mid-bite. She snorted. "Is it safe?" she repeated around the large bite of muffin. She chewed and swallowed, washing it down with a drink of milk. "Would I be eating it if it wasn't safe?"

"You might be one of them. Maybe it's fine for you, but for me, it would…" Julian cast around for something creative. "If you eat food in the underworld, it binds you there."

"You're not in the underworld."

"But maybe it could bind me here."

"Aren't you already bound to this world?"

Eventually, Julian nodded. He helped himself to a bear claw. "This… nice of your godfather to supply all of this food."

"He can be handy to have around."

Julian ate a few bites of the bear claw before sitting down and trying to clear more space for himself and his yellow legal pad.

"You remember meeting him before?" Reg asked.

His pale complexion had returned to normal, but at Reg's question, he flushed.

"I… don't know. Maybe. It was a long time ago, and we were just kids. I'm not always sure what I remember from back then and what I've just made up to fill in the holes."

"Yeah." Reg nodded. "I just try to forget all that stuff."

"That stuff?"

"Foster care. Anything else… unpleasant from when I was a kid. Or even later. I guess I didn't change much as an adult either. I'd rather not think about unpleasant stuff."

"Which brings us back to your trip to the Everglades."

He sat with pen poised, ready to make more notes.

"It wasn't that unpleasant," Reg said. "Some of it was nice. I mean, it's beautiful out there… some parts of it. And… interesting."

"What happened the first night?"

Reg tried to think of what to say.

"The truth," Julian prompted. "I'll know if you lie to me."

But Reg didn't think he was a diviner, like Damon. She was a pretty accomplished liar. He might know if he had evidence to the contrary, but if he weren't a diviner, she figured she could probably tell a convincing tale and he would believe her.

"We set up camp. Went to bed."

"Ah, you were camping. Not staying at a hotel?"

"I guess they don't have any that are actually in the park. And if you have to add all that time going back and forth to get there... Damon figured it was better if we just camped over in the park."

Reg wondered if they had somehow damaged a plant where they had set up camp. They hadn't lit a fire because of how wet everything was. There was really no dry firewood. Reg could have lit a fire anyway, but she didn't want to get in trouble and wasn't supposed to be "playing with fire" without Davyn's supervision.

"You brought all of your camping gear."

"I didn't have anything. Damon didn't tell me that it was a camping trip, so I was kind of out of luck. But when I opened my bag... there was a sleeping bag in it. That kind that crushes up really small, so you can carry it anywhere."

"Who put it there?"

"I didn't know for sure. I thought maybe it was Tybalt. Corvin and Damon had said they didn't have any extras, and I was with them all the time. Tybalt was the only one who had separated during the lunch break, so I thought he must have gone shopping during that time."

"And how did that affect your feelings about him?"

"I thought it was really nice of him. That even though we hadn't really talked to each other, it was nice of him to have done something like that for me and he didn't even mention it."

"Did you thank him?"

"Corvin said I shouldn't. That since Tybalt didn't present it to me, there might be awkwardness if I said anything to him. He's the one who understands magical etiquette, not me, so I assumed he knew what he was talking about."

"And what happened that night?"

Reg shrugged. "We went to bed."

"And what happened? Something happened, because in the morning, you were gone, and your companions reported you missing, saying you must have wandered in your sleep."

"Well, we found each other again."

"Apparently."

Julian waited for an explanation. Reg wasn't sure she wanted to tell him anything about her disappearance.

"And at that point, you apparently decided to seek another guide instead of Tybalt."

"I did? I wasn't there, remember?"

"It wasn't your choice to switch guides?"

"No."

"Where were you? Clearly, you had not wandered into the swamp."

"Well, I woke up somewhere other than the camp."

"Where?"

"Some other place in the swamp. So I guess you're wrong; I *did* wander off."

"Did you?" His eyes were sharp.

Reg said nothing. It was time for him to fill the silence. To tell her what he knew. Was this part of the reason she was being investigated? For what had happened that night?

"Where did Tybalt go?"

"I wasn't there," Reg repeated.

"You and Tybalt both disappeared at the same time. I assume that means that you left together."

"I think he left before we made camp. Before we went to sleep, anyway. He didn't stay with us."

"But he retired nearby. You didn't expect him to take his boat and abandon your company. He was supposed to be guiding you the next day too, wasn't he?"

"You would have to ask Damon or Corvin. I didn't make the arrangements. I was just riding along to provide my services when they were required."

"He was supposed to stay with you for the entire trip," he maintained. "But that obviously is not what happened. What made him change his mind? Or what made your company decide not to keep him on?"

"Like I said, talk to the others."

"I think you know."

"What makes you think that?"

"Because you disappeared at the same time."

"You don't know that. You don't know what happened that night."

CHAPTER TWENTY-ONE

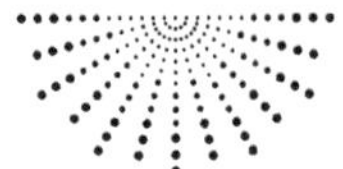

Julian shook his head. "I think I do. And I know you do. Quit pretending you don't know what happened to Tybalt."

"What happened to Tybalt?" Reg echoed.

"You know what happened to him. I want to hear you say it."

"Tybalt disappeared. When Damon and Corvin got up in the morning, he was gone."

"And so were you."

"And I eventually met up with them again. Tybalt didn't. So they had to get a new guide."

"What happened to Tybalt?"

"I guess he had a change of heart. Decided he had a better gig somewhere else. How would I know?"

"Because you were with him."

"No."

It was a bald-faced lie, but Reg held his gaze steadily, counting the seconds until she let her eyes slide away. Long enough to be taken for sincerity. Not long enough for him to think she was being aggressive or evasive.

"Are you a shapeshifter?"

That one blew Reg out of the water. She choked on a piece of muffin. "What? A shapeshifter?" She coughed and took a drink of orange juice. "Is there even such a thing?"

"I haven't seen one—that I know of—but that doesn't mean that they don't exist. Many of the creatures that we have cataloged and tracked through the MI databases are things I have never seen."

"Well… no, I'm not a shapeshifter." Reg laughed. "Is that what you came here to ask me?"

"You were with Tybalt. I'm sure of it. The evidence all indicates that you were."

"Say what you like; that doesn't make it true. I can't change into other forms. Like what? I can't even imagine what you think I changed into."

"A panther. Mountain lion."

"A panther? No." She gave him a guileless look. "That would really be something. A mountain lion in the middle of the Everglades? That would be weird."

"There are panthers in the Everglades. The Florida panther is an endangered species. There are still a few of them left in the protected areas."

"And you think I killed one of these panthers?"

"What makes you say that?" Julian questioned, confused.

"Well, you said they were endangered, And you said that you were with something like the endangered species department. So I assume this is what you were talking about. Someone hurt one of your panthers and you're trying to figure out who."

"No. No one hurt one of the remaining panthers." He spoke slowly and clearly, enunciating his words and being sure not to say one of "his" panthers. "But there are indications that a panther was involved, which is why I asked you if you could shift into a panther."

"Oh. Well, the answer is still no. I didn't change into a panther and hurt—" Reg cut herself off quickly, "or hurt anyone."

He sat there looking at her, his eyes triumphant. Of course he knew what she had almost said. *And hurt Tybalt.* And she hadn't. She had not, definitely not, turned into a panther and hurt Tybalt. She didn't have the ability to shift into anything other than herself.

"You know what happened to Tybalt," Julian said.

Reg shrugged. "What happened to Tybalt?"

"He was killed."

"Killed?" Reg widened her eyes as far as she could. "I thought he just took off. Who killed him? That's horrible."

"I think you did."

Reg made a noise of disgust. "Me? Why would I kill him?"

"Maybe you want to take the opportunity to explain it to me. Give me your story first; get out ahead of this thing."

"Why would I kill our guide? That's ridiculous."

"You and he both disappeared. And only you came back."

"So? Just because he disappeared, that doesn't mean I had anything to do with it. He could be anywhere."

But he had said there was a panther involved in Tybalt's death. He wasn't just assuming that something had happened to Tybalt because he had disappeared. He already knew Tybalt was dead.

"You killed him because you discovered he was a swamp goblin."

"A what?" Reg let her jaw drop open.

"I don't need to repeat myself. You found out what he was, and you decided that his life wasn't worth anything. You didn't want to be traveling with a swamp goblin. You decided he was evil and needed to be eliminated, so you waited until everyone had fallen asleep, and then you did it."

"Did what?"

"Killed him."

But Tybalt hadn't been killed near their camp, and Julian knew it. Julian knew there had to be something in between. Reg would have to have lured him away. And Julian knew that it hadn't been Reg who had lured Tybalt because Tybalt had been killed in his own lair, not close to their campsite.

"I killed him. Let me get this straight. I didn't like him because he was a goblin. So I waited until everyone was asleep, and then I shifted into a panther, went to his campsite, and killed him?"

Julian watched her carefully. He was going to have to be highly skilled to see past her deceptions. And he was going to have to try a whole lot harder to catch her in a lie.

"Why don't you tell me how it happened, then?"

Reg shrugged. "I walked in my sleep. I woke up in another part of the swamp, didn't know where I was. It took all day to get back to civilization and contact the guys. They picked me up." She shrugged. "And that was that. We went on with our search."

"And you never asked them what had happened to Tybalt?"

"They said he took off. They got a new guide."

"You just took their word for it."

"Why wouldn't I?"

"You didn't look into it yourself? Ask questions?"

"No. Why would I? Corvin was in charge of finding a guide. It wasn't anything to do with my role."

Julian leaned forward. "What gifts do you have?"

Reg shifted back, keeping a bubble of space between them. "That's a personal question. I thought it wasn't polite to ask."

"We are beyond being polite. This is a magical investigation."

"That doesn't mean anything to me. I'm not really magical, just psychic."

"Gifts are gifts. You are a witch."

"A psychic," Reg insisted.

"You have a lot more power than any other psychic I've ever met."

"So? I'm good at what I do. What's that to you?"

"Tell me about your powers. You predict the future?"

"Sometimes."

"Find lost items? Or people?"

"Yes."

"What else? Can you move physical objects?"

Reg hesitated. Julian waited.

"No."

"No? Why didn't you answer right away? Because you *can* move items telekinetically?"

"No. And I don't want to play twenty questions about my gifts. I'm a psychic. That's what you know."

"I don't think that's the whole story."

"That's your problem."

"Can you talk to animals?"

Reg narrowed her eyes at him, thinking about it. "Anyone can talk to animals," she pointed out.

"Let me rephrase. Can you talk to animals in a way that they understand? And can you understand them?"

"I have a cat. He comes when I call him—sometimes—and I know when he wants to be fed or to play. So yeah, I guess I can."

"More than that. Can you understand their thoughts?"

Reg lifted her hands, palms up. "Sometimes. Can't you?"

"No. I can't."

Reg sat back, considering him. "But you can't understand the thoughts of other people either, can you? They're a mystery to you."

"I have been trained in recognizing deception."

Yet he hadn't called Reg on hers.

"But you can't put yourself into someone else's place. Get inside their head." Reg pushed harder. "You don't have any idea what I'm thinking about right now."

Julian's face tightened. "I'm good at my job."

"And I'm good at mine. I can read you, but you can't read me."

And what she read were not happy thoughts. He stared at her, jaw tight, eyes blazing. His aura was red.

Reg didn't remember much about him from when they were young, but she remembered his anger. She'd known to avoid him when he was angry.

Julian held his pen like a weapon. Did he intend to stab her with it? Or to use it as a wand to channel some kind of spell or curse at her? Either way, she could see how close to the edge Julian was. She couldn't push him any further without putting herself in danger.

CHAPTER TWENTY-TWO

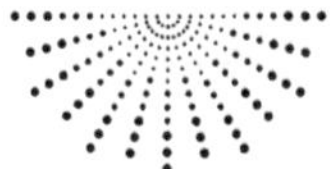

Reg said nothing. Julian looked down at his notes, struggling to keep himself under control. He looked back at her after a few minutes.

"Could you command a cat to attack?"

Reg chuckled. "I don't think you know cats very well. You really can't command them to do anything."

"Was this your first visit to the Everglades?"

"Yes."

"When did you decide to kill Tybalt?"

Reg massaged the space between her eyebrows. "Look, if he was a goblin, then why does it matter? I would think that goblins would have a lot of enemies. What makes you think that I had something to do with his death?"

"Swamp goblins are an endangered species." Julian was back to over-enunciating his words. "They are protected. The death of any swamp goblin is fully investigated and we evaluate what measures need to be taken to prevent it from happening again. And what consequences need to be imposed on the perpetrator."

"What consequences? What are you going to do if it was just a natural enemy?"

"Goblins have few predators other than humans."

"And panthers, apparently," Reg pointed out.

Julian glared at her. "Swamp goblins and panthers have lived together in the Everglades for hundreds of years. I'm not aware of any other cases of a panther attacking a goblin."

"Then maybe... there's no other prey around and it was desperate. Or maybe it was a mama with cubs and she thought the babies were in danger. Or maybe you just never heard of any before because there aren't many goblins around now."

"There were signs of a human at the scene. Things had been disturbed. There were indications of magic having been used. You were there."

Reg thought quickly about what things might have given her away at the scene. She had not been able to take anything with her; there were no personal possessions at the scene. It wasn't like she had gone willingly. The only items she could think of that she had left behind were the ropes that had bound her. But if they saw those ropes, they would know that she'd been there against her will and had only been protecting herself.

Did the magical laws allow for self-defense? Reg wasn't willing to guess after what Corvin had said. She couldn't assume that the magical rules were the same as the laws of the land. No one had given her any warnings before she went to the Everglades. She knew some of the magical world's mores, like reading someone's thoughts without their permission. Now she had to worry about whether the creatures who attacked her were endangered? What about Corvin? She had been told that his magical bloodline was dying out. Did that mean that she couldn't protect herself against him too? How far would the rule be taken?

"I don't know how you would make a panther attack a goblin," she said with a shrug, returning to the line of questioning that Julian had been following earlier. "Good luck figuring that out. Why is it that sometimes a cat will chase a catnip mouse and sometimes it won't? They have their own minds."

"You think that this panther just decided to attack a swamp goblin. For no reason."

"No. I gave you some reasons. I guess you didn't like them."

"You are trying to avoid the question."

"What question? I think I've answered all of them."

"The question of why you killed Tybalt."

"Well, you're going to have to go back to Magical Investigations without the answer to that one. I've told you everything I can. I don't know what else I can do for you."

Julian stood. He leaned over the table laden with food, pointing his pen at her, his face turning red again. "I know you, Reg Rawlins. You can't lie to me. I came here to get answers to these questions and you'd better cooperate!"

"I have cooperated. Now I think it's time to go. We're just going to keep going in circles, and I don't have anything to share with you."

"How did you get back to civilization to find your friends? It's like a labyrinth out there. If you don't know the swamp, you could wander for days. People do wander for days. And then they die."

"And you'd be happier if I had just died? I just kept going. I found a couple of homes, which led me to a larger settlement where I was able to get my hands on a phone. That's it. Nothing special. I didn't use my magical guidance system if that's what you're asking."

"You are making light of something very serious."

"I don't know what else to do. What you're asking is ridiculous. You expect me to just tell you that I happened to kill this goblin because I decided I didn't like goblins, and I commanded a panther to kill it, and then what, I transported myself out of the Everglades telekinetically. Is that it? Does that cover all of the points?"

"Quit playing games with me."

"I don't play games," Reg said coldly. "And I don't like being accused of something you can't even back up. You thought you could come out here and get some story out of me because you knew me back when we were kids? Because you bullied me back then and you figured you could bully me into confessing whatever you wanted now? I'm stronger than I was then. So don't try it."

He looked triumphant. "You admit you have powers."

Reg vacillated between telling him she was powerful so that he would be afraid and back off, and telling him, as she previously had, that she had practically no powers, in the hopes that he'd give up on her as a suspect and leave her alone.

"You can't bully me," she said instead, not giving him an answer one way or the other. "I'm not a little kid anymore."

He pointed the pen at her with a sudden jerk, and it appeared to channel electricity toward her like a lightning bolt. Reg nearly fell out of her chair dodging out of the way. She put a psychic shield up in an instant—something that she should have done before—and snatched the pen out of his hand.

"What did I just say?" she demanded.

Julian looked at her wordlessly, his body vibrating with anger or the unspent energy he had been channeling. His face was suffused with blood. Even his eyes had turned red, giving him a demonic look. Reg kept the shield up around her.

"Who do I report you to?"

"You don't report me to anyone. I am the one who reports you," he snapped.

"You must have a boss. There must be some kind of process for complaints."

"You don't have anything to complain about."

"You're allowed to shoot lightning bolts at me?"

"It's your word against mine. Who are they going to believe? The witch who just killed a swamp goblin against magical laws, or the investigator they trained and trust?"

"They'll believe me. I'm sure it's not the first time you've stepped over the line."

She read guilt in his features and was satisfied that she was correct on this point. Of course Julian wouldn't be able to follow all of the rules and would have stepped over the line in his enthusiastic pursuit of justice. That was the kind of guy he was. Some cops joined the force because they wanted to help people and do good, and some wanted the power and authority over others, to be able to beat down the lawbreakers. She knew which camp Julian fell into. And he had never been able to follow all of the rules.

"We're done," she told him. "I hope you're ready to explain to your superiors exactly what happened. If not, you'd better start thinking up your story."

She turned her back on him, being sure to keep her shield in place, and walked out of the room. She heard Julian moving, knew that he was looking for something to use as a weapon against her. She continued to move, presenting him with her back and letting him know that she wasn't afraid of him. That would be the thing that galled him the most, that he hadn't even cowed her with his threats.

She walked quickly down the empty hall where she had once encountered Harrison, but he wasn't there this time and she didn't want to call him. She had handled her own problem. She didn't need anyone else to help her out. Then through the door back into the public face of The Crystal Bowl.

There were a few more people gathered now. Late breakfasters or early lunchers. A person or two drinking at the bar, maybe drunks or maybe just starting their day with an orange juice or a mimosa. Reg wasn't hungry after the muffin and the other food she had picked at, but she lingered for a moment, looking around. The restaurant was a warm, safe, familiar place, and she wasn't quite ready to walk out into the open, unprotected outdoors. Maybe she would stop for a drink—just something small to clear her head and relax her.

"Reg. Hey."

Reg turned her head and saw Davyn approaching. He was dressed for his day job—as an accountant, or whatever he was, he wore dress slacks, a white shirt, and a tie rather than his wizarding robes.

"Hey."

"How are you?" Davyn greeted. "We need to set up an appointment for a training session. I'm sure you're eager to get back at it."

Reg nodded. "Yeah, of course. I don't have my schedule here…" She was too lazy to put it into her phone and relied solely on the hard copy datebook at the cottage. "But if you give me a call when I'm at home, we'll figure out what works."

Davyn was her mentor, another firecaster. While she hadn't initially thought much of him as the leader of Corvin's coven, she had grown to respect him and enjoyed the lessons he taught her about how to use her power. She would have liked to be able to move faster and do more with her fire, but he kept her moving at a slow plod, encouraging her to practice each skill until she was proficient, but only in their time together. He said it was too dangerous for her to practice alone yet; she might end up burning the house down. They were friends now, or something like it, even though she couldn't imagine herself being friends with him under any other circumstances. He just wasn't her type. Rule-oriented, careful, always in charge, all the things that drove Reg crazy in a relationship.

"You've been following the rules?" Davyn asked, studying Reg carefully. "Even though we haven't been able to get together in the last little while, you still need to be sure to follow the rules I've given you."

"Yeah, of course."

"You haven't used your fire at all since we last met?"

Reg tried to remember how long ago it had been. She had definitely used her fire since then, but she hadn't had any choice. And it hadn't all been intentional.

"Uh…"

He gave her a look. "Reg…?"

"When we were in the Everglades, I used it for light. You said I could do that when we were going to the mountains."

He nodded slowly. "Yes. That should be fine. As long as you are careful. Did you light the campfire too?"

"No, we didn't have one. Everything was so wet that we didn't even try. Though I bet I could have lit one, no matter how wet the wood was."

"Yes, you probably could," Davyn agreed. This made Reg feel warm and validated. Like he'd just told her how well she was doing. "And is that all?"

"Uh… yes… I had trouble, though. I went to the opening ceremonies for the Spring Games."

He nodded immediately. "And they had a fireworks display."

"Yeah."

"We should talk about that, do some exercises. I can give you some pointers on controlling yourself in a situation like that. Were you… okay? I didn't hear about any incidents."

"I was there with Sarah." Reg wrinkled her nose. "She made me drink until I practically drowned."

He chuckled. "Not the most pleasant remedy. But it does work."

"Kept me from lighting anything on fire."

They both smiled and shook their heads. Reg wondered how many times Davyn had to go through a similar exercise. While he was very strong and well-conditioned, she imagined that when he was a youngster, he might have been put through it at some point.

Davyn looked over Reg's shoulder. Turning, she saw that he had spotted Julian, who was coming out of the door she had just used.

"Who is that?"

"Oh. Uh…" As Julian drew closer to Reg, then slowed, seeing that she was with someone else, Reg motioned to him, making introductions. "This is Julian Sabat. Julian, this is Davyn Smithy; he's the leader of the warlock coven here. Or one of them."

Julian's eyes went from Reg to Davyn. He gave a brief nod of greeting

Reg tried to warn Davyn with her eyes not to say anything about their mentor-mentee relationship. She thought it clearly, trying to push the words into his head. *Don't mention firecasting.*

Davyn gave Reg an uncertain look and she wasn't sure whether he had gotten the message or not.

"What brings you to Black Sands?" Davyn asked politely. "Are you here for the Spring Games?"

Reg broke away from them. The best thing was for her to just leave Julian behind. Davyn would engage him in polite small talk for at least a few minutes, giving Reg the chance to get back to her cottage.

CHAPTER TWENTY-THREE

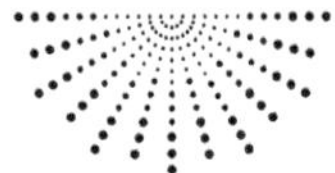

Reg was glad that she had insisted on taking her own car. In a couple of minutes, she was home. It took three tries to get her key to work in the lock. She concentrated on it hard, trying to encourage the lock to just release, and in a few moments, the key turned of its own accord and she was in. Reg stepped in and pushed the door shut behind her. She twisted the deadbolt, something she didn't usually do during the day. But Sarah would have to deal with it. Reg wasn't going to leave it unlocked while Julian Sabat was running around free.

Starlight greeted her with trilling meows and jumped onto the table to nudge the mini terrarium Reg had made the night before. It was lying on its side. Reg picked it up and looked at it. Surprisingly, she could already see the first leaves sprouting up through the dirt. Maybe she shouldn't be surprised. She had been assisted by a garden gnome, after all. She knew the kind of magic that Forst had performed in Sarah's garden. In mere days, it had gone from neglected and broken-down to one of the most beautiful gardens Reg had seen. Forst still worked on it regularly. Reg didn't know how many other gardens in Black Sands Forst worked on. He must earn his living from more than one little plot. But he seemed to be there every day and at random moments through the night.

Zinnia was a garden gnome and clearly, she had those same powers. She had helped feed the seed just the right soil and given it just the right amount of water to drink. A few words of a spell or whatever other magic Zinnia had performed, and of course it would begin growing immediately.

Reg meditated for a few minutes, focused on the little leaves of the seedling. It seemed to grow before her eyes. Reg put it back down. There had only been two leaves when she had picked it up, but now there were several. It was growing at a remarkable rate. Maybe even faster than normal gnome magic.

She turned it around several times and could see white roots against the edges of the cup. Could it have grown that many roots so soon? Shouldn't the root system reflect the same amount of growth as above the surface?

She picked the terrarium up and left the cottage, going around the back to the garden. She looked around for Forst. He could sometimes be hard to find, even with his red cap among the greenery. She reached out to him mentally, projecting her words to him.

Forst? Are you here?

There was movement to her right, and then she saw him. Forst bowed deeply. *I am honored, Reg Rawlins.*

Hi. I brought something for Sarah's garden. Reg held the little terrarium toward him. *I don't know if it is the type of plant that wants to go in this garden, you'll have to ask it.*

Forst, of course, knew and talked to his plants all the time. He said that they had feelings, and Reg had no doubt that he could have told her what any of the plants in the garden required for light, water, and nutrients.

Forst took the small terrarium from her carefully. He gave a crusty smile. *Is this one of Zinnia's?*

Yes, how did you know?

She was doing them at the equinox celebration.

Yes. Were you there?

No. I don't go... too many people. Loud voices. He shook his head as if pained. *Not good for gnomen.*

Zinnia seemed to enjoy it.

She is much better with humans and outside words.

Reg nodded.

Forst looked back down at the little plant. *But you did not plant this at the equinox celebration.*

Yes.

He shook his head, studying the growth. *This is six… seven days' growth.*

No. I just planted it yesterday. You can ask Zinnia.

He brought it right up to his eyes to look at it. *It will need to be transplanted soon. The roots are overgrown.*

I noticed that. I don't know why they're growing so much faster than the top.

Forst sighed. *There is much going on in Black Sands. Many magicals… they upset the balance.*

And equinox is supposed to be a time of balance.

He nodded and gestured to the garden. *You see how wild it is right now. Very unruly. I should be planting, but with everything disrupted… it would not be good.*

It looked perfectly fine to Reg. *Can you plant this one? Before it gets too big for the terrarium?*

Yes. Of course. I will find out where it wants to be planted.

Great. Thanks. So… are Fir and Zinnia…?

He raised bushy gray and white eyebrows at her. *Are they…?*

Are they together? In a relationship?

Oh. We do not… discuss such things.

Not at all? You and he are twins.

Still. We do not. If they announce their nuptials… He shrugged. *Then we know.*

Gnomes don't discuss it with anyone if they're dating? Gnomen, I mean, Reg made the effort to refer to Forst's race with his own language. *If they are seeing each other, they do it without anyone knowing?*

Gnomen be private creatures.

Yes, I guess so. I shouldn't ask you about your family, then? I didn't know whether you are a bachelor, or…

Forst handed the terrarium to Reg. He took out his curvy pipe and tamped tobacco down into the bowl. He lit it and took a long draw on the smoke, puffing it back out in rings.

That's so cool, Reg told him.

He gave her a smile and a sideways look. *Am not a bachelor,* he told her.

Oh. So you have a wife? Any children?

We have kindern, he agreed. *One set. Boy and girl. And our kindern have kindern.*

She remembered that the gnomes always had twins. *So you are a grandpa! How many grandchildren do you have? Four?*

His eyes twinkled. *Six!*

Six!

My son. His wife has two sets! Very productive. He chuckled to himself.

Well. The gnomen race won't be dying out soon with numbers like that.

He nodded his agreement. For a few minutes, they just stood there looking at the garden, Forst smoking his pipe and Reg holding the plant. Eventually, Forst was finished. He put the pipe carefully back away and took the plant from her. *Thank you. I will find a place for your seedling.*

Reg gave a little bow, sensing that he was ready to get back to his work. *Thank you. If you see Zinnia, you can tell her how well it is doing.*

CHAPTER TWENTY-FOUR

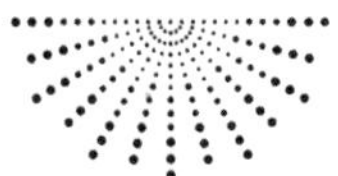

Reg hoped that Julian would go back to Magical Investigations to report his failure to find anything out from her. They would decide that the investigation wasn't going anywhere and would let it go cold. Or they would send another investigator out instead, one that Reg didn't have a personal relationship with and could feel more comfortable with. Someone who would explain to her exactly what was going on and work with her rather than making accusations and threats. Because Reg hadn't done anything wrong. Protecting herself against a goblin that had targeted her could not be against the law.

Someone tried to open the front door, and then there was a knock. Reg got up from the couch, yawning, and went to see who it was. Starlight trotted over to the door to welcome the new arrival, so Reg had a pretty good idea that it wasn't anyone to be worried about. Starlight had good instincts about who was safe and who was not.

Looking through the peephole, she saw it was Sarah. Sarah had the key for the deadbolt, of course, but she probably understood that Reg locking the door was counter to her usual practices and meant she didn't want anyone walking in on her. Sarah had managed to interrupt a couple of Reg's sessions in the past, and that wasn't good business. An interruption could completely derail a reading or seance.

Reg unlocked the door and let Sarah in. She shut it and relocked it. "I'm not locking you out," she explained. "I just don't trust Julian Sabat."

"Of course not," Sarah agreed. She went over to Reg's datebook to skim through it and added a couple of new notations. "You're okay for me to add a few appointments, as long as they don't interfere with the Games?"

"Sure. I'm not even sure that I'm going to go to many of the Games. I don't want to run into Julian again. Or more fireworks."

"It's an opportunity you don't want to miss. Who knows when they will ever be held in town again? They move all over the world. It's very special to have them held here."

"Do you think it is worth it? With the negative stuff that is going on right now? The imbalance?"

"Oh, I don't think it's that bad. I haven't heard of any negative effects."

"Forst was just complaining about the garden and how wild it is when it's supposed to be balanced and peaceful and ready for seeds right now."

"Forst was complaining? The man never says a peep."

"Not aloud, maybe. But telepathically."

"Yes, I suppose. Well, you know how sensitive gnomes are. They will always have something to complain about with their gardens. You remember how upset he was about the key that he found buried out there." Sarah made a motion toward the back of the lot and rolled her eyes.

Reg couldn't exactly forget.

And Forst had been right about that dark key. Reg had been taken in by it, and the consequences had been much worse than Sarah would ever know.

"Yes… so you don't think there is anything to be worried about? All of those protesters that were there…"

"People will protest anything. It's their way of celebrating and proving that they aren't just sheep. Even though they follow each other like sheep. Half the time they don't even know why they are there. Whoever is in charge hands out the signs, and everyone marches around protesting something they didn't even know about before."

Reg nodded. She wondered which were true—that the Spring Games were causing a magical disruption in Black Sands, or that everything was in harmony as it should be?

With the way she had been feeling lately, anxious and unable to sleep, she had to think that it was the former. But maybe that wasn't because of the Spring Games. Maybe that was because of Julian Sabat. Maybe she had known he was there to cause trouble for her even before he had first appeared. Her body had remembered his presence from back when she was a child.

"Is there somewhere I can direct a complaint about Julian Sabat and the way he's treating me during this investigation?" she asked Sarah. "The guy is driving me crazy, and he's not being professional at all. Shot me with some kind of lightning bolt today." She took his pen out of her pocket and looked at it, as if visual examination might prove that it were something other than a regular pen. But it looked like a perfectly normal ballpoint to her. Sarah peered at it.

"I can pass the word along for you. It will have more of an impact coming from an old crone like me than a phone call from someone who is being investigated."

"Okay." Reg didn't object to Sarah's use of the phrase "old crone," knowing it was used as a term of respect for an experienced witch like Sarah. Most of the time. "I'd really appreciate that. If they can call him off, that would be great."

"Do you know what it is they've got their shorts in a knot over?"

"Something that happened in the Everglades," Reg said vaguely. "There was a swamp goblin."

"A swamp goblin." Sarah made a face. "Nasty creatures. Why anyone would *not* want that race to become extinct, I don't know."

Reg nodded. "Exactly. Why are they bugging me about it?"

"They have their reasons. But swamp goblins…" Sarah shook her head. "What did you tell Julian?"

"Nothing, really. I just said I didn't know what had happened."

"And how much do you know?"

Reg raised her eyebrow and didn't tell Sarah any details.

"Nothing," Sarah confirmed with a nod. "Got it."

Reg's phone rang. She looked at the screen and saw that it was Davyn. She motioned to her appointment book. "When is my next opening?"

Sarah flipped pages. "Tomorrow afternoon. Unless you want to do something tonight. And I assume you would rather attend the Games…?"

"Tomorrow afternoon." Reg swiped her phone to answer the call. "Hey. Davyn."

"Reg!" Davyn's voice was different. Bouncier and more cheerful than usual. "Are you home?"

"Yeah. My next opening is tomorrow afternoon. Is that good?"

"Perfect. Three?"

Reg looked at the page Sarah had open. There was nothing written in the block for three o'clock.

"Yes. That looks good."

"We're on, then."

"What's up?" Reg asked. "You sound… I don't know. Excited. Something going on?"

"No, nothing." Davyn let the words sit for only a fraction of a second before contradicting himself. "That friend of yours. Julian. What a charming fellow."

Reg swallowed. "Charming? Really? I don't think I would have used that word."

"He is. We had a very nice chat. He has led a fascinating life."

What exactly had Julian told Davyn about his life? Had he mentioned being in foster care? Knowing Reg? Or had he made a bunch of stuff up? What exactly would Davyn find interesting?

"He's not exactly a friend," she told Davyn cautiously.

"No, I understand that, but the two of you seem to get along well enough."

Reg looked at Sarah, who, although pretending not to eavesdrop, could clearly hear Davyn's voice from the phone. Sarah gave her head a little shake.

"He's not the kind of guy I would get too close to," Reg cautioned, trying to pull Davyn back.

"We're going to meet for drinks later," Davyn said, oblivious to her warning.

Reg sighed. "Okay. Well, I'll see you tomorrow afternoon."

* * *

Reg slept better that night after attending some of the Spring Games with Sarah. She was exhausted after several nights of poor sleep and dealing with Julian.

The Games were interesting. She was glad she had let Sarah talk her into going. Reg had seen magic acts before, always trying to spot the sleight of hand and figure out how each of the tricks was performed.

It was different to watch the Games and believe that what she was seeing was real. Maybe some of it was. But all of it? It all seemed so unbelievable. People and objects appearing and disappearing, being transformed before her eyes. Moving across the table or the stage. Most of the magic that she had seen since her move to Black Sands had been understated, things that were hidden or difficult to see. The showy magical performances had been very different. More like what she had seen from Harrison.

The air buzzed with magic and it seemed to take a lot out of Reg to watch it. She was inordinately tired after a few performances. She wasn't the only one, as she saw a number of the members of the audience snoozing in their seats. Reg didn't want to be vulnerable, dropping off in public where she was an easy target for anyone. Or to be more exact, an easy target for Julian or Corvin.

"I don't like to leave early," Reg told Sarah, "But do you think if there's an intermission, we could sneak out?" She rubbed her eyes. "I know it's still early, but I'm really wiped."

Sarah looked toward the field, then nodded. "Of course."

"If you want to stay, I can take an Uber. You don't have to drive me."

"I have seen most of this before. There is only so much you can do to show magic off visually, and one does get tired of all of the conjuring and telekinesis." She made a gesture toward the field. "You could do most of what they are showing off."

"No, I couldn't."

"You have done much of it already. It wouldn't be hard for you if you tried some of the other bits."

"But I don't really do magic. I'm just a psychic."

Sarah smiled. "Yes, dear. Well, there are two more heats, and then we will be able to sneak out."

"Great." Reg rubbed her eyes and watched the witches and warlocks gathering on the field.

CHAPTER TWENTY-FIVE

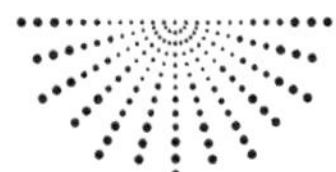

Davyn was more animated than Reg had ever seen him before when he showed up for their appointment. While he had her demonstrate her skills and gave her new exercises to do, he chattered on about his conversation the night before with Julian. They had apparently gone to the Games together and then stayed up talking most of the night. Davyn had a day job to go to, so Reg didn't imagine he'd gotten very much sleep between the late-night visit and going to the office. And with a three o'clock afternoon appointment with Reg, he would have had to leave the office early. But maybe he was senior enough to dictate his own hours. Or he had taken the week off for the Spring Games. Reg imagined a number of people had probably done that. Maybe some of the local offices had even closed during the Games to allow their employees to attend.

"You know I don't like Julian, don't you?" Reg asked finally, after Davyn dropped yet another "Julian said."

He looked at her. For a minute, he didn't say anything. He looked away, frowning. "I really think you should give him another chance," he said finally. "He's a good guy."

Reg shook her head. "No, he's not."

"You don't know him like I do—"

"You've known him for a day! I've lived with the guy."

"That was when you were kids. It was a long time ago. He could have changed during that time."

"You have no idea what kind of person he is. He hasn't changed. I've seen him, I've talked with him. Not as much as you have, maybe, but enough to know that he *hasn't* changed, not one bit."

Davyn opened his mouth to argue.

"Okay, maybe he's gotten sneakier. Maybe he's able to charm people better now than he could when we were kids, but he's still the same guy."

"I think you're misjudging him," Davyn said earnestly. "You're adversarial because he's investigating you. But there's no reason to be that way. He's just trying to find out the truth. He doesn't have an agenda. He's not out to get you."

Reg shook her head, her lip curling in distaste. "I know Julian. You don't. And you haven't been in the room when he's been interviewing me. There's a reason I'm 'adversarial.'"

Davyn rubbed his chin. "Maybe you *should* have someone in the room. A witness, and someone who can give you some advice and insight. It's hard to see things clearly when you're so close to it all."

The flames in Reg's hands flared up, causing them both to flinch back, despite being firecasters.

"Stay in control," Davyn warned.

Maybe that was it. Maybe he was just trying to provoke her to see if she could keep her attention and control. It wouldn't be the first time he'd resorted to something like that. Reg hoped that was the case, rather than that he just really liked Julian and wanted them to be friends.

Reg focused, trying to let go of her feelings about Julian and the way Davyn was poking at her emotions and to focus only on the flame. She stared into the dark center of the ball of fire, feeling the warmth of it going over her in waves, letting herself become the fire.

She let Davyn fade from her view. It was just her, a singular flame in the darkness.

"Keep it focused," Davyn warned. "Don't feed it. Don't let it get so big."

Reg hated to pull back. It felt so good when she let the flame burn and just watched it, from the inside and the outside. That was when she felt at peace and balanced.

"Bring it down," Davyn said. She could feel him squeezing it, pushing the flames back and compacting them into a ball.

Reg groaned. She let the flame go out.

"You're distracted today," Davyn observed.

"No kidding. And I'm sure you have no idea why I would be so distracted today."

"I know it's hard to concentrate with the Spring Games going on. You would rather be there. You're probably anticipating seeing them tonight."

Reg shook her head. "It's not the Spring Games. I can take or leave the Spring Games. It's you."

Davyn's brows went up and his eyes widened. "Me? I'm here to help guide you and keep you focused on what you're doing. Without me, your experiments would get too big. You would end up killing yourself or burning the house down before you learned how to control it."

"And how do you think it is helping to come in here chattering on about Julian?"

"Chattering on?" Davyn looked taken aback. "Reg…"

"You have been. You've got a serious crush on this guy."

Davyn's face flushed. Reg laughed in disbelief. "That's it, isn't it? You *like* him."

"I told you I like him." Davyn's breathing had sped up. He sounded a bit like he had been running. "He's an interesting person. I enjoyed talking with him."

"Uh-huh. And you can't wait to get back together with him, can you?"

"It's not that bad." Davyn scratched the back of his neck. "I just thought he was interesting…"

"When are you seeing him again?"

"Uh… I don't know."

"When?" Reg pressed. Even though they were talking about Julian, she was enjoying herself. She liked seeing Davyn squirm.

Liked the way he got flushed and embarrassed and wasn't sure what to say.

"Tonight," Davyn admitted, looking down. "We're going to go to the Games together again."

"Second date already! He moves fast."

"It's not like that," Davyn sputtered. "We just really clicked."

"Well, I'm all for you having a good time, but watch yourself. Because Julian is not what you think he is."

CHAPTER TWENTY-SIX

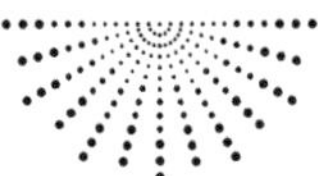

Reg decided that she would not go to the Games again. That way, she could be sure that she wouldn't run into Julian and Davyn. She could have the cottage to herself and not worry about any appointments because everyone else was at the Games.

"We're just going to veg in front of the TV," she told Starlight. "No clients. No readings. No Julian. Just you and me and the silver screen."

Starlight purred and rubbed against her legs. Reg thought she'd better make sure they had ice cream and whatever other snacks she would need before beginning her couch potato marathon. She looked in the cupboards, fridge, and freezer. There was a severe lack of junk food. A situation that would need to be remedied immediately.

"Any requests?" she asked Starlight.

He butted his head against her leg, and Reg was assailed with a very strong mental image of a can of tuna.

"Okay, then. I think I can manage that." Reg laughed. She remembered Julian asking her if she could communicate with cats. Cats were easy. They almost always wanted just one thing. Even without an image of tuna in her head, she would still have known that Starlight wanted fish. What else would he ask for? Other than seeing his friend Nicole, of course.

She was still chuckling to herself when she added a couple of cans of tuna to her shopping cart at the store half an hour later. Ice cream. Root beer. Cookies. She was going to make it a proper party. And she would pick the shows or movie. No having to make sure it met with anyone else's approval. Sometimes it was nice just to be by herself.

"What are you laughing at?"

Reg whirled around. She had not expected to see anyone at the store, thinking all of her friends would be getting ready to go to the Games.

Julian stood behind her, watching her thoughtfully. "They say to be careful of people who laugh at their own jokes."

"What are you doing here?" Reg demanded, her voice harsh.

He displayed a bottle of wine. "Just picking up some necessities." He looked down at her cart. "Looks like someone is going to be home alone tonight," he taunted.

Reg's anger erupted. She was looking forward to being alone. Being alone was her choice. What she wanted. She didn't care if he were buying the wine to share with Davyn. He could do what he liked with Davyn. But Reg could do what she wanted, and she *wanted* to stay at home.

"Leave me alone!" she growled, not caring about who saw and heard her. "It's none of your business what I do. Get your groceries and get out! Don't even talk to me!"

The bottle in Julian's hand burst. He stared down at his red-stained loafers in dismay, mouth dropping open.

"How could you!" he fumed.

He dropped the neck of the bottle to the floor and went for his pocket. Reg didn't know what kind of weapon he had there. She was sure that he would have a license, whatever it was. But a person couldn't just pull a weapon in a grocery store. She tried to freeze Julian in place and get whatever he had in his pocket, but he resisted. He was moving slowly, but he was still moving, and if he had a loaded gun, he might still be able to get off a shot before she could get it away from him.

"Stop!" Reg tried again to freeze him. She grabbed his arm, but it was his left instead of his right and he continued to move his right freely. Maybe even faster than he had done just a moment before. Reg gripped his arm harder and pulled him toward her. She was an instant faster than Julian and grasped for what he had in his pocket.

It was, at first glance, a slender stick. But Reg saw it for what it was. A wand. None of the other witches or warlocks she knew used wands, at least they hadn't around her. Maybe it was special issue for Magical Investigators. Perhaps they were allowed to carry around a dangerous weapon and others were not. Any of Reg's friends might have a wand that they usually left at home. She had never asked.

Having never seen one used, she wasn't sure how it was done. But she'd seen enough TV, and she'd already dealt with Julian using his pen as a wand. She pulled it back and kept it out of his reach, putting a wall of protection around herself.

"Give that back!" Julian snapped. "You think you can attack an investigator for MI without consequences? Give me my wand!"

"You're the one attacking me. I'm just defending myself. You were going to use this on me!"

"You blew up my bottle!"

"I didn't have anything to do with that." But despite her denial, Reg had a sinking feeling that he was right. She hadn't yet been able to get control of the things that happened around her when she got angry. She had been hoping that her work with Davyn would help in that regard, and maybe it had helped a little, but that all went out the window when she saw Julian and he started to taunt her. "You can get another bottle. Just leave me alone."

Julian stood staring at her, his face all twisted up in anger. She knew that he would attack her if he could, but with her protections up, there was nothing he could do. She was stronger than he was. It gave her a flush of pride, a warmth that spread from her stomach outward to her limbs and cheeks. He was a trained agent of some kind, and she was stronger than he was. She had taken his weapon and he couldn't do anything without it. He couldn't even get close to her.

"You have no idea what kind of trouble you are in," Julian

growled. "This is unacceptable. You could be bound. Held for a hundred years! How would you like that?"

"That would be fine if it meant I didn't have to see you for a hundred years!"

He snarled at her wordlessly.

Reg looked down at the wand, sobering. She had pushed him too far. He would be coming after her in earnest now, if he hadn't been before. He would show no mercy. It didn't matter whether she tried to excuse herself with self-defense. He was going to do whatever it took to take her down.

"Look. Julian…"

"I'm not Julian to you. I am Investigator Sabat." His eyes burned scarlet.

Reg swallowed. "Investigator Sabat," she repeated, hating that she was bowing to him. "I just reacted. I was upset. I didn't mean to do any harm. And I didn't mean to…" She looked at the wand. "I never… You can have this back. Just don't use it on me. I was… afraid."

His face relaxed slightly. "You're in deep trouble."

"I get that. I'm sorry. I just reacted, and I should have better control."

"You never did have any," Julian sneered. "Back in foster care, you were… feral. No one had ever taught you how to control your powers. None of them knew what to do with you. What do non-practitioners know about disciplining a child with powers?"

She didn't want to think about the discipline in her foster homes. They might not know how to treat someone with paranormal powers, but they had known how to punish her, how to drive it out of her. How to keep hurting her until she stuffed everything down.

Until she felt exactly how she was feeling. Trapped and beaten and backed into a corner, and it had to come bursting out.

"Maybe you can give me a break, then," she suggested. "I didn't mean any harm. I was just reacting. Take this back. Just don't…" She stopped herself before begging again for him not to hurt her. She was stronger than that. She could still walk away from this, go home, and have her movie night all by herself.

She held the wand out to him, pointed down slightly, just pinching it at the very tip in hopes that she wouldn't trigger something. She didn't know exactly how wands worked, but she imagined it would magnify the powers she already held, like a megaphone or a microscope. And she didn't want her anger to find a way out through the wand.

Julian looked at her, grinding his teeth. Just when she thought he was going to object, he snatched it out of her hands.

Reg jumped, but she let him take it. Julian turned it around to point it at her. Reg watched it, queasy, waiting for him to zap her with lightning or to hit her with some spell that would drop her to her knees.

He kept it pointed at her, his hand shaking. Reg still had her shield up. If he tried to bind her or take her into custody, she hoped it would prevent him.

"Get out of here," Julian said finally, his tone flat.

Reg looked at the food in her cart. It wasn't worth it. There was no way she was going to wait patiently in line for her turn and watch the cashier ring up her order. She needed to leave.

She left her cart in the middle of the aisle. Let the store employees worry about putting the ice cream back away before it melted. She backed away from Julian one slow step at a time, her eyes on his wand.

When she was out of his sight, she turned and fled, running until she got to her car.

CHAPTER TWENTY-SEVEN

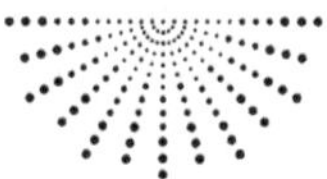

Reg hesitated about even going back home to the cottage. Julian would know where she was. He could have people there waiting for her. Going where she was expected to go would be a grave error.

But how could she leave Starlight there without arranging for his care, even if it was just to ask Sarah to feed him until she and Francesca were able to find a home for him? She couldn't. She just couldn't do that to him. She knew how much he had mourned when he lost his previous owner, and she couldn't abandon him as if she didn't care. She had come to care for him a great deal.

She went back to the cottage, startling at every sound and unexpected movement out of the corner of her eye. She was sure that Julian would be there ahead of her or would have sent someone else. But she didn't see anyone lurking in the shadows as she drew up to the house.

Reg looked around. She reached out with all of her senses and tried to feel if anyone were there. Sarah was gone, having already left for the Spring Games. The only presence Reg felt was Starlight. And of course, the night birds and animals around the house. Forst was gone too, home to his own plot, Reg assumed. He didn't seem like the type who would want to watch the Games. There had been gnomes there, but Reg assumed they were the most extroverted of the species, which Forst was not.

Reg blew out her breath slowly. Then she held her breath and listened, trying to pick up every sound around the cottage. She still couldn't sense anyone there waiting for her. But if she waited forever to act, she would end up getting caught.

She walked along the grass border in the shadows of the trees rather than walking on the cobblestone pathway that led to her door. She watched the darkest of the shadows for any movement. But there didn't seem to be anyone there waiting for her.

Reg inserted her key shakily and unlocked the door. Starlight jumped down from the couch and hurried over to her, yowling hungrily and nudging her legs to encourage her to produce his tuna.

"We have to go," Reg told him. "I'm sorry, there's no tuna. And we have to run."

He stopped stock-still and stared at her.

"We are in danger."

Starlight sat back and began to wash. Reg was comforted that he would take the time to do something so ordinary. He didn't keep begging for food, but he didn't rush her to the door either. There was still time for grooming and thoughtful consideration.

Reg went to the bedroom and grabbed her duffel bag. She rifled quickly through the drawers and the bathroom to gather the items she would need for several days and nights, then zipped it shut. She grabbed the cat carrier from the closet. She took it out to the living room and placed it on the floor, door open, near Starlight.

He looked at it and continued to lick his paw and groom his face.

"We need to go," Reg encouraged. "I don't know how long we have. I was surprised there wasn't anyone here already."

But Starlight wasn't ready, and Reg figured if she tried to force him into that carrier, he would take off her hand.

"What else is there to do?" Reg asked. "You can still wash in the carrier. I need to go."

He paused to look at her, his gaze steady and calm, and then he resumed.

"Okay." Reg looked around. What was she forgetting? She picked up the crystal ball and slid it into her bag. There was still enough room for it, and it was a tool of her trade, so why not take it with her? It clinked against something else in her bag, and the sound brought a flash of revelation into her mind. Her box of gems. She was acting in such a panic that she'd forgotten all about her wealth. She could stay under cover for a long time with those gems. Without them, she would have to set up somewhere close by and start offering her psychic services right away. It would be much easier for them to track her down.

Reg went back to the bedroom and retrieved her hidden stash. She even had the presence of mind to put a couple of gems into her pocket so that she could liquidate them quickly without having to open the box in front of someone else.

When she returned to the front room, Starlight was nowhere to be seen.

"Starlight? Star, where did you go?"

There was an answering meow and Reg found him inside the cat carrier.

"Oh. Right."

She shut and latched the door on the carrier. "Sorry about this. But it will keep you safe on the drive."

He was quiet. Reg picked everything up and walked out of the cottage.

CHAPTER TWENTY-EIGHT

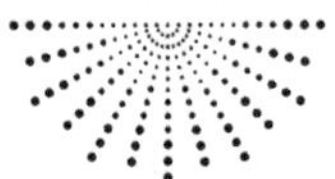

Reg couldn't shake the feeling someone was watching her as she left the cottage. She looked around quickly for anyone, but everything seemed just as still and quiet as it had before. She needed to stop looking for spooks and get herself out of there.

Reg forced herself to move quickly out of the yard and to her car. She should have had the gas tank filled, the oil changed, and the engine serviced before going any distance. But since when did she plan her getaways like that? The gas tank was never full. She was lucky if she had enough fuel to get out of town.

And this time, it was three-quarters full. Reg thought that was a good omen.

She opened the map app on her phone once she was sitting down and had the door locks engaged. She pinched and zoomed and panned around the map, looking for a good place to hide. There was never a perfect place to run to, but she had enough money this time that she didn't have to worry about depending on friends or even looking for a job right away. She could afford to just lie low for a few weeks until everything had blown over.

Julian would forget about her soon enough. And how long could Magical Investigations watch her cottage and wait for her to show up again? If Julian could talk them into it, maybe they would provide an agent to watch it for a couple of days, but they wouldn't start a nationwide manhunt for her. What had she done wrong, after all? She had accidentally broken a bottle of wine and had taken Julian's wand from him for two minutes to protect herself. She hadn't threatened him with it. She had given it back. He didn't have anything on her.

Not really.

And the stuff that had happened in the Everglades? What happened in the Everglades stayed in the Everglades, right? There were no witnesses to testify against her. All they had were suspicions. So what if they had the ropes she had been tied with? What did that prove, other than that she had been bound? There was no evidence to connect the panther attack to Reg. She was no skin walker. She couldn't command panthers. She wasn't responsible for what had happened to Tybalt and no one could prove that she was.

She found a small town a couple of hours' drive away. They had a few motels and B&B's. She would use cash and a fake name. It would take time for anyone to track her there. She would be safe for a day or two at least.

Hopefully, they were pet-friendly.

* * *

Starlight snoozed in the cat carrier while Reg drove. He'd been with them on the road trip to the dwarf mountain, and the new carrier was much more comfortable than the cardboard box she'd had for that trip. When Reg pulled to a stop at the B&B, he yawned and stretched and looked around, sniffing the air with interest. Reg grabbed the carrier and her bag and went up to the front door. She hadn't registered ahead. Hopefully, they would have a room free. She didn't know how often they were fully booked, but hopefully with the Spring Games, they would lose some of the bookings that they might normally have had, leaving space free for Reg.

A woman came to the door. Older, hair turning from a strawberry blond to gray, round coke-bottle glasses blurring her eyes.

"Hello," she said in a welcoming voice. "Are you looking for a room?"

Reg nodded. "Yes. Sorry, I didn't call ahead, but things happened… sort of suddenly."

"Don't worry. I have two rooms free right now. You have your choice."

"Great. I'm so relieved. And… I know this is a stretch, but… it will only be a couple of days—I have my cat with me…"

The woman peered into Reg's cat carrier, squinting through the thick lenses. "Oh, and isn't he a gentleman? Of course. That's not a problem. The larger room has an attached bathroom and you can set up a litter box in there. He can't have run of the house, in case others have allergies, but I don't think there will be any problems. You'll be just fine, won't you, honey?" she finished, querying Starlight directly.

He just looked back at her. At least he didn't hiss or try to scratch her through the grill of the door.

"Good boy," Reg breathed.

"This way," the woman led the way into the house, and Reg had to jump to keep up with her. She moved much more quickly than Reg would have expected.

The larger room was located on the main floor, near the kitchen. Reg looked around the room, made cozy with handmade quilts and little plaques with sayings hanging on the walls or propped on the dresser or tables.

"This is perfect," she said, even before opening the door to the bathroom to verify that it was large enough to put a litter box into without crowding.

She started a list in her head. Box, litter, cat food. It was too late to get anything that night, so she would have to get out early in the morning to make sure that Starlight had everything he needed to be comfortable.

The old lady, Mrs. Agnes, chattered on about the schedule and rules of the house. Reg nodded and thanked her repeatedly and, eventually, the woman left. Reg let Starlight out of the carrier, and he stepped delicately out onto the quilt-covered bed.

"How are you doing?" Reg asked him. "Can you wait until morning for your litter box? Or should I take you outside?"

Starlight strolled across the bed to the nearest window and peered out into the darkness. Apparently deciding that he didn't need to go outside, Starlight lay back down on the bed and curled his tail around his nose.

CHAPTER TWENTY-NINE

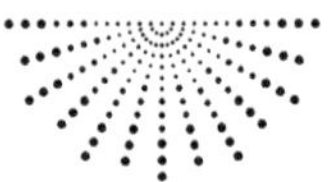

Reg slept with Starlight cuddled against her, which helped her feel more normal. Like she wasn't sleeping in a bed and breakfast, miles from home. As long as she had Starlight with her, she was fine. Being away from the Spring Games and Julian didn't hurt, either. She was away from the anxiety that they both produced and could finally relax to sleep.

She got in a few hours of sleep, but then Starlight insisted that she wake up, and Reg couldn't put off taking care of his needs. She might be able to steal some fish from the kindly Mrs. Agnes, but she didn't suppose there was any kitty litter lying around unused. She hadn't seen any sign that the old woman had cats of her own.

Morning was not Reg's best time. There was no way she would have been up that early if she were at home and didn't have to worry about her familiar. She would have been sleeping for several more hours.

But she wasn't at home, so she had a shower to wake herself up and explained to Starlight that she would be back as quickly as she could with his kitty litter and food. He wandered around the room a little, meowing conversationally and sniffing at everything. She turned the bathroom faucet to a dribble and he had a drink. Reg headed out, asking Mrs. Agnes where she could buy kitty litter so early in the morning. There was a 24-hour department store. Reg tapped it into her GPS and hoped that they had a counter where she could buy hot coffee.

Her phone began to ring.

Reg hadn't properly thought through what would happen when people discovered her absence. Or how she would handle the phone calls. Of course, it was best to disappear without a trace. She had left friends behind before. But she didn't want the police involved. Especially if some police detective started doing country-wide searches on her history and warrants.

The number on the screen was Sarah's. It made sense that she would be the first to notice Reg's absence. Reg took a deep breath and tapped the answer button on the phone.

"Hi, Sarah."

"Oh, Reg. I'm glad I reached you. I just wanted to make sure everything was okay. I came in to check your schedule this morning, and you and Starlight were both gone. I know it's none of my business, but you hadn't said anything about going on a trip…"

"Yeah. It was kind of… an impulse."

"Are you okay? Did something happen?"

"I'm all right."

"Are you coming back?"

Reg considered the question. If she wanted to keep the police from investigating, then Sarah would have to know something. She would have to reassure Reg's friends that even if she never returned, she was okay. Reg couldn't talk to them all. It was probably the last time she would answer her phone.

"I don't know."

"What happened, Reg? Is it this investigation? I told you it is nothing to worry about."

"It's more than that. If you can hold the cottage for now… I'm paid up for another month, right? If I'm not back by the end of the term, you can get rid of anything I left behind and find another tenant."

"Reg, I don't want to do that. You can come back. Everything will be fine."

"I don't know that. And neither do you. Right now… it could go either way. It doesn't feel very safe. Maybe if it all blows over…"

"Can I call you? Will you keep this number?"

"No. I don't want anyone to be able to trace me. I'll dump this phone. I'll find another way to get in touch with you if things settle down."

"How will you know if they have settled down if I can't contact you?"

"I have to be sure that no one has followed me or can find me. Then… we'll see. I have ways to reach you."

"You are overreacting," Sarah said sternly.

"I hope so. If anyone asks questions about me disappearing, can you head them off? Say that you're in contact with me and I'm just fine. Make sure no one starts a missing person investigation."

"Yes, of course," Sarah agreed. "But I don't understand why you think this is necessary."

"Keep an eye out. See what happens."

"Okay. I guess someone will need to contact the people that you have appointments set up with as well."

"Oh, yeah. Could you do that?"

"I will. You take care, Reg."

"I will. You too." Reg touched the red button to end the call.

The silence in the car was deafening.

* * *

Reg picked up what she needed for Starlight and added a pint of ice cream to her cart. She hadn't gotten her ice cream the night before, due to the complication of running into Julian.

She couldn't put her whole life back to rights, but she could have her ice cream. Knowing that her load would be heavy with kitty litter and cans of cat food, she didn't bother to get anything else. She had what she needed to survive. She would get breakfast at the B&B and maybe go out for dinner in the evening. It wasn't a big deal if she missed meals. She'd missed plenty before and could stand to lose a few pounds. It was more important to stay safe and out of sight.

Reg returned to the B&B and breathed a sigh of relief. Hopefully, Starlight had behaved and had not destroyed anything or had an accident while she was gone. He knew where she was going, but a cat couldn't be expected to be in control of all of his bodily functions or instinctual behavior.

CHAPTER THIRTY

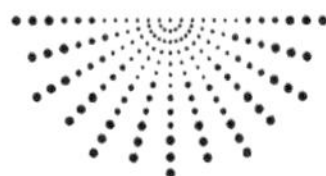

The bags were heavy and Reg wasn't paying attention to anything around her as she walked up the sidewalk to the front door. She shifted her load to try to free up one hand to knock or try the door. She wasn't sure what the proper protocol was at a B&B. Did she ring and wait for the owner to let her in, or just go in as if she lived there, which she currently did?

"Regina."

His voice went through Reg like an electrical shock. She spun on her heel and found herself face-to-face with Corvin.

"What are you doing here?"

"Shall we go inside?" he gestured to the door, making a motion to open it for her. Reg swallowed and looked around her to consider her options. At her house, she had wards set to prevent Corvin or anyone she didn't give permission to enter her home. But she hadn't even thought to protect her room at the B&B. She had been too tired, too distraught, and although Sarah had given her some instruction, she'd never attempted it by herself before.

She was able to shield herself from Corvin, though. She had done it before; it wasn't really a problem as long as she was strong and well-rested. But she'd barely gotten a couple of hours' sleep under her belt.

"To talk," Corvin said, raising his brows at her. He looked around as if there might be people listening to them on the street. "I'm sure you would like some level of privacy."

Reg scowled at him, the muscles across her forehead tight. "What are you doing here?"

"Waiting for you to return."

"How did you know I was here?" She shook her head. "Did you follow me?"

He gave a little shrug, as if embarrassed.

"How did you find me?"

"You know that we are connected." He spread his hands apart. "I don't know how to break that connection."

Even if he wanted to. Which Reg was sure he didn't. He had been delighted to follow her there, away from the protections and Sarah's watchful eye. He was happy to get her by herself.

"So you… spied on me psychically?"

"No more than you have done."

Reg swallowed. That much was true, but she hadn't thought he had been aware of it.

"You really want to talk about this outside?" Corvin asked. "We are safer indoors, where we can put up a shielding spell."

Reg set down one of her bags and rubbed her forehead. "Corvin… I don't want you here. You shouldn't have come here!"

"If you are in danger, I can help."

"What makes you think I am in danger?"

He motioned again to the door. Reg gave in. She gave the knob a twist and opened the door. Corvin picked up the bag she had set down, and Reg led the way through the house to her room. Reg saw Mrs. Agnes peer at her from the kitchen.

"We didn't talk about you entertaining men here," she said, warning in her voice.

"He's not staying."

She didn't stay to hear what else Mrs. Agnes had to say about it. She used the key she had been given to unlock her door and ushered Corvin in.

Starlight was sleeping on the bed. He stretched and yawned,

squinting in Reg's direction. Then his mouth shut with a snap. His ears folded back and he snarled at Corvin.

"Cat," Corvin sneered, not liking Starlight any better than Starlight liked him.

"Both of you be civil. Corvin is not staying."

Corvin shut the door behind him. Reg decided she'd better take care of Starlight first. He had been waiting patiently for her, and she didn't want him to be crabby about not being fed or being able to relieve himself and to take it out on Corvin. Although Corvin could probably use a little comeuppance. She ignored Corvin's presence while she unpacked her bags and got everything set up for Starlight. Starlight went immediately to the litter box and Reg pulled the bathroom door shut most of the way to give him some privacy. She put some kibble in a bowl for when he was done, ducked out to put her ice cream in the freezer in the kitchen, then finally faced off against Corvin.

"You shouldn't have come here."

"Probably not," he agreed. "But I wanted to make sure you were all right."

Or to take advantage of her distressed state.

"As you can see, I am just fine."

"I'm not sure I would call this fine." Corvin looked around the room with its homey, feminine decorations. "This isn't exactly home."

"It will do until I sort things out."

"You are not planning to return to your cottage?"

"I don't know yet. Have you been talking to Sarah?"

"No." He frowned. "About what?"

"She called me. I just wondered if the two of you were in cahoots."

"You know how Sarah feels about me. Suffice to say, we are not collaborating."

Reg stared at him for a minute, trying to figure out what to do next. She folded her arms across her chest. "What do you know?"

"What do I know." Corvin rubbed his whiskered chin and leaned back against the closed door. "I know that you are in the middle of this Magical Investigation, but I'm not sure what it is all about. I know that you and the investigator have… not been getting along. That there was an incident last night. And I know you left home and came here." He displayed his hands palm-up as if to show he had nothing else. "That's it."

"Hasn't he talked to you? Julian?"

"Yes. He has talked to me. But he didn't want to give me any information about what concerns they have. I would have put any worries they have to rest, I can assure you."

"Davyn seems to like him."

Corvin raised an eyebrow thoughtfully. "Indeed. Well, I did not find anything to like about him. What is it he's investigating in the Everglades?"

"What did he ask you? What did you tell him?"

"He just asked about where each of us was on each day. The progress of our search. I've answered in generalities. No details."

"What did you tell him about me? About what happened while we were there?"

"I told him… that you were helping us to locate a missing person. Your arrangement was with Damon, not me… and as little as possible about our movements."

"You told him that I sleepwalked and disappeared?"

He surveyed her unemotionally. "You did."

"You know I wasn't sleepwalking."

"I told him that we thought you had been sleepwalking. It was the only explanation we could come up with at the time for your absence."

"And after that? You didn't tell him anything I told you?"

"I said that you couldn't tell us very much. That you were confused and disoriented, and we didn't have any idea what had happened to you while you were away."

Reg nodded. She hadn't thought that Corvin would give Julian any details. Damon might. He was a security guard and was far more likely to be open and honest with what he perceived to be a legitimate investigation. But she had told Damon even less about the missing time period than she had told Corvin.

Neither of them said anything for a while, gauging the options and weighing their words. Reg sat down on the end of the bed, tired. She wanted to crawl back into bed and sleep the rest of the day away. She didn't want to think. She didn't want to have to deal with her problems. She thought she had left everything behind, and there was Corvin, following her and sticking his nose into her business.

"Julian is with the Endangered Species department," she told Corvin finally.

He probably knew that already. If not, it probably wouldn't be hard to find out.

Corvin nodded slowly.

"He wants to know about Tybalt."

Corvin groaned. "Are they seriously concerned over the disappearance of a swamp goblin?"

"Death," Reg corrected.

"And MI thinks it's their job to find out what happened to him and put additional safeguards in place."

Reg nodded.

"You really don't need to be worried about them. They are… they don't have a lot of power. They are mostly bureaucratic."

"Tell Julian Sabat that."

"He's young. He's just cutting his teeth."

"Well, I don't want to be the case he teethes on."

Corvin snorted.

"Sarah is going to complain about him," Reg said. "She figured that would go farther than me doing it."

"I'm sure she's right. She probably knows half of the department over there. The older staff, anyway."

There was another period of silence. Reg didn't offer any more information.

"What happened last night?" Corvin asked eventually.

"What do you know?"

He pursed his lips. "I wasn't there," he said slowly, feeling his way through the conversation.

"But you know something happened. Who talked to you and what did they tell you about it?"

"No, no one said anything. I felt something from you. Your…

emotions carried through our connection. I wasn't eavesdropping, but your emotions were very strong and I couldn't help knowing something was happening."

Strong emotions. That was one way to put it.

"I had a confrontation with Julian."

"But not at your house."

"In the grocery store. I'm sure it's all over town this morning. All you had to do was stay in Black Sands and you would have heard all of the details."

"Why a confrontation in the grocery store?"

"I was picking up some treats. He was picking up wine for him and Davyn."

The raised brows. Silence, waiting for her to go on. Reg could hear Starlight chowing down on his dry kibble. At least he wasn't yowling at her about serving him substandard food. She couldn't manage anything better at the moment. She would give him some canned food later in the day when she could summon up the energy.

"Julian was bugging me," Reg said, her voice sounding juvenile in her own ears, like the kid in the back seat on a car trip. *He's bugging me. He's in my space. He's looking at me.* "I might have… *accidentally* exploded his bottle of wine. And then… things kind of escalated from there."

It sounded trivial and ridiculous when she recounted it. It was hard to explain the fury she had felt at being the brunt of his bullying. Again. She wasn't going to take any more from Julian Sabat.

"Escalated how?"

"There was shouting… he drew his wand…"

"He drew his wand?" Corvin repeated, aghast. "In *public*?"

Reg nodded. "Right there in the grocery store."

"Unbelievable. I would complain to MI too. If I didn't tear his head off first. Drawing a wand on you." His eyes swept over her as if looking for an injury. "You seem to be in one piece. I gather you handled it."

"Yeah. I kind of took it away from him, kept him from doing anything else."

"Where is the wand now?"

"I gave it back," Reg assured him quickly. "I wouldn't take something like that with me. I don't even know how to use it. I wouldn't want to have an accident."

"No. You wouldn't. You are quite powerful enough without wand magic as well."

"I just… I didn't know what else to do. I had to get out of there. I can't deal with him or his questions anymore, and now there's going to be some kind of investigation into me taking away his wand. I don't want to get clapped in some smelly prison or bound for a hundred years."

"I think he would be more likely to get into trouble than you, but…"

"I'm not going to take that chance."

"So you're not coming back."

"I can't. Not right now."

"You should have the chance to tell your story. Contact his superiors. Let them know what happened. They're not going to lock you up, trust me."

Reg hadn't managed to stay out of jail thus far by giving her side of the story to the police. She avoided contact with them wherever possible. She recognized when she was in a bad situation and she left. She got to where she was by using her brain, not by telling sob stories to the cops.

"You won't reconsider?"

Reg thought about what she had told Sarah earlier. To hold her cottage for another month. Wait and see what happened. But Corvin was less of an ally than Sarah. And if he thought she was slipping away from him, leaving Black Sands for good, he might be even more desperate to steal her powers than ever before. And she didn't want to have to fight him.

"I can't say. I don't know how this is all going to turn out."

"Some fortune-teller you are."

Reg laughed. It was the case, though, that fortune-tellers could rarely see anything about their own futures. When she thought about Julian and his investigation and about her empty cottage in Black Sands, all she could see was the way he had attacked her in the store, drawing his wand, just as he had used the pen at The Crystal Bowl.

Red eyes, lightning streaming from his wand. Fury written all over his features. She didn't know what he was authorized to do if he decided she was guilty of something, or if she attacked him. Could he kill with his wand? Or was that only TV? It was hard to know what was really real. She hadn't grown up in a magical community like Corvin had.

"I don't want to have to deal with Julian Sabat. I've told him I don't know what happened to Tybalt. Unless they can prove otherwise… that's all I'm going to say. I'm done."

Corvin nodded. "That's probably the best course of action."

She was glad he hadn't told her that she should go back, explain everything that had happened, and throw herself on the mercy of MI. Because she wasn't going to do that.

"So… you're staying here with the cat for how long? Until the investigation is closed? That could be a long time."

"I don't care if they close the case or not as long as I don't have to talk to Julian again."

There was a tap on the door. Both of them flinched, and Corvin moved away from the door.

"Breakfast time," Mrs. Agnes invited from the other side. "And if you want to bring your guest… you can."

Reg wasn't ready for breakfast. She looked at Corvin. His eyes lit up. To get there so early in the morning, he had probably left Black Sands just hours after Reg and consumed nothing but gas station coffee or chocolate bars.

Reg rolled her eyes. "Fine. We'll do breakfast."

She looked at Starlight to make sure that he would settle. "We're going to go get our food. Are you okay here by yourself? Go to sleep?"

He looked at her and then turned his head to stare at Corvin.

"He's going to have breakfast and then go back to Black Sands," Reg told Starlight. "Right?"

"I don't want to leave you alone here, defenseless."

"I'm hardly defenseless." Corvin knew that she was strong. She had a lot of power she could draw on if something happened and she was in danger. Julian didn't know where she was. Corvin was the only one who had any idea.

"It's better if you don't stick around here," she told him. "Two people are a lot easier to find than one. You're not exactly inconspicuous."

"Neither are you."

"Well, I'm going to stay undercover. I'm not going to go wandering around town. If I don't go out, no one will see me." She shook her head at him. "Come on, two new mysterious strangers in town? Two unknown vehicles on the street. People will talk, even if it is just speculation. Word will get out. Next thing you know, Julian and his cronies will be crawling all over this place."

"I think you're giving him too much credit." Corvin sighed. "Yes, I will go home. But you call me if you need me."

"I don't need you."

"But if you do."

"I won't."

"Reg."

"No. Just go home. Don't follow me anywhere else. Don't talk about me to anyone. Don't let anyone get crazy and file a missing person report. Just keep everything quiet on the home front."

This appeal seemed to suit him better than just being sent back home. He would take care of business in Black Sands. He wouldn't be abandoning her, but he didn't actually have to do anything.

He opened the bedroom door. "I bet you'll be back in time for the closing ceremonies."

"I wouldn't take that bet."

They adjourned to the dining room, where Mrs. Agnes had lain out a large breakfast spread. Corvin sat down and ate a couple of plates full of food. Reg did the best she could, but wasn't hungry. There was plenty she could filch that would hold off hunger for the rest of the day, but with Mrs. Agnes right there watching, Reg couldn't exactly wrap it up in a napkin on her lap. Reg had a feeling she saw more than she should through those thick lenses.

Corvin turned on the charm and Mrs. Agnes fell for him hook, line, and sinker. She leaned toward him, fluttering her eyelashes at him and preening, smoothing out her shirt and readjusting the neckline to the best advantage. But Reg couldn't smell any scent of roses from Corvin, which told her that he was just using his good looks and smile. He wasn't using magical charms on Mrs. Agnes.

There was also an older couple at the table. They were staying in one of the other rooms. It sounded like they had been there for a few days already. Everybody was polite and friendly and, eventually, Reg couldn't stand it anymore. She pushed herself back from the table.

"I need to lie down for a while. I'll see you later," she told Corvin.

He looked at her for an instant too long, leaving the query *Will you?* floating in her head. She blinked and looked away from him. She needed space and to catch up on her sleep. He'd eaten and now he needed to go back to Black Sands and act as if everything were normal and he didn't know where Reg had gone.

CHAPTER THIRTY-ONE

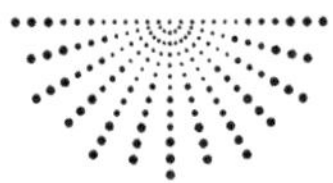

Despite her exhaustion, sleep eluded Reg. She lay in the bed in the brightly-lit B&B and couldn't stop thinking about Julian and his investigation, Tybalt, the Spring Games, Davyn… and everything else that was whirling around her head.

She wished she could sit in the garden and look at the greenery and budding flowers that Forst had planted and cultivated and babied. Even if Reg had never had a green thumb or an appreciation for the great outdoors, it was relaxing there.

There were gardens around the B&B. It had been very nicely landscaped. But she didn't exactly want to be seen there, and it wouldn't be the same as being in the garden cared for by a gnome. They had even been visited by elves during winter solstice when Starlight had been sick.

Eventually, she got sick of trying to sleep and of being cooped up in that one room. She needed to be able to get out and get a feel for the place. She could gas up the car so that she was ready to go anywhere at a moment's notice. She should know where the various stores were and her escape routes out of town. Despite everything she had told herself about staying in and under cover, she just couldn't stay there anymore.

"Oh, hello, there," Mrs. Agnes greeted, nodding to Reg as she put in an appearance. "And how is this lovely day going for you?"

"Uh… just fine. Thought I'd get out and see the sights, get a breath of fresh air."

"Of course," Mrs. Agnes agreed. "Anything in particular? I can make recommendations, give you directions."

"No… I am fine. Just going to wander."

Reg could feel the woman's eyes on her. She was self-conscious as she walked away, feeling like she couldn't remember the right way to walk anymore. Very awkward.

"Where did you say you came from?" Mrs. Agnes asked before she could escape the room.

"I've been all over," Reg said truthfully. She kept going, then paused with her hand on the doorknob. "Northeastern seaboard, mostly," she said. "The ocean is a lot colder there than it is here!"

"I could never live in such a place," the older woman said with a shudder. "If you follow that path behind the house," she gestured in the direction she spoke of, "it leads you right down to the ocean. As warm as any bath."

Reg looked in that direction, feeling the ocean's pull on her, even though she couldn't see it through the walls. It was there, waves lapping, salt in the air, something she could sense even if she couldn't see it.

"I'll see it later," she said lightly. She had told herself she was going out to reconnoiter, and she would stick to that plan. She didn't need to put her feet in the warm water. She could do that back in Black Sands anytime she wanted to.

"You like the ocean, do you?" Mrs. Agnes asked, her voice a little sharp.

"Yes. Of course I do. I love the ocean, especially with how warm it is here. I'll go down later."

Reg could feel Mrs. Agnes's eyes on her all the way down the sidewalk to her car.

* * *

The little town had a different feeling from Black Sands. Maybe because Reg already knew Black Sands and everything in Sandy Cove was still new and foreign to her. But there did not seem to be nearly as many magical practitioners there as in Black Sands. They were only a couple of hours apart; what was it about Black Sands that attracted the magical community's attention? Was it just chance, that one family had moved there and then had invited their friends? And then they had invited others, had used each other's services, living separate and apart from the non-magical community?

Or maybe both towns had once had large magical communities and then a threat of some sort had scared the townspeople away, or some disease or curse had wiped them out. There were a lot of possibilities when Reg thought about it.

She drove through the small downtown. None of the stores she saw had the cute double-meanings that she was used to in Black Sands. The Crystal Bowl. Witch's Brew. Instead, they all seemed to be boring and empty, not enough people to keep the little town's economy going. It would be a ghost town if things kept progressing as they were. And not the kind of ghost town that Reg had seen in the Everglades. It would be empty and sad, and there wouldn't even be any ghosts there for Reg to visit with.

She filled her car's tank at the gas station, eyes alert for anyone who shouldn't be there. Anyone paying her too much attention. Even with her red box braids and a head-dress and flowing, colorful fortune-teller skirt, they should only give her a cursory look. The kind of look that took her in, then discounted her as just another crazy person they didn't want to acknowledge. She might ask them for money. Offer to tell their fortunes. Say crazy things. People didn't like crazy.

CHAPTER THIRTY-TWO

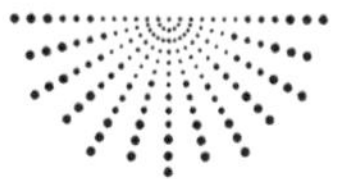

Reg returned to the B&B feeling out of sorts. She had hoped that getting away from the house again would clear her head and settle her down, but she felt like the B&B was a prison instead of a safe house. She didn't want to go back in her room to watch videos on her phone to pass the time. She felt like she had left her whole life behind in Black Sands. She had never felt that way when running away before. She'd always had a sense of excitement and adventure. Escaping from trouble and starting a new life was always a thrill.

This time, it seemed like she was giving up. She had begun to build a life in Black Sands and had just given up on it, denying the person she had become.

Rather than going back into the house, she decided to take Mrs. Agnes's advice and go down to the ocean. She liked the water. She could just sit there and watch the waves and, like watching a fire, it would calm her and help her focus and relax and know what she should do next.

She wandered down the cobblestone path behind the house through Mrs. Agnes's garden. She didn't have a gnome so it was not nearly as nice as Sarah's. Reg would have to remember to tell Forst that and compliment his work when she got back to the cottage.

The thought gave her a pang. When? Would she ever go back to the cottage? She might never be able to go back there, even once the investigation had cooled down.

The cobbled path led to steps going down the back of the hill to a sheltered beach. Reg descended and walked through the sand, as white and soft as baby powder. The sun in the clear blue sky warmed her skin. It was perfect. She should be happy there. It was a great place for a vacation, or even to stay longer-term. She was sure Mrs. Agnes wouldn't mind if she decided to stay more than a few days. It would be good for her pocketbook.

But her heart wasn't in it. As much as she liked the perfect little beach, she didn't want to stay there. She walked to the water's edge, scanning the sand for a shell or rock to throw into the water. But there wasn't even a piece of driftwood.

Sand was getting into Reg's sandals, so she slipped them off. Looking at the water lapping against the shore, she had conflicting feelings. She knew that the water might trigger her siren instincts. But there wasn't anyone with her; she wouldn't be putting anyone in danger. She was by herself and could just let the warm water cover her toes and bring her comfort.

Why not?

She stepped into the water and let it cover her foot. Mrs. Agnes was right. It was like stepping into a warm bath. She could luxuriate there all day. Forget hiding in her room watching YouTube videos. She could just float in the warm, clear water in the little cove and let time wash over her.

She took a couple more steps into the water until it was nearly up to her knees. She took a long breath in and released it. That was where she belonged. She didn't want to go anywhere else. Maybe she had left her life behind in Black Sands, but she could start again. She didn't need friends or her own house or anything else that she'd experienced there. She could soak in the ocean all day. With the gems, she had all of the money she needed. She didn't have to work. She didn't need any clients. She could just rest and meditate and feel the wonderful warm water around her every day.

But as Reg took another step into the water, her dress starting to float around her, she realized that she had miscalculated.

She was *hungry*.

She hadn't been able to eat much of anything at breakfast, but time had passed since then, and hunger gnawed in her belly. She couldn't just laze around in the water all day. She needed food.

She closed her eyes, trying to push it out of her mind. She had skipped plenty of meals. It was just a matter of will. If she ignored the hunger, it would go away. But when she closed her eyes, she saw Julian. She remembered his being in the grocery store when she was picking up snacks. She hadn't been able to get her snacks. She'd had to run home and then had packed her bags and left. She was still hungry. She wanted that ice cream.

She hadn't bought ice cream in Black Sands, but she had purchased some when she had picked up Starlight's food and kitty litter. She hadn't even touched it yet. That's what she would have.

She regretted having to leave the water, but she could go back later. She needed to take care of her physical needs. Reg grabbed her sandals and pulled them on, then mounted the wooden steps and hurried up to the house. She followed the path and, in a moment, was at the front door again. She didn't bother to knock, but went straight in. Mrs. Agnes was in the living room doing a cross-stitch picture on a hoop. She looked up as Reg entered, giving a reserved smile.

"Hello, Reg, dear. Did you have a nice time?"

Reg could barely stand to answer her. She was on a mission. She needed that ice cream, and nothing was getting in her way.

"Yes, very nice," she agreed.

Mrs. Agnes followed her into the kitchen. She looked down at the wet border of Reg's dress clinging to her legs. "You went down to the water."

"It was really nice," Reg said. "You were right."

She opened the freezer and pulled out her pint of ice cream. She opened and closed several drawers before Mrs. Agnes pointed out the one for the cutlery. Reg grabbed a spoon, ripped the top off of her ice cream, and started to eat.

"You're hungry."

"Starving."

"If you're starving, ice cream isn't going to satisfy you."

Reg had already noticed that the chocolate and caramel were not giving her the usual rush. She could barely taste them. It was like eating sawdust. If sawdust were an ice cream flavor.

"Ugh." She took a few more bites of the ice cream, then looked down at it, disgusted. "What's wrong with this?"

"There isn't anything wrong with the ice cream."

"You didn't taste it."

"You don't want ice cream."

Reg thought about it. Her stomach was still practically turning itself inside out, a deep ache, almost like when Corvin had forced her to feel his hunger. Hunger that made her so desperate she wanted to cry. But it wasn't ice cream she wanted. It was something else. Back in the Black Sands grocery store. There had been something else that she wanted, but she couldn't think of what it was.

"You have to go," Mrs. Agnes said.

Reg nodded. She did. She had to go back to Black Sands to get… what it was that she wanted. She couldn't understand why she had left in the first place. There had been no reason to leave. It was her home. Her territory, not anyone else's.

"I'd better pack."

"Do you even need to pack? You could just leave everything here." Mrs. Agnes's eyes were blurry behind her thick lenses, but she was studying Reg intently.

"No. I have my cat. And my… things. I have all of my necessities with me. I need to take them."

"Maybe you could come back for everything else another time."

"No." Reg shook her head. No matter how hungry she was, she couldn't leave Starlight behind. She couldn't leave her gemstones or the few other things that she really needed to survive. "I'll pack and then I'll go."

She shoved the remaining ice cream back into the freezer. She fumbled at the door of her bedroom with the key, her hand shaking in her impatience to get in. Starlight jumped down from the bed and made an inquiring noise. Maybe wondering where she had been for so long. Or maybe he sensed the change in her and wondered what was going on.

"We're going home," Reg told him. "Back to Black Sands." She grabbed her bag and started throwing things into it. "I'm sorry for the change in plans. I know this is crazy, but I can't stay here. I have to go back."

She hadn't worked out why she needed to go back in a satisfyingly logical way. There was no way she could tell Sarah or Corvin or one of the others why it was suddenly so important that she get back to Black Sands. She just knew that she had to.

She was hungry. She needed to get back to the grocery store in Black Sands.

She couldn't explain it; she just knew that things had not ended the right way in the grocery store. Leaving her groceries there and running away to Sandy Cove was not the way it was supposed to turn out.

Starlight sat down and watched her curiously, his ears pointing forward and his head cocked to the side.

"I'm not crazy," Reg muttered.

When she had gathered all of her possessions, she opened the door to the cat carrier for Starlight. She hoped it wouldn't be a fight to get him inside.

But he seemed amenable to her plan and when she swung the door open, he walked in and lay down as if it were his royal coach.

"Good boy. Let's go home."

CHAPTER THIRTY-THREE

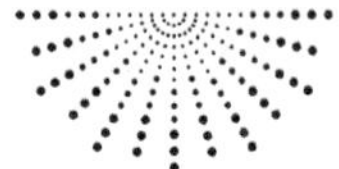

The trip back to Black Sands sped past. Looking back at it later, Reg had no recollection of actually being on the road. She didn't know what route she had taken or how fast she had driven. She had gotten into the car, intent on getting home, and the next thing she remembered, was rolling into town.

She smiled at the friendly lights of the little town. The sky was just twilight, but people were turning on their lights and the streetlights were starting to come on as well. She felt happy returning to Black Sands. It was home, in a way that no other place had ever been home to her. She felt warm. She felt possessive. It was *her* town. It was where she belonged.

Reg waffled over what order to do things in. She wanted to get over to the grocery store right away before it closed. But she also wanted to get Starlight home and check on everything at the cottage. It really wasn't a good idea to leave him in the car. He could get too hot or too cold, or someone could snatch him. He might think that she had abandoned him, or someone walking by might think her a negligent owner and call the police or animal control.

So leaving Starlight in the car was a non-starter. She would have to go home first. The grocery store would be open when she was done. Lots of places in Black Sands were open late or at odd hours because so many of the residents were night owls, practicing their magic or holding seances after dark or around midnight, the witching hour.

She zipped over to the house. She would be quick. She could drop her stuff there with Starlight and be on her way in five minutes. As long as she didn't get interrupted.

But of course, as soon as she opened the door and turned on the lights, Sarah knew she was there and hurried out to talk to her.

"Reg, is that you?"

"Yeah, it's me."

"Is everything okay?" Sarah peered in the door, unsure whether to enter. Reg nodded, setting down the cat carrier and releasing the catch on the door so Starlight could get out. She put down her bag on the kitchen floor, but then decided she couldn't leave it there. If Sarah decided to help her by putting away her things, she would know that the box of gems was still in the cottage. Reg should have put them in a safety deposit box or somewhere else they would be less accessible, but harder to steal. Sarah wouldn't want Reg to keep them in the cottage where something could happen to them.

But Sarah was one to talk. Reg had seen the big emerald pendant that Sarah kept in her house. She had to be near it to reap its health benefits. So she couldn't put all of her valuables away where they were safe either.

Sarah had Frostling, her African Gray parrot to help guard her precious jewel. Well, Reg had an animal too. Starlight could help to guard her gemstones and keep them safe.

"I'm fine," Reg said, carrying her bag into the bedroom and depositing it in the closet. She shut the closet doors and returned to the front room, where Sarah hovered, wondering what Reg was doing back.

"I just wondered, because you said that you weren't going to come back until this investigation had gone away, and… well, of course they are still asking questions. It's going to be a while before it's safe to come back without having to worry about it…"

"I'm not worried. I had to come back here to…"

Reg had been about to say "to eat," but that sounded kind of weird. Sarah would point out that she could eat wherever she went. There was plenty to eat no matter what town she hid herself in.

"You just had to settle things?" Sarah filled in her own thought.

Reg nodded in agreement.

She looked at her phone, wondering again what time the grocery store would be open until.

"Are you expecting someone?" Sarah asked.

"No."

"There she is! You're back!" Julian appeared in the doorway, flanked by a couple of other men in cloaks. "I thought you had left town."

"I had some things to do," Reg said vaguely. Suddenly, her impetus to go back to the grocery store was gone. It wasn't the groceries she wanted. It was to see Julian. To settle things with him properly.

"You can't come here without an appointment," Sarah objected, holding up her hand to stop Julian and his cronies from entering. "If you want to ask Reg more questions, you will have to set up a time."

Reg waved Sarah's words away. "It's fine. They don't need an appointment."

Sarah opened her mouth to argue. But it was Reg's schedule, not Sarah's. Sarah was always ready to help her out, but if Reg didn't want her help? Sarah couldn't exactly force her.

Looking suspicious, Julian entered the room.

Sarah gasped. "He broke the wards."

Reg shook her head. "No. I released them."

"Why would you do that? Reg, this is a bad idea and could turn very wrong. Anyone could come in here. And he may have evil intentions. You can't protect yourself if you release the wards."

"I want him to come in," Reg said irritably. "I don't need the wards."

Julian looked around as if expecting something to jump out and attack him. He looked at Reg, puzzlement evident on his face.

"You're cooperating now? I don't understand. Is this some new kind of game? What are you up to?"

"I'm not playing games," Reg said. She took a step toward him.

She longed to touch him. She had no interest in talking or answering his questions to establish the facts. She took a couple more steps, her heart beating harder and faster. She felt a warm flush, like diving into a deep, warm ocean. It spread from her head down to the rest of her body. Her hands were reaching out toward Julian. "Come with me."

He took a step back, startled by her sudden change in behavior.

"Come on," Reg urged. "There's nothing to be afraid of. You and I need to… talk."

"Are you ready to tell me what happened to Tybalt, your guide?"

Reg smiled, showing her teeth. "I don't want to talk about that. Put all of your other agendas aside for a while. Let's just get together and talk, you and I." She flicked a glance at the two other men with Julian. "Send them away. Sarah was just going back to the house."

Julian looked at the two other warlocks and shook his head. Sarah seemed rooted to the spot. She didn't take the hint and go back inside either.

A wind picked up outside, blowing in the bewitching smell of the sea, along with green leaves and flower petals. Reg smelled something that reminded her of Corvin at first, the way that she could smell roses whenever he was trying to charm her. It wasn't roses, but it was floral. And the rainy, earthy smell of spring. Rabbits followed the blowing leaves and petals into the cottage. Reg's jaw dropped in astonishment. What was going on? Was it because she had released the wards? Did that mean she was going to have to fight to keep nature out of her cottage now?

Before she had a chance to ask Sarah anything about the strange guests, a woman swept into the room.

She was very tall and wore an outfit of green and white. It looked like a cross between what the elves might wear and a wedding dress or elaborate Easter gown. She had a circlet of flowers in her head, like the ones that Reg and the other women had worn at the spring equinox celebration.

Reg's mouth was open, but she couldn't seem to muster up the ability to ask a question.

"I am the goddess Eostre," the woman said in a smooth, melodious voice that filled the room with its resonance.

"You're… a what?"

"I am the goddess Eostre," the woman repeated, an edge of irritation in her voice this time. She made a grand gesture to indicate everything around herself. "Goddess of Spring."

"Oh." Reg blinked. "Well, what are you doing here?"

"You must stop." The goddess changed her mind, rewording. "I am here to tell you that you must stop. You must not go forward with your plan."

Reg looked at the others in the room, thinking that one of them might know what she was talking about. She spread her hands wide, palms up. "What? What plan?"

"You came back here to claim your prey."

Reg's eyes went inadvertently to Julian. "What are you talking about?"

"Are you going to try to deny the hunger within you? The hunger that's eating away at the pit of your stomach, you crave it so badly."

Reg's stomach twisted. Her hunger was a deep pain gnawing at the inside of her belly.

"How would you know that?"

"Don't believe her, Reg," Sarah said.

"What?"

"Eostre. Goddess of Spring. Really?" Sarah shook her head at the strange woman. "There was no Goddess Eostre. She's a creation of the neopagans, something they created from the mistake of that idiot Bede and the drunken ramblings of the brothers Grimm. There is not and never was a Goddess Eostre."

"How could you say such a thing?" Eostre objected, her voice getting screechy. "I stand here before you!" She made a grand gesture. "I am *right here!*"

"I don't know who you are," Sarah said with a shrug. "But you are not Eostre. There is no Eostre."

The goddess's face glittered when she moved in the dimming light, a ghostly, lustrous shine. Or cheap glitter makeup picked up at the nearest Wal-Mart.

"Those who deny me shall die!" Eostre shouted, taking a step toward Sarah.

Sarah took a step back, but it was clear from the grim expression on her face that she was not backing down and was not afraid of what the intruder might do. She looked at Reg, shaking her head. "What did I tell you about releasing the wards? You never know what is going to come in here if you disable them."

Reg didn't like Eostre getting so close to Sarah. She advanced, hands clenching into fists, glowering at the fake goddess. "What are you doing here? This is my home. You leave my friends alone."

"Your friends? Or your prey?"

"Don't be ridiculous. Why would I attack Sarah? I have no interest in her." Reg licked her lips, startled by the words that had escaped her lips before she could stop them. "She's just my friend. And I don't want anything to happen to her."

"Reg…" Sarah frowned. "What is she talking about? Your prey?" Her eyes flicked around the room, looking for some kind of explanation. For someone to tell her that it was just a joke.

"You're not my prey," Reg insisted. "I don't know why she is saying that. You're my friend."

Sarah nodded, but her eyes were narrow and suspicious.

"Your prey?" Julian echoed. "What is all of this? I don't know if this is some kind of joke, Reg, some kind of bizarre attempt to scare me away, but it's not going to work. I'm not afraid of you."

Reg was distracted from protecting Sarah. Eostre had no intention of harming Sarah. She was just there to disrupt things. To prevent Reg from proceeding with her plan. Reg wheeled and instead stalked closer to Julian. He stood there like a deer caught in the headlights, thinking that he was perfectly safe from her.

Reg kept getting closer. The two men in the cloaks stepped back, eyeing her with suspicion.

CHAPTER THIRTY-FOUR

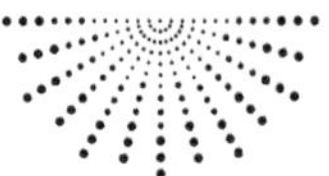

The goddess flounced across the room and put herself between Reg and Julian, eyes blazing. "You don't have the right!" she insisted.

"What are you talking about? This is my house. You can't make rules for me in my own house."

"There are still rules. Whether you like it or not. This man entered under your hospitality. And you do not have the right to take him here. This is not your territory."

"It is," Reg snapped.

There was a brilliant burst of light and, for an instant, Reg thought that she had blown something up. Maybe Eostre's head. That would serve her right. Coming into Reg's home and acting like she could control what Reg did there.

The light burst outward like a supernova, and then focused into one bright form, about the size of a person, beside Eostre. Had Eostre called upon another god to help her? This one seemed to be much more powerful than Eostre. A pure white light, whereas Eostre seemed like she had only some sparkle makeup and a dramatic dress.

"What—or who—is that?"

The light gradually faded until Reg could make out another

woman. She had to squint and only look at her sideways, she was still so bright.

"I am Kybele." The woman's voice was as deep and resonant as a cello, sending a shudder through Reg. "Mother of all the earth." She turned her face toward Eostre. "Abandon your disguise."

For a moment, nothing happened. Then the air around Eostre shimmered. She sparkled and wavered, then transformed in front of Reg.

Reg blinked, still dazzled by the light of Kybele. She tried to make out what Eostre had been changed into, and frowned, confused. "Mrs. Agnes?"

The woman stared back at her through thick glasses. No longer friendly, her face hard and chiseled with anger.

"Who is Mrs. Agnes?" Sarah asked. She studied the woman before her.

Reg thought she understood. Mrs. Agnes was a witch. Of course Reg had ended up in a B&B run by a witch. That's just the way the fates aligned. She would be drawn to magical places and people, even when she didn't realize it.

But why had Mrs. Agnes followed her back to Black Sands? She had known where Reg was going. There was no reason to follow her. Had she wanted to keep Reg safe?

But she hadn't. She had used the disguise to try to stop Reg from carrying through with her plan. Which was what…? Reg couldn't even form it into words. She was being driven by feelings, emotions that had been building ever since she had stepped into the ocean on the beach below the house.

"She's the owner of the B&B I stayed at," she told Sarah, shaking her head as she tried to fit the rest of the details together in a way that made sense. "But I don't understand…"

"You don't have any right to be here," Mrs. Agnes insisted.

"This is my house."

"I don't care about the house," the woman argued. "These are not your waters."

Reg rubbed her eyes, trying to remove the afterimages produced by Kybele's brightness. "Not my waters?"

It was the echo of something else she had heard. She could hear another voice in her head. Someone else who had stood in this very cottage. *You claim these waters. This is your territory.* She rubbed the back of her neck, trying to remember. Her head was pounding. She could detect Julian's scent even though he was several feet away from her. And he smelled entrancing. She wanted to be close to him. And more than that.

"These southeastern waters are mine," she told Mrs. Agnes.

"No! This is my territory. You cannot hunt here."

Reg shook her head. Norma Jean, her mother, had told Reg that the waters were to be hers. She wasn't going to give them up to some other siren who thought she had the right over them.

Mrs. Agnes let out a howling, a keening that made everyone but Reg slap their hands over their ears in pain.

"This is mine," Reg repeated, raising her voice over the shriek. "None shall hunt here but me!"

"You have no claim. I have been here for a hundred years—"

"And now, you shall leave. Go somewhere else. Find other waters."

Reg was sure that if the other siren insisted on a physical fight, Reg would come out victor. The woman was old, half-blind, and slow. Reg could fight her with one hand tied behind her back.

"It is mine!" Mrs. Agnes insisted. "I knew what you were the instant you showed up on my doorstep. I hoped I was wrong, that you had not awakened, but I knew… once you stepped into the water, you could no longer deny what you were."

CHAPTER THIRTY-FIVE

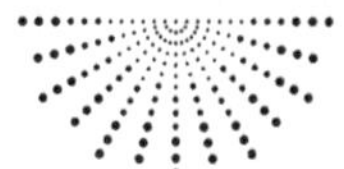

Reg took long, deep breaths. It was difficult to concentrate with the rival siren on one side of her and her prey on the other. She wanted to fight to protect her territory and to feed at the same time.

She turned her gaze toward Kybele again. "You are a real goddess?" Reg turned the question back to Sarah as well. "Is Kybele a real goddess?"

"A proto-goddess," Sarah agreed. "One who existed before the immortals that peopled this earth." She studied Kybele thoughtfully. "But I have not heard of Kybele walking the earth in millennia."

Kybele's light dimmed a little more. Enough that Reg could look straight at her face. And Kybele winked.

Reg's jaw dropped. She was more confused than ever. What did that mean? What was that signal? She thought fast. She was good at thinking on her feet, but the situation was enough to throw anyone off their game.

"Kybele banishes you," she told Mrs. Agnes. "She is Mother of the earth and all that, so this was her territory long before it belonged to a single siren. Right?"

Kybele gave a grave nod. Mrs. Agnes shrieked again. Reg winced.

It wasn't as painful to her as it was to the rest of the house's occupants, but it still annoyed her like fingernails on a blackboard.

"I won't go," Agnes insisted.

"You will."

"This is wrong! It is my territory."

"Not anymore."

She shrieked and howled and stormed out the door, scattering the leaves and petals behind her in little swirling whirlwinds. Reg didn't see any sign of the rabbits. She watched Mrs. Agnes until she was out of sight and then shut the door. No point in inviting any more strangers into her home than she already had.

"Well. That was fun."

"I don't understand what just happened here," Julian complained. His eyes were wide, and though he looked worried and frightened, there was a certain amount of excitement in his features that he just couldn't hide.

"Aren't you supposed to be an expert in endangered species?" Sarah asked caustically.

"I am," Julian snapped. "I know all of the endangered magical species."

"Then I would think you would be able to recognize a siren. How many of them are left on the earth? Half a dozen? And you don't recognize when you have two of them in the same room together?"

"Sirens." Julian looked at Sarah and then at Reg. "You two?"

"No!" Sarah laughed. "I am just a witch."

"Reg?" Julian's eyes clouded with confusion. "And… that old woman?"

Reg took a couple more steps toward Julian. She smiled, trying to look as warm and welcoming as she could. "Of course. And now that she is gone, we can relax. How would you like to go for a swim?"

"What…?" Julian's brows came down. "Are you serious?"

"Yes. I'm sorry I was so antagonistic toward you before. I want to make it up to you. Let's go down to the ocean. If you don't want to swim, we can just walk beside the water. And after we're all nice and relaxed, we can come back here, and I'll answer all of your questions."

Reg stepped toward Julian again, getting inside of his personal space. She touched his cheek with the tip of her finger.

He inched toward her, eyes focused somewhere far in the distance. His scent enticed Reg. She could sense the warm, throbbing pulse in his neck, the movement of blood singing through his body. She smiled at him.

"Reg," Sarah warned. "I don't think you want to do this."

"I do," Reg breathed. "I'm *so* hungry."

"I think there's something in the fridge," Sarah tried to tempt her with human food. "Or we could order in. I could run to the store and get you anything you want and you don't have to wait for delivery."

"I already have what I want."

"You can't, Reg."

"Yes, I can." Reg touched Julian's shirt collar, slipping her finger behind it and tugging him toward her. "Tell her, Julian. It isn't against the rules. You can't make a law that I can't take my natural prey."

"Of course not," Julian agreed. "But the treaty between the sirens and humans specifies that the sirens cannot hunt on land."

Reg's hand was shaking with her proximity to Julian. "I wasn't part of that treaty."

"It binds all sirens," Sarah said. "You don't get the opportunity to agree with it or not. You have to abide by it, like any other law."

The two cloaked warlocks had apparently recovered from their shock and got up enough courage to act. They stepped forward together, angling to separate Reg from her prey. "Let him go."

"Why?"

Her hand was so close to his pulsing carotid that Reg could feel the rush of blood beneath her fingers.

"Investigator Sabat is right. You cannot take him on the land."

"That's why I invited him to go down to the water," Reg explained impatiently. It wasn't, of course, but she would look like the good guy, someone who was willing to follow all of their stupid rules.

"You can't hunt on the land and take him down to the water. You can only hunt on the water."

"That's ridiculous."

"That's what the treaty says."

"A treaty written by humans," Reg said hotly. "Imposed on sirens unfairly. It can't be enforced."

"Reg," Sarah cajoled, "this is going to wear off, and you're going to be glad that you didn't do anything rash. I understand that what you're feeling right now is real, but it will pass. You'll go back to yourself once you've had a chance to relax."

"He is mine," Reg insisted, pointing at Julian. "He was taken away from me once before. I won't let it happen again."

Sarah gave a slow blink. "When was he taken away before?"

Reg turned her eyes toward Kybele, still watching the scene before her with interest, her face and whole body shining. "Somebody took him. Was it you?"

CHAPTER THIRTY-SIX

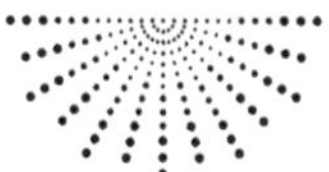

Kybele smiled serenely. "Why would I take your prey?"

"Someone did it before—someone like you. I don't know why. It wasn't fair."

Julian frowned, turning his gaze toward Reg. "This happened before? When? You're not talking about in the grocery store…?"

"Yes," Reg agreed. Then she shook her head. "No… that wasn't it. You were…" She looked Julian up and down. "You were bigger."

"I was bigger?" His brain already fogged by her touch, Julian couldn't sort this out. "What does that mean?"

"Maybe Regina was smaller," Kybele prompted.

Memories flooded back so fast that Reg was unable to sort them out. They were fragmented and confused, all mixed together.

"When I was a child," she said, trying to sift through the memories. "You were there."

Julian nodded his agreement. "We were together," he said with a dreamy smile, "when we lived with the Newburgs."

"We were not *together*," Reg said, not wanting the others to think that they had been romantically involved. "We were both in foster care with them."

With the memories flooding her brain, her need to feed was starting to pass, the hunger gradually lessening. Julian was still making cow eyes at her, charmed by whatever happened when she touched him. It was incredibly irritating.

"We were in foster care," she repeated, raising her voice as if that would help him to process what she said better. "What happened?"

"I didn't do anything," Julian said in a slightly petulant tone. "It wasn't my fault."

Of course it was. He had been older than Reg. He had tormented her to no end. Whatever had happened had definitely been his fault.

"You're lying."

"It wasn't me."

Did he remember what had happened, or was he just generally denying that he could have done anything wrong?

"Julian."

"What?"

"Look at me."

He didn't at first, unfocused, staring off into the distance. Reg shook his shoulder.

"Wake up. Forget everything else. Look at me. At my eyes. I want to know what happened."

Eventually, Julian was able to draw his eyes back over to Reg. He looked reluctantly at her. Reg looked at his eyes, still vague, and tried to enter into his thoughts. If he had memories of what had happened, she wanted to share them. Put them together with the bits and pieces she could recall and build a full picture.

"Let me in," she urged.

It was against the rules to force anyone to connect. But Julian wanted to, didn't he? He wanted to remember what had happened just as badly as Reg did. If he allowed her into his thoughts, there would be no need for force.

"This is just…" Julian's voice faded out. Reg felt her way through as his barriers dropped.

"Yes. Let me see."

She explored, trying to understand how his brain worked. She had connected with other minds in the past, especially since she had moved to Black Sands. But Julian was different. Things seemed fractured and unconnected. There were orphaned memories that didn't flow into each other or didn't have any emotions attached. It was a noisy, chaotic place. Usually, when Reg went from her mind into someone else's, she found it peaceful, momentarily leaving the clamoring voices of her own mind behind. But it wasn't like that with Julian. He didn't hear the voices that she did, but things were unsettled, in a constant state of reprocessing and hyper-vigilance. She wanted to raise her hands and make everything stop and be still.

When we lived together, Reg prompted mentally. *In foster care with the Newburgs.*

A lot of mental indexing. Scene after scene of their time together in the Newburg home. Reg hadn't been able to remember it very clearly. Sorting through his memories was like watching long-forgotten family vacations in a slide show. It was disconcerting to see herself as a child from the outside. She'd had that experience before when Weston and Harrison had taken her back through time to when she was four.

But seeing herself through Julian's eyes was different again. Her view was filtered through his perception. Everything seemed darker and a little fuzzy at the edges. As if his memories were faded film. He had watched her a lot—more than she had ever known.

CHAPTER THIRTY-SEVEN

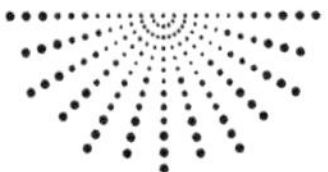

Julian had arrived at the Newburgs' home on a chilly spring morning. While the social worker talked about how nice it was that the weather was warming up and the snow was melting, Julian saw only the dirty remnants of snow revealing the mud and layers of dead, decaying leaves that had remained hidden during the long freeze.

The Newburgs had several children. Julian was fourteen and there were a couple of kids just a little younger than he was already in the home. Julian was irritated by them before they even opened their mouths. They looked so… boring and bland and stupid. A lot of the foster kids that he'd run into were stupid. He didn't know why. Maybe they were brain damaged by alcohol or drugs they had been exposed to before they were even born. Maybe from being beaten by their parents or Johns or gangs on the street. Maybe it was because they rarely went to school, and when they did, they didn't pay any attention or bother to do the classwork or the homework. Whatever it was, he hated encountering the same boring, stupid brains over and over again as he was moved from one home to the next.

And then he'd seen Reg.

When she had been a child, Reg's hair had not been braided in the tiny box braids that she sported as a medium. Her shoulder-length red hair was always frizzed, tangled, or greasy, depending on how long it had been since someone last forced her to wash it and brush it into some order.

She was eleven. Her skin was as pale as snow and her eyes were enormous. She looked like a wraith. Or a witch.

Reg played on the floor with several toy cars, dollhouse furniture, and Smurfs. She was talking quietly to herself, describing the little scene she was laying out, the characters asking questions of each other, or occasionally growling at someone and swiping her hand through part of the scene to wipe it out.

"Who is that?" Julian asked Mrs. Newburg.

Mrs. Newburg's lips pressed tightly together. That look that foster parents and social workers always gave Julian when he asked a question he shouldn't have or that they didn't want to answer. Julian didn't see why it should be wrong for him to ask the name of one of the other foster children, so he had to assume it was because Mrs. Newburg didn't like the girl or didn't like to talk about her.

"That's Reg," she said eventually, her lip curling in distaste. "Reg. Reg! Regina!"

The girl didn't look up, completely engaged with her game. Mrs. Newburg marched over to her and grabbed her arm, yanking her to her feet.

Reg squealed a protest and tried to writhe away. Mrs. Newburg kept a tight hold on her.

"Reg. You stop that now. Listen to me. I'm talking to you."

"I was playing with Odette!"

"You were not paying any attention to me. I was talking to you."

"Didn't hear you," Reg pouted.

"You need to listen to me. Or you're just going to end up in more trouble." Mrs. Newburg gave Reg's arm another shake. "Do you want to be in more trouble?"

"No."

"This is our new foster child." She shook Reg again, still trying to get her full attention. Reg was looking down at her toys, her body reaching and drooping toward them, hoping that Mrs. Newburg would give up and let her go so she could continue with her game. "Look! Pay attention! This is Julian."

Julian waited. Reg's eyes eventually moved from her toys to him. She looked him over and shrugged her thin shoulders.

"Hi."

"Hi," Julian greeted. He felt something different around Reg. Not that same stupidly boring crap that he got from most of the other foster kids. There was something very alive about Reg. Her eyes sparkled with intelligence and curiosity. "What are you playing?"

"I'm playing with Odette." She repeated what she had said a moment ago.

Julian looked around. There didn't appear to be any other children in the near vicinity. Another little girl might have gone to the bathroom or been sent to clean her room or go run an errand.

Mrs. Newburg shook her head angrily at Reg. "Quit making up nonsense. Now you need to get your stuff picked up. You have chores to do before supper and you're not going to get to eat if you don't get them done."

"We just got everything set up."

"And now it's time to put them away. You've had hours to play. Now it's time to get to work."

She released Reg's arm. Reg returned to her place on the floor, painstakingly setting up more doll furniture and Smurfs.

Mrs. Newburg had apparently finished showing Julian around. She left without a word to him, leaving him alone with Reg.

Julian crouched down to look at the scene Reg had set up. "What are you playing?"

"Me and Odette are playing. Go away."

"Missus said you have to clean up."

"I don't have to."

"She said you have to clean up and do your chores before dinner."

"I don't want to."

Julian grinned at her defiance. He could understand the sentiment. Grown-ups were always telling him to do this or do that. He wished he were grown up so that he could do whatever he wanted to.

Julian picked up one of the Smurfs to look at it. Reg squealed.

"No! Put that back. I need him over there," she pointed to the spot Julian had picked it up from.

"You have lots of Smurfs. I don't have any. I think I'm going to keep this one," Julian ventured, goading her to see how she would react.

"You can't! That's mine!"

"This is yours?" Julian repeated. He recognized Reg as the type of child who likely got moved from one home to another every few months. And a kid like that didn't have very many possessions. She'd have to leave everything behind when she went to a new home, and just take the clothes on her back and maybe a few other clothes that would fit in a plastic shopping bag to hold her over until the next foster parent could get everything she needed. Not much room for toys or collections. "I bet it isn't. I bet it's Odette's."

Reg's eyes snapped to Julian's face. She didn't have to be coached into making eye contact this time. She stared into Julian's eyes as if trying to read him. "You see Odette too?"

Julian raised his eyebrows. So she had an invisible friend. Someone she'd made up so she would have someone to play with. No wonder Mrs. Newburg had said she was talking nonsense. There was no Odette.

"Sure, I see Odette," Julian said, playing along. "She's right there, isn't she?" He nodded toward the toys Reg had set up as if there were another child there.

Reg's eyes widened. She looked at the toys and then back at Julian. "Really?"

Julian snickered. "Not really, you moron. There's no one there. You're a freak."

Her face tightened into a mask. "I'm not a freak." She clenched her teeth, not saying anything else, even though Julian could tell that she wanted to.

He was going to have fun with her. Reg was going to be a ton of fun to wind up; he could tell that already.

"Well, freak, it's time to clean up your toys. Do all of these go into the bin?" He indicated a box standing nearby that was partially filled with small toys that had seen better days.

Reg turned her back to him, ignoring the question. She continued to set up the figures, her voice a sing-song as she talked about what she was doing.

Julian knelt beside her and started scooping up toys and putting them into the toy box. Reg protested, grabbing at his hands and arms to stop him.

"No! No, I'm playing with those. You can't take them away."

"Missus said if you don't put them away and do your chores, you don't get to eat. You don't want that, do you?"

"I just want to play for a few more minutes. Then I'll clean up."

"You won't get done in time if you don't get started now." Julian grabbed a couple more handfuls of toys and dropped them into the bin.

"Stop!" Reg screeched and hit his arm.

Julian just kept going.

"Stop!" Reg picked up one of the bits of doll furniture and hit Julian with it. The pointy little legs of the table scratched his arm and it stung.

"Ouch. Don't you know you're not allowed to hit?" Julian pulled the small table from her hand and tossed it into the bin.

"Stop it! Don't touch my stuff!"

Julian used his powers to pull more of the small toys into his hands and he dumped them into the box. Reg looked at him, her eyes wide.

"Hey!"

He didn't mind using magic in front of her. She had an imaginary friend. He suspected she told the Newburg's about a lot of other "nonsense." No one would believe her if she told them what she had seen. Adults who didn't practice magic themselves didn't even believe that it existed. Even if the most stable foster child were to tell them that Julian moved things without using his hands, they would laugh and tell him to quit making things up.

Reg tried to pull toys out of Julian's hands. When he wouldn't release them, she grabbed the bin and pulled it toward her to retrieve the toys that she "needed" out of it. Julian grabbed the other side of the container and pulled it away from her.

"Give it!" Reg insisted through clenched teeth.

Julian tried to hold on to it, but even with his physical strength and magic put together, he was having trouble keeping a grip on it. That feisty little redhead was strong! After calculating for a moment, Julian released his grip on the bin and Reg toppled over backward, the toys showering everywhere.

Reg screamed and threw herself at Julian, pounding him with her fists, knocking him from his knees to the floor.

It was at that moment that Mrs. Newburg returned, disturbed by the noise of their altercation.

"Julian! Reg! Cut it out. What's gotten into you? Stop it now!" She waded into the fray and pulled the two of them apart, grabbing ears to pull them off of each other, and then shoving their heads back together so that they clonked against each other in the middle.

"Ow!" Julian protested. He rubbed the spot on his forehead where they had connected. "She attacked me! Why are you punishing me?"

"It takes two to fight. I don't know what's going on in here, but you know it's time to clean up. Reg… look at this mess! I said it's time to clean up."

"I didn't do it! It was him!" Reg pointed her finger at Julian.

"Who?"

"Him!" Reg pointed again, furious.

"You'd better learn names if you're going to start blaming things on other kids."

"Him," Reg repeated.

"Julian."

"Julian took my toys away and he made me spill them all over."

"They aren't your toys, are they?" Mrs. Newburg countered, confirming Julian's guess. "Those toys belong to me, and if they are going to cause problems, then I will take them away and you won't have any toys to play with. How does that sound?"

"Julian spilled them."

"No, Julian did not. Now the two of you…" She looked at Julian. "You go to the kitchen and find the plates and cutlery and set the table. Put a plate at each place there is a chair. You can do that, right?"

Julian nodded. What was he, six? He knew how to set the table the right way. And he certainly knew how to put a plate at each place setting.

He got to his feet slowly, his head a little dizzy from the collision with Reg's. She was one tough cookie. She hadn't even cried out.

"And Reg, it's time to put these toys away. And you'll do it now unless you want to lose them for two weeks. How would you like to just sit on your bed for two whole weeks?"

"That's not fair."

"Life isn't fair. Get them picked up."

"But Julian dumped them."

"And you are better at picking up toys than he is, aren't you?"

Reg's face brightened slightly at this. She grabbed hold of the offered compliment immediately. "I can pick them up faster than he can," she bragged.

Julian wanted to go back and teach her a lesson. He was older than she was and he could do anything better than she could.

But it was his first day at the Newburgs', and he didn't know the lay of the land yet. He would have to wait another day to teach Reg a lesson.

CHAPTER THIRTY-EIGHT

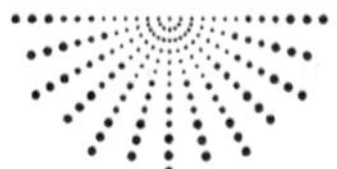

Reg could barely remember the incident herself. It didn't stand out among her other memories. Children had come and gone in all of the families that she had stayed with. She couldn't count them all, let alone name them. She couldn't have remembered half of them. But apparently, she had made an impression on Julian.

She flipped through the memories, trying to put them in some kind of order.

She saw herself walking home and into an empty house. Mr. and Mrs. Newburg were both gone to some foster parent training thing. The older children were supposed to be taking care of the younger. The other children were still at school, taking part in extra tutoring or after-school activities. Neither Julian nor Reg had tutoring or was interested in participating in anything.

Julian followed Reg without her being aware of his presence. When he arrived home, he took a look around the house to confirm that they were alone. Reg was already climbing up on the counter in the kitchen to reach the cookie tin. It was supposed to be far above anyone's head, but Reg was a little monkey. Climbing up on the counter, extending her reach with a wooden spoon, and jumping, she was able to knock the tin off of the top of the cabinets and catch it deftly in her hands.

Julian watched her get a cookie out. Reg startled and her eyes narrowed at him when she realized that he had caught her at it.

"You can have one if you put it back up for me," she suggested.

Julian took the tin from her and took a handful of cookies out for himself. "I don't need your permission."

"She'll notice if you take that many."

"I'll tell her you took them."

Reg's mouth pressed together into a long, thin line. For someone so young, she looked like a disapproving old woman. "I'll say that you did," she countered.

"She already knows that everything that comes out of your mouth is a lie."

She blinked and didn't answer.

"You could just throw them back up there," Julian said.

Reg looked at the height and angle and shook her head.

"Then how were you planning to put them back?"

She shrugged and didn't tell him.

"You could just do this." Julian made a tossing motion, and the cookie tin floated up out of his hands and inserted itself into its allotted place.

He expected astonishment out of Reg. A dropped jaw and wide-eyed disbelief. But she just looked at him, her eyes wary. "How did you do that?"

Julian raised his brows. "Can't you do that?"

She didn't answer. Julian gazed at her, wondering if maybe this wasn't a surprise to her because she could do the same thing. He hadn't caught her doing any magic, but he had his suspicions.

Reg jumped down from the counter and took a bite of her cookie. Julian snatched it out of her hand and shoved the whole thing into his mouth. He would have laughed at her if he weren't afraid that he would choke. The look on her face was priceless. She had worked hard to get that one cookie and had intended to get every ounce of enjoyment out of it. He had taken a whole handful of cookies with no work and then stolen hers too.

Reg tried to grab one of the cookies in Julian's other hand, but she was too short and couldn't reach them when he held them higher.

"Come and get it, Reg," he teased, after swallowing his mouthful. "Come on, reach… reach… you can get it!"

He lowered it slightly so that her fingers just brushed his hand, but she couldn't get the height necessary.

"Give me one! One of them was mine."

"Well, you should have guarded it better."

"Julian! Give it!"

He continued to shake his head. Reg kicked his shins.

"Ow!" Julian kicked back, aiming higher, retaliating not with a kick to her shins but burying the toe of his shoe in the middle of her stomach.

Reg went down and writhed on the floor, gagging and choking, trying to get her breath back again. Julian waited, making sure that she was really hurt and she wasn't just going to jump back up the instant he let down his guard. He smiled at her and took a bite out of another cookie.

"Oh, these are so good. I'm going to eat them all and then tell Missus that you ate them. I'll tell her that's why you have a stomachache."

Reg sniffled and gasped. She rubbed at her eyes with her fists but didn't let him see any tears. Julian just watched her and ate more cookies.

Eventually, Reg pushed herself up and leaned back against the cupboards, putting her hands over her face so that he couldn't see her expression. He assumed she was still trying to stop the tears. She knew that if she cried in front of him she would never hear the end of it.

There was a loud pop and the kitchen light went out. It made Julian jump. He looked up at the bulb to confirm that it had burned out, laughing at himself for being scared by a light burning out.

Reg didn't move. Her breathing was slowing, steadier. Maybe next time, she would remember not to fight back against him. He was bigger and stronger. He wasn't going to let anyone beat on him. Never.

There was another pop, this one louder, and the bulb over the kitchen table shattered, raining glass down on the tabletop. Julian looked at it in surprise. He'd never seen that happen before.

"Weird."

"If you hurt me, bad things will happen to you," Reg warned in a raspy voice.

Julian forced a laugh. He was a little concerned about the light bulbs suddenly burning out. There was obviously something wrong with the house's electrical wiring. Could that be dangerous to them? Maybe he should go out of the house. At least for a while, until they were sure that no more lights were going to blow up. But one thing that he wasn't worried about was that bad things would happen to him if he hurt Reg. She was showing her teeth, but that's all it was—a wild animal's attempt to appear threatening before turning tail and running away.

"You're the one who had better look out," he returned.

Reg lowered her hands from her face. Her expression was not tearful, but angry. And Julian would have been mad too, if someone had treated him that way. But that was the whole point. He wasn't going to let anyone hurt him. He was going to be the one who did all of the hurting.

Whoever and whenever he could.

CHAPTER THIRTY-NINE

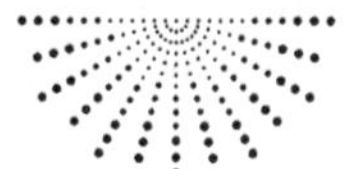

Reg didn't immediately dive into another memory. Many scenes had played out similarly, Julian bullying her, getting her in trouble with Mrs. Newburg, stealing from her, and using her as a pawn. Sometimes light bulbs broke. Sometimes something else happened. Once there was a fire, but it was contained in the kitchen and Julian was quick to put it out.

But all the time, Julian stayed in control; he was on top.

Whenever they were alone, Julian was on the lookout for ways to bully and harass Reg.

The Newburgs hadn't been the most awful foster parents. Certainly, she'd had worse—those who were more abusive or negligent. But after the way Reg's own mother had been, how could Reg expect someone who wasn't her own blood to treat her any better? The Newburgs had done their best to get her into therapy that would make a difference in her behavior. Mrs. Newburg was always reading up on the latest advancements in parenting and in behavior modification. Ways to reclaim wayward and rebellious children or to force them to make better choices. It had been a confusing time for Reg as they hopped from one therapy to another, chasing after the elusive pill, meditation method, or discipline technique that would make a difference and keep Reg under control.

Julian had therapy too, of course, but he was better at appearing to be compliant and only disobeying or showing his true colors when they were out of the room. Reg and the other foster children quickly learned to avoid being left alone in the same room with him for even just a few minutes.

Julian was supposed to be at football practice that afternoon. But Julian hated football. He was a skinny kid, not very well-coordinated, known to be a nerd. No one wanted him on the team and Julian himself had no intention of putting himself in a position where he could be injured on the field. So he wrote himself a note and was dropped from the team.

The Newburgs had no idea he was no longer participating. Usually, he stayed at the school until practice was over so that they wouldn't catch on. But that day, Julian knew the Newburgs weren't going to be home after school. The kids were supposed to get their own suppers and work on their homework independently until evening, when Mr. and Mrs. Newburg would be back.

The two middle kids were in the house. They were not working on their homework as they were supposed to be, but they stayed quiet and out of the way, playing electronic games or doing other things they were not supposed to.

Mrs. Newburg's newest attempt at reforming her foster children was water therapy. There was an aboveground pool in the back. Not a big one, but not a little kid wading pool, either. Big enough to kick around in and to do a bit of swimming. Reg loved the water, and whenever it was warm enough, she was out there, playing, floating, and swimming. The others had quickly gotten bored of the pool, but she hadn't, and the Newburgs held out hope that it was working and would prove Reg's salvation. Reg's behavior had been better. She was more focused. Her grades were gradually improving, slowly but surely. Maybe she would become an Olympic swimmer and her story would be told on TV as an inspiration to other foster children and parents everywhere as to what could be done if they put their minds to it.

Julian went out to the yard and watched her. She didn't see him and wasn't expecting him to be home. Reg swam around the pool, pretended to dive to the bottom—it was only about three feet deep—and, as always, talked nonstop to her invisible friends.

Then suddenly, she stopped. She said "What?" and turned around quickly, spotting Julian before he had a chance to duck back.

Reg knelt on the bottom so the water came up to her shoulders. She frowned at him suspiciously. "What are you doing here?"

"I live here."

"I mean out here. Why are you watching me?"

"Maybe I came out to swim. It's not just your pool, you know."

Her eyes flicked over him. "You're not wearing your swimsuit."

"I could skinny dip."

Reg's nose wrinkled in disgust. "Gross!"

Julian grinned and pretended he was going to take his clothes off. Reg backed up, her eyes alert, but she had a pretty good idea that he was only teasing. He didn't like swimming like she did. The water was too cold for him. He enjoyed lazing around in the water on hot days, and other than that, eschewed the pool.

"Who are you talking to out here?" he demanded.

Reg's eyes slid away from him. "No one."

"I heard you talking. Who are you talking to?"

"There's no one else out here." She looked back at his face. "*You* don't see anyone else, do you?"

She said it in a way that suggested he might be able to see someone else there, but she was pretty sure he couldn't.

"You think I can't see them?" Julian challenged.

Reg's eyes darted around. Julian got a disquieting feeling that she was looking around inside his head. He shook it, trying to get rid of the feeling. Of course she couldn't get inside his head. He kept his thoughts safely hidden from everyone. He didn't tell his friends or his parents the thoughts and fears he harbored. He didn't tell his therapists. He kept them all carefully wrapped up where no one could see them.

"You think you're so special," Julian growled at Reg. Why did she get special treatment? Why did she get a swimming pool when he didn't get anything? They catered to Reg's interests, and Julian got football, which he hated. "You think you can have whatever you want. They don't like you any better than the rest of us."

"I never said that," Reg said, frown lines appearing between her brows. "I just like swimming."

"So they got you a swimming pool. You think they like you like a biological kid? Because they don't. They just think you're more messed up than the rest of us."

Reg didn't seem as shocked and hurt by this as he had expected. She shrugged and went from kneeling to sitting so that her head disappeared under the surface of the water. He felt her shutting him out, telegraphing to him that she didn't care about Julian or his opinion. She could spend all afternoon in the pool and not have a single thought about him or what he wanted. Under the surface of the water, she was in a whole different world, one she didn't have to share with him.

Rage blossomed in Julian's memory, startling Reg and nearly throwing him out of his head. Everything was just red rage and darkness. In the memory, eleven-year-old Reg sat serenely under the water and didn't have a clue what was coming.

CHAPTER FORTY

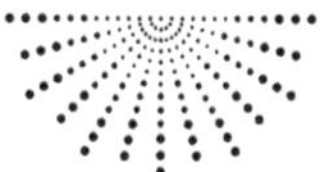

Julian dropped his schoolbag, stripped off his shirt, and kicked off his shoes. He wasn't wearing any socks, so he stood there in just his pants, the cool air tickling his skin but not doing anything to cool the blinding rage Reg had triggered by disrespecting him. He strode over to the swimming pool and waited for Reg to pop her head out for a breath.

She stayed under for a long time; then, looking up through the water, she saw him there. She bobbed back up to the surface.

"What?"

"You're stupid! No one likes you! You know at school they all talk about you behind your back? Talk about how weird you are? And Mrs. Newburg wants to get rid of you. She keeps telling your social worker that they need to find a new family for you, because she doesn't want to keep you."

Reg shrugged, resignation in her eyes. Like she already knew all of that and it came as no surprise to her. Julian knew how much it hurt to be rejected by his peers and his foster families, however much he hated them. He expected her to be angrier about it.

But Reg had been in the system almost her whole life. She knew that she was always going to leave the family she was with, either to be transferred to another family or facility, or when she aged out and was on her own. She didn't have a forever family and she didn't expect to. She lived in the moment, swimming when there was a pool.

Reg knew that was just Julian's lens. He didn't know about ghosts that always dragged her into the past or visions of the future. Reg did try to live in the moment and be happy with what she had, but she wasn't nearly as successful at it as he perceived.

Julian reached out and grabbed a handful of Reg's red hair, darkened by the water. He yanked her toward him and she cried out. Julian was happy he hurt her. Glad to hear her protest. He hated to be ignored.

Reg tried to pull free, but pulling her hair out of his hand was impossible and just hurt her more.

Reg's scalp burned with pain, her memory merging with Julian's, everything suddenly becoming another layer deeper and richer.

"Let go!" She knew there was no point in screaming. There were no adults home to hear her. She wouldn't even have cared if Mrs. Newburg knocked their heads together for fighting; at least Reg would get away from Julian. But Mrs. Newburg wasn't there to put a stop to it. There was no one to give her a hand unless Uncle Harrison showed up, and he was unpredictable. She never knew when he would come and when he wouldn't.

"You know what you are?" Julian demanded. "You are a spoiled brat."

He plunged her head into the water. Reg didn't even have time to take a deep breath of air before going under the surface. She struggled to escape his hold and to get above the surface again. He held her there while she fought back, desperate to break his hold, her scalp on fire and not sure how long she could hold her breath and keep from sucking water into her lungs.

After what seemed like forever, Julian pulled her head back up so that Reg could hurriedly gasp for one breath, and then he pushed her under again.

Was he going to drown her? Was it just a game for him and he would laugh at her when he eventually let her go?

His rage didn't allow him to think clearly, or Julian would not have held her under the water for so long. He would hold his own breath to gauge how long he could keep her under before he had to let her back up to take a breath. But he was too angry. Julian just held her under the water, relishing her struggle, feeling the power of holding her life in his hands. It was his to do what he wanted to with. He could hold her there longer, until she was pulling in the water and went limp under his fingers, or he could let her snatch just one more breath of air, enough to tantalize her into thinking he was going to let her live.

Julian jumped at a bang like a gunshot, but didn't release her. Looking around, he realized that the buzzing motor of the filter had stopped. A thin stream of acrid smoke streamed out the top.

He pulled Reg back up out of the water to look at her face and to see if she were crying. She struggled to free herself, flopping around and clawing at his arms. But he was tough. He had put up with a lot of abuse; he could certainly handle a little girl having a temper tantrum because she wasn't getting what she wanted.

Reg was getting more and more desperate. Every time he pushed her under the water, he seemed to hold her under for longer. She knew that if he kept it up, she would never survive to see Mr. and Mrs. Newburg come home. She put all of her strength into breaking free from him.

He shifted his grip on her hair, and Reg snapped her head around and sank her teeth into his arm. Initially, he hit her under the water and tried to shake her free, thinking it wouldn't take any effort. Reg clamped down her jaw and ground her teeth, digging into the flesh of his arm as deeply as she could.

Julian was shocked by her attack. He tried to wrench away, pulling his arm back out of the water, but Reg stayed attached to him like an animal—a viper or a pit bull with its jaws locked in a death grip.

"Let go!" Julian shouted, hitting her in the face with his other hand. "Stop it! Let go of me!" His voice was breaking, a fact that made him even more furious. A little girl! He wasn't going to be hurt by a little girl!

But he was. Her teeth caused searing pain. He wanted to pull her away with the other hand, but was afraid that all of his flesh would come off with her, like pulling the meat off of chicken bones.

"Stop it! Stop it! Let go!"

Reg felt something she had never felt before. A kind of power and desire rose up in her. She tasted his blood, and instead of being the awful, metallic taste that she got when she was hit in the face or the nose and ended up with a mouthful of blood, it was sweet and warm like an elixir.

She tried to pull him over the edge and into the pool with her. Julian was already off-balance and she nearly succeeded. But he reared back, trying to pull away from her, his feet gripping the dry ground and giving him more purchase than she had in the slippery pool.

Come for a swim.

Reg wanted to say the words out loud, but she couldn't open her mouth and risk losing her grip on him. She projected them into his brain instead, hoping that he was aware enough to hear them and to understand what she wanted.

Come swim with me. Come into the lovely warm water.

He tried to hold on to the edge of the pool. Reg pulled, gripping him with her teeth, trying to inch him into the water where she could control him.

He tried using his gifts, those powers that she couldn't understand. Reg felt his power trying to push her back, to force her down under the surface of the water. If he could keep her there long enough, she would drown, and then her jaws would loosen and he would be able to get free. He worried about the bruise and the bite mark that she would leave behind. How was he going to explain that to anyone? Could he get away with saying that Reg had attacked him for no reason? Or for something trivial like trying to get the TV remote from him so that she could watch her favorite show instead of his?

Julian knew he was stronger than she was. Physically he was stronger. Adding his magic on top of that should have meant that he could overwhelm her without any problem. He shouldn't have been having so much trouble controlling an eleven-year-old. But he could feel her power battling his. He felt a triumphant rush that he had finally forced her to use her magic, proving to him that he had been right all along about her abilities. He had proven she had magical gifts.

Reg gave Julian a sudden, unexpected yank downward, and his face collided with the hard side of the pool. Julian yelped unintentionally at the blast of pain that radiated out from his nose.

She'd broken it. He was sure it was broken; it wasn't the first time he had sustained a broken bone.

That little girl had broken his face! It was unforgivable.

Blood ran down his face and into the water, sending out little tendrils of red, stretching out into the water until they dissipated.

Julian lost control of the situation, trying to grab his smashed nose, trying to free himself from Reg's teeth, shocked and in pain and no longer able to fight against her effectively. Reg rose up to her feet and grabbed his other arm, the one that she didn't still have her teeth sunk into. With a hand under his armpit, she boosted him up and over the edge of the pool. He slid gracefully into the water and she finally released her clenched jaw.

Julian's body sagged with relief. The mortal struggle was over. He was going to be okay.

CHAPTER FORTY-ONE

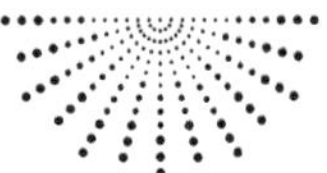

Reg's memory became clearer, while Julian's faded. Overwhelmed with pain and with the relief of her releasing his arm, his recollections became blurred. He floated in the water, which was exactly the right temperature. He felt comfortable there with Reg. Everything would be okay. She would take care of everything.

Reg's hands moved over him, clumsy as she tried to follow the directions her instincts dictated. Her calming venom was already in his bloodstream. Her hands traced over his body uncertainly, and she pushed him under the water, watching his face, wary that he could be trying to trick her by simply appearing to be compliant. But he didn't struggle. Either the blow to the face or her hold over him had taken down all of his defenses.

The knot of hunger grew in her stomach. She put her face in the water and drew it into her mouth. Although his blood was very diluted by the water, she could still sense it. She'd heard sharks could sense just a drop of blood a mile away. She probably could too.

She lowered her face toward Julian's throat.

"Regina."

Reg paused. She turned her face to see Uncle Harrison standing beside the pool, looking down at her with an expression she couldn't quite fathom. She cocked her head at him.

"Why are you here now?"

"You needed me."

Reg shook her head. She had taken care of the situation without him. She hadn't needed him after all. She looked back down at Julian, his body floating just a few inches off of the bottom of the pool, eyes clouded, still bleeding from both his nose and his arm.

"I don't need you."

"Reg. You don't want to do this. Give him to me."

Reg bit her lip and pouted. "No, I don't want to."

"He was damaging you and you stopped him. Now it is over."

"No."

Harrison reached to take Julian out of the water. Reg pulled Julian away from him, snapping her teeth at Harrison in warning.

Harrison allowed a small smile. "It's okay, little one. You are safe. But you are too young to do this. You need to wait until you are an adult and know your mind."

"I'm grown enough."

He shook his head. "It's an instinctive reaction. You are not old enough." He again reached for Reg's prey. She snapped at him again, but he made a pocket of thicker air around him that she couldn't get through, and he was able to reach in and pull Julian out of the water without Reg being able to reach him.

CHAPTER FORTY-TWO

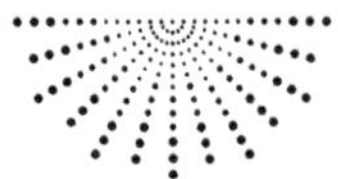

Reg withdrew from Julian's memories and stared at him.

He stared back, her powerful hold on him gradually fading and the shock of their shared memories overcoming them both.

Sarah was watching closely. "What is it? Did you remember?"

Reg nodded slowly. She looked at Julian, then tore her eyes away from him to look at Sarah. "He was… it must have been the combination of the water and his blood that made me…" She shrugged, not wanting to put it into words. She hated this part of herself, the dark instinct buried within her that resurfaced at unexpected moments. "I… had him in the water. Harrison took him away. Said that I was too young to… have him."

"You're probably both lucky that he did."

"Yeah." Reg licked her lips. They were dry and salty. "I had called Harrison… but I wasn't happy when he came and stole my prey." She released Julian. Sarah was right. Once the instinct started to fade, she was glad that she hadn't followed through on the temptation. She didn't know a lot about sirens. Not enough, clearly. But she sensed that if she gave in once and had her fill of human blood, she would never be able to go back. Her only hope of retaining her humanity was to resist the instincts.

Julian took a step back from Reg and then two. "He didn't warn me off because I could harm you," he said slowly. "It was because of what *you* could do to me."

Reg nodded. She, too, had misunderstood Harrison's reference. She hadn't remembered what had happened way back then. She thought that Harrison had saved her from Julian, when it was the opposite way around.

She looked at Kybele, who didn't seem the least bit surprised by what had just happened. "Who are you?"

"I am Kybele, Mother of the earth—"

"You are not. Kybele hasn't walked the earth for millennia," Reg repeated Sarah's words, "...Uncle Harrison."

Kybele smiled at Reg, her smile beatific. Then she was gone and Harrison stood in her place, twirling the ends of his mustache and giving her a rakish look.

"I don't understand how all of this works," Reg said slowly. "Are you also Kybele, or did you just dress up as her?"

Harrison pressed his hands together. "Indeed."

Reg made an impatient noise and tried to figure out another way to ask him. A way to make him spill the beans. But she should know Harrison well enough to understand that he would never give her a straight answer to something she really wanted to know. It would always be a riddle of some kind.

"Why did you decide to stop me from... *taking* Julian that day?" Reg asked. "Why were you concerned about him?"

"My only concern was you, Sirens who are awakened too early tend to have... sanity issues. And you would be active in your mother's territory. She would try to kill you."

"But my mother was dead."

"Not in this timeline," he reminded her.

"But the first time—didn't the same thing happen the first time? Or did you only change things in this time? Maybe it didn't even happen before." But all of Reg's memories were of the former timeline, and that meant Harrison had appeared and saved Julian in that timestream too.

Reg rubbed her temples. Her head was pounding and making her nauseated, like she was hung over. Siren hangover. Overindulging in salt water and exhausting herself chasing down her prey.

"I hope this doesn't mean… that you'll always consider me your prey," Julian said slowly.

"No," Reg assured him. But she wasn't sure if that were true. When the hunger hit, would her primitive siren brain always go back to the moment she had lost Julian? She hoped not.

Julian rubbed his eyes, looking a little like a child who had just gotten out of bed. Still trying to sort everything out and to think about where he was and what he should be doing. He started to smile.

Reg didn't like that. His smiles had never boded well for her before.

"What?"

"I had an encounter with a siren," Julian said self-importantly. "I had a face-to-face, life-and-death struggle with a real siren."

Reg laughed and nodded. "Yep. You did."

"When I was just a teenager. It's no wonder I decided to go into Magical Investigations and ended up investigating endangered magical species."

"I guess it was only natural. Your destiny."

"I always knew there was something special about you, Reg Rawlins. I just never knew what it was."

He knew there was something special about her? He had tormented her, had tried to kill her. If she had been anything but a siren, he would have succeeded. Now he was all happy about it.

Reg shook her head.

CHAPTER FORTY-THREE

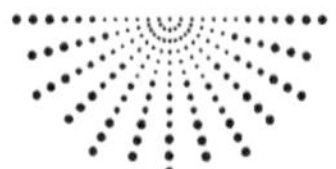

One of the other cloaked men met Julian's eyes and jerked his head in Reg's direction. Reg didn't suppose they were her welcoming committee. Julian had brought in reinforcements to arrest her. He was done with asking questions and was now ready to lay down the law.

Julian looked over at Reg, rubbing the back of his neck. "Are you ready to tell me what happened in the Everglades?"

Reg shook her head. "I don't see how it's any of your business."

"It is my business," he said emphatically. "That's exactly what I do. That's my job. I'm here to find out the truth of what happened in the swamp. And of course... I was curious to see you again, to find out what you're really all about."

"You wanted to arrest me. To make an example of me and… I don't know… bind me for a hundred years for what you thought I did."

"I couldn't figure it all out, to begin with," Julian admitted, speaking slowly. "I didn't understand the burned ropes. I knew you used magic to defeat Tybalt. Maybe you didn't strike the death blow unless you shifted into a panther, but I knew you were involved."

Reg stirred uneasily. He hadn't known to begin with? She wasn't sure she wanted to hear it. It wasn't good news for her if he had put everything together.

"I remembered some of the stuff from when we were kids. How things happened when you were upset. Lights blowing or other equipment failing. Sometimes moving things telekinetically. I didn't *think* that I was doing it, but I couldn't prove that I wasn't, either, because it was always when the two of us were together."

Reg shrugged. She had looked through his memories. They were clearer than hers, for the most part, but they didn't prove her abilities.

"But one time… I do remember a fire," Julian said.

"That could have been an electrical short. It could have sparked and started a fire."

"I thought maybe that was the case. Until I met Davyn."

And Davyn was a firecaster. He was Reg's firecasting mentor. She knew she should have talked to him. Explained that he couldn't say anything that would lead Julian to the conclusion that Reg was a firecaster herself. It would come too close to proving what had happened in the Everglades that night.

"He told you?"

"Let's say… I got it out of him in a private moment." Julian smiled proudly.

"You're despicable," Reg snapped. "I can't believe you would use him like that. He really liked you."

"And I like him," Julian said, shrugging. "Without that connection, I never would have figured it out."

"When he finds out that the only reason you were spending time with him was to find out details about me, he's going to be devastated." Reg didn't actually know whether Davyn would be devastated or just disappointed. But he was not going to be happy to learn that the warlock he had a crush on had only been trying to get information out of him.

"He already knows that," Julian pointed out. "I told him from the start that I was here for an investigation."

"And that you were investigating me?"

"Well… no, I probably didn't tell him that."

"Of course not, or he wouldn't have told you about me."

"He didn't tell me about you. He only told me about himself. We were talking about childhood experiences, growing up with powers in a community where no one else had any, the difficulty of that."

"Davyn grew up in the magical community, didn't he?" Reg was surprised. She'd always assumed that, like Sarah or Letticia, Davyn had been around for many years, growing up in a home where he was trained in magic.

"Not in the beginning, no. He was lucky enough not to be taken into custody by Child Services for being a fire setter. Instead, his abilities were discovered by a teacher who was a practitioner and he was apprenticed to an experienced firecaster."

"Lucky for him."

Julian nodded. "So when we exchanged stories about our childhoods and what it was like growing up in homes where our powers weren't understood, I learned that he was a firecaster. And then I knew that his relationship with you had to be that of a mentor."

Reg said nothing. He hadn't asked a question.

"We knew from the necropsy that the goblin had extensive burning on his chest and upper torso." He waited for Reg to react. "A human would never have survived that kind of blast injury."

"I guess swamp goblins are tougher."

"They are. It's not easy to kill a goblin. That's not the reason they are endangered."

"They've probably killed each other off, like the sirens."

He shrugged. "So you were the initial cause of his death. The injury that disabled him."

"Disabled?" Reg repeated in astonishment. "He wasn't disabled! He was still…"

She bit her lip, trying to silence herself. She had promised herself that she wasn't going to tell Julian anything about what had happened in the swamp, but he was tricky. A better investigator than she had given him credit for.

Tybalt had still chased her, fought her, and tried to kill her even after she had blasted him with a fireball. He had seemed unconquerable. If she had been left to her own devices, it would have been her body they found out there instead of Tybalt's. Only they never would have discovered her body because he would have consumed her and placed her bones, or at least her skull, in his vault with the dozens of other human skulls she had seen.

As far as Magical Investigations was concerned, humans were disposable. Goblins were not.

"And then there was the panther." Julian's eyes were alive with interest. "I still don't know how much you had to do with the panther attack. Maybe you aren't a skinwalker, maybe there isn't even such a thing in existence, but I still think you had something to do with the panther attack. An animal wouldn't have just attacked him without provocation. If goblins were the usual prey of panthers in the Everglades, there would be no goblins left. But they've co-existed there for hundreds of years."

"Maybe they're like wolves and go after the weak and injured. Maybe it was just because he was injured that the panther attacked him." Reg shrugged and shook her head. "I wouldn't know."

"You were there. I have no doubt of that."

"But you can't prove it. You can't prove any of this."

"I don't need to prove it. Just show enough evidence to persuade a reasonable person as to what likely happened."

"Seriously? How can that be the standard? You punish people who just *might* have committed a crime against your precious creatures? How is that just?"

"We are careful. We have a very low rate of false conviction."

"That doesn't make me feel any better," Reg complained. She eyed the two henchmen Julian had brought with him, who were just waiting for his signal to take her into custody.

"Well, as it turns out, there's no point in me pursuing this investigation any farther."

Reg had to play Julian's words back in her head several times before she was sure that he had said what she thought he had. "You're *not* looking into it any farther?"

"There's no point in it."

"Because you've already decided that I did it."

"Well, yes."

Reg's stomach clenched. She held her breath and tried to find her center. She had known it was too dangerous to come back. That Julian was too close to knowing the whole truth. But she had come back to the cottage. Mrs. Agnes had persuaded her to go into the water as a test to see if she was really a siren. It was Reg's own fault that she had let herself be talked into something, and that she hadn't had the willpower to resist a return to Black Sands to hunt for her lost prey.

Reg looked at Sarah, trying to divine whether she would be willing to help Reg or to cover her retreat if she were able to run. Sarah looked back at her without any concern. Maybe she had already talked to someone else in Magical Investigations who had assured her that nothing would happen to Reg. But something was going to happen to Reg. Julian had already made the decision.

Julian was looking at Reg expectantly.

Expecting what? For her to give up and surrender herself into his custody? That wasn't going to happen.

"I can't do anything to you," Julian pointed out. "You're a siren. *You're* endangered. We have no recourse if one endangered magical species kills another or contributes to the death of another. I can't do anything to restrict your movements or your ability to find a mate and raise offspring."

Reg stared at Julian, trying to convince herself that Julian was telling the truth. They weren't going to do anything about her contributing to Tybalt's death? Not even a reprimand?

"Sometimes we relocate individuals," Julian said apologetically. "To somewhere they are more likely to be able to mate or reproduce. But you seem pretty stable here. As stable as sirens ever are. I don't think Mrs. Agnes will be a problem, but if she hunts in your territory, we will probably relocate her rather than you. She is past her... uh... productive days."

"You want me to produce baby sirens?"

Julian chuckled. "Well, yes. You're not much good to us if you don't reproduce."

Reg rolled her eyes and shook her head. "I don't know if I'll ever have kids. It was never part of my plan."

"Biological imperative is a funny thing. You might find yourself changing your mind in the future. A species that has to fight so hard for existence has to have a strong drive for reproduction."

"My mom never wanted me. And sirens often kill their kids."

"None of that negates the need of the individual to reproduce for the continuation of the species."

Reg rolled her eyes. "Is that it, then? You have everything you need for your report? You're going to go back to wherever you came from and report that they can't take any action against me if I was the one responsible for Tybalt's death?"

Julian nodded. "And now that you know that, will you tell me the whole story?"

"No. I want to put what happened behind me." Reg shuddered. "I never want to talk about it again. I don't even want to think about it."

But she couldn't stop thinking about Tybalt's repulsive smell and the grinning skulls on the shelves of his vault.

Julian sighed. "Well, if you ever want to get it off of your chest…"

"I won't be calling you," Reg finished for him.

He grimaced and shook his head.

"But I will tell you one thing."

Julian looked at Reg expectantly.

"There are skinwalkers. And there are more things going on in the Everglades than you can imagine."

Julian grinned, looking like a child who had received an early Christmas present.

Maybe he wasn't so bad after all.

Who did she think she was kidding? Of course he was.

CHAPTER FORTY-FOUR

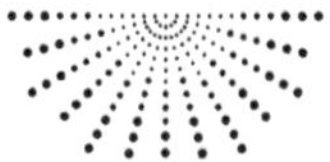

Harrison had vanished. Everyone else had left. Reg was tired, but sleep eluded her. She knew that her body needed to recover from everything she had put it through the last few days. And her brain needed time and rest too. But she just couldn't seem to slow it down enough to get to sleep. As the sky began to brighten, she gave up and left her bedroom. If she pretended that she no longer cared about sleeping, then she was sure her brain would decide that it was finally time. A breath of fresh air and some distraction was all that she needed.

Starlight stretched and squeaked at her but stayed on the bed, eyeing her sleepily. "You just stay there," Reg said. "I'm going out for a walk, but I won't be long."

He closed his eyes again, purring.

Reg slipped on some sandals and left the cottage. She wasn't walking for exercise; she just needed a change of scene. She went around the back of the house and gazed at the garden. Despite Forst's complaints about how much the Spring Games were affecting the garden's growth, it was a riot of color. Reg was sure that some of the flowers were twice the size of their counterparts in other gardens. That was the benefit of having a garden gnome.

Reg Rawlins. The voice came into her head. Reg looked around and eventually spotted Forst. He must have just arrived, because his clothing, usually grubby with dirt and smears of green, was spotless.

Oh, sorry. I didn't know you were here already. I didn't mean to disturb you.

Reg Rawlins does not disturb us, he said heartily. *It is right you should be here.*

Reg blinked at him. Why should she be there? And he didn't usually use the plural to talk about himself.

The garden looks beautiful. You've done such a nice job with the spring flowers.

After I planted Reg Rawlins's, the garden was happy, Forst explained. *Thy seedling has had a beneficial effect.*

Oh? Reg smiled. *This was all because of the seed I planted with Zinnia at the equinox celebration?*

He nodded, giving a deep bow. He pointed to one of the plants that had produced tall stalks topped with white lilies. *This be it.*

That's not my seedling.

It is. This is canna.

Wow. How did it grow so fast? It shouldn't be that big already, right?

He didn't answer her question *When white canna appears in a garden for the first time, it means there will be a wedding.*

Reg laughed. The folklore of the plants and flowers was interesting. She could never keep track of what each symbolized or what their histories were. *A wedding, huh? Maybe you'd better tell Sarah. But I don't think she is interested in getting married again.*

In fact, Reg knew for a fact that Sarah did not want to get serious with anyone, let alone be married again.

No, not Sarah, Forst agreed.

It took a moment before Reg started to make the connections. She looked around the garden, searching for another flash of white, and found a stout little woman with a poofy white dress and a pointed white cap.

Zinnia?

The gnome woman nodded, her cheeks flushing a duskier red.

You are beautiful. Such a lovely bride! She searched the foliage and finally spotted Fir as well, in a spotless black suit and hat. *And there is the groom. I've interrupted you all. I'm so sorry.*

No, Fir insisted. *Sit. Stay with us.* He gestured her toward the bench. Reg took a seat hesitantly. She was wearing her housecoat over a pair of shorts and a t-shirt. Not exactly wedding attire.

I'm not…

You planted the canna, Zinnia said. *You are meant to be here.*

Reg still felt awkward, but she sat down and drew the housecoat around her so that her ragged pajamas wouldn't show.

If I'd known it was a wedding, I would have dressed up.

Reg Rawlins is welcome here, Forst insisted.

Reg looked around the beautiful garden. As if her eyes were adjusting to the dark, Reg started to see other gnomes through the garden, some holding flowers, some with the cutest little gnome babies or children. She relaxed back into the bench, trying to remain inconspicuous so they could continue with their ceremony.

The smell of the flowers and the gentle breeze soothed her soul. She needed that. She needed to know that nature would proceed in its proper order. Spring flowers would bud and blossom, and the march of time would go on as it always had. It didn't matter what she found out about her past or her heritage. Nothing that had happened would change that. She was still the person she had always been and, so far, she had been okay.

Zinnia wore a circlet of the white canna flowers and the daisy-like fleabane Reg had worn at the equinox celebration. Even though Zinnia was not a young girl and was embarking on her second journey into marriage, she was still a beautiful blushing bride. Her eyes shone when she looked at Fir.

The ceremony was plain and simple, the wizened little officiator taking each of the gnomes by the hand and drawing them together to hold each other's hands. He pronounced a blessing on them. Gnomes waved their flowers and whispered congratulations in their inside words.

Reg felt that everything was in balance, as it was supposed to be at the equinox.

CHAPTER FORTY-FIVE

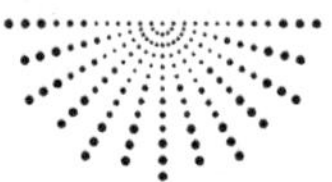

"I don't know if I should go to the closing ceremonies," Reg told Sarah. "I probably shouldn't."

"Why not? You're feeling better. You may never get a chance like this again. You should take it while you can."

"I just... with the fireworks, and just... everything that has happened... I don't know if I want to be around all of those crowds."

"Come with me and watch the last of the Games and the closing ceremonies. We will leave before the fireworks begin. And you can make sure you've had plenty to drink before then."

"I'll end up having to listen from the bathroom."

Sarah laughed. "They have screens on the insides of the stall doors."

Reg couldn't help chuckling and shaking her head. "Like it was built with firecasters in mind."

Sarah nodded. "You have to come. Don't make me go alone."

"You have plenty of friends. You'll know half the people in the arena."

"But I want to go with you. It's different going with someone who has never been there before or who is new to magic. Like taking a toddler to the zoo. It's just more exciting through their eyes."

"I'm a toddler now?"

Sarah smiled. "You are new to magic."

"At least I'm not an infant anymore. That's an improvement."

"You will have many years to grow and mature. What's important is not where you are; it's where you're going. Face forward and just keep taking another step."

Reg nodded. "I am… but it's all so much more complicated than I ever thought it could be. I don't know. I guess when I was a kid, I thought that magic was just a few spells, a few tricks, and that was all there was to it. All of these different species, and complications with treaties and laws, and finding out that I have different gifts than I thought I did in the beginning."

"Or more gifts," Sarah corrected.

Reg nodded, allowing that. It wasn't that she had lost her ability to read people or to talk to the ghosts. She still retained the powers she'd struggled to control since she was a little girl, but there were other things that she hadn't known about or had suppressed, not understanding what was going on.

"I just wish it was all simple."

"Then your journey would be over as soon as it started. The world is a dark, complex place, and so is magic. Now come to the Games."

"Okay." Reg nodded. "Fine. I'll come. But I'm not responsible for anything that happens while I'm there."

"We'll look after you. You don't need to worry about that."

So Reg found herself seated in the arena once more. She sat beside Sarah and sipped her water as people assembled in the stands and set up on the staging area. The big screen made it so that she didn't need to worry about seeing what was going on. Even the slightest detail would be broadcast in front of her, bigger than life—kind of like the big screens in the dwarf mountain. The dwarfs didn't do anything small.

"Please welcome the final contestants," the amplified emcee boomed, introducing each of the practitioners who was there for the final games. Reg recognized a few of them from the first day. She had lost track of what had gone on in between. She knew that Sarah followed the results carefully and had told her about the progress of the Games several times, but she hadn't been paying any attention.

None of it impacted Reg and she had been too worried about Julian's investigation to enjoy it.

Now the investigation was finally behind her, and Reg could watch the displays of magical prowess without continually thinking back to whether they were going to take her away.

The demonstrations were breathtaking. Reg found it hard to convince herself that they were not being performed using sleight of hand, mirrors, and misdirection. Not like when she had watched magic shows as a child and had tried to figure out how each one was done. She could feel the magic shivering around her, playing over her skin. It was incomprehensible that it was all real, and yet it was.

There was much pomp, bands, cheers, and eventually, the winners of the competition were announced. Reg watched them elevate the three medalists without any kind of dais and make the final pronouncements. Reg shifted in her seat.

"We should probably get going. They'll be setting off the fireworks any time."

"Wait another moment." Sarah put a hand over Reg's arm to prevent her from getting up immediately. "We don't want to miss any special appearances."

"Special appearances?" Reg asked, thinking about Wilson. She certainly hoped that he would not be showing up. He had been warned away from the Games, but would he keep his word? Would he stay away from the Games and Reg and her family and friends?

She focused on the emcee's overly dramatic voice just as he announced, "Mother of all the earth," in ringing tones.

Reg looked at the jumbotron screen. "Oh, no. It isn't, is it?"

Sarah laughed as she saw the proto-goddess's image floating in the air, the very same visage as Reg had seen when Kybele-Harrison had sent Eostre away from the cottage.

"Is it him?" she demanded, covering her face and then peeking out between her fingers.

"You mean is it her?" Sarah asked.

Reg took another peek through her fingers. "Harrison?" she asked.

"You should call her by the name she appears as."

"But he—she—isn't really Kybele, is he? I mean, not the original Kybele? He's just playing a game. Acting out a part."

"I don't know, Reg. The immortals are very long-lived. I have no way of knowing if she is the original Kybele or not. But what does it matter? She is today."

"It's just hard for me to wrap my head around. I don't understand how he could also be a female goddess from centuries ago. And if he is, then what is he still doing around today? And why is he… hanging around me? Why does he care anything about me? I'm insignificant. I'm like a bug to him."

"Clearly you matter more to Harrison than a bug."

Kybele declared how happy she was with the Spring Games and all of the valiant contestants. For the spirit of cooperation, even when they were trying to beat each other. For the peace and balance that had surrounded the Games. It sounded to Reg like she was reading from a script. None of it was true.

But there was thunderous applause and cheers. A sense of goodwill rose up and enveloped them, washing the doubt away from Reg's mind. She closed her eyes, wondering at the feeling.

"And now we had better slip out," Sarah said.

Reg found it difficult to rouse herself and get up from her seat. She wanted to just sit there forever, remembering all that had happened during the Games. She felt as if it had all been planned, even the magical investigation and her reunion with Julian. It had somehow all been meant to be.

Sarah tugged on her arm. "Come on, Reg. We don't want to get stuck out here when the fireworks start."

"I think I'll be okay."

"I'm sure you'll be fine. But come anyway. Humor an old woman."

Her grip on Reg's arm was surprisingly strong. Reg managed to get to her feet and Sarah guided her out, informing the guard at the nearest door about Reg's condition. He allowed them to leave together.

As Reg stepped onto the concourse, she could hear the fireworks beginning to go off. She felt the pull, but she had been drinking water, so it wasn't as bad as it had been at the opening ceremonies when they were caught off-guard. And maybe she had grown a teeny bit too, and was a little more relaxed or in control of herself. She still had some of her feelings of balance and peace from the wedding that morning. She was glad they had asked her to stay.

A couple of warlocks were walking toward her. Reg didn't realize until they were closer that one of them was Davyn. And the other, with a shock of white hair, was Julian. She looked for a way to escape before she had to talk to them. She really didn't want to have to talk to Julian again, and she didn't want to hear how things had ended up between the two of them. Had Davyn been devastated to learn that Julian had only been friendly with him in order to find out Reg's secrets? Though the fact that they were walking together suggested that there were no hard feelings over the investigation.

There was no easy escape. Reg pasted an awkward smile on her face and tried not to look either one of them in the eye.

"Avoiding the fireworks?" Davyn asked with a knowing smile.

"A lot of people don't like fireworks," Reg pointed out. "And these ones are quite… dramatic."

Davyn had given her an opening to announce her status as a firecaster to Julian, but Reg hadn't taken it. Hopefully, that would be enough for Davyn to realize that she didn't want to talk about it and still intended to keep those gifts to herself.

"That's true," Davyn agreed. "We saw a few people leave before they started."

Reg looked around and could see a few other practitioners who had opted to leave the stadium bowl for the fireworks demonstration. How many of them were firecasters? Any of them? Or maybe they had PTSD or sensitivities to sound. Or maybe werewolves or other shifters whose animal halves did not like the thunderous noise and the fiery tails of the fireworks.

"I thought you would be… gone back home," Reg said to Julian.

"I couldn't miss the opportunity to see something like this. Who knows when I might have another chance? I extended my stay for a couple of days."

Reg looked at Davyn. "And you had a nice time, I guess."

Julian looked at Davyn as well, smiling. "Yes. We've had a good time together." He returned his gaze to Reg, waiting.

Reg didn't want to wreck whatever enjoyment Davyn was getting out of knowing Julian, but she didn't want him to get hurt either. He should know who Julian was and what he had done. What kind of person he really was, behind the charming facade.

"You guys have gotten to know each other pretty well."

Davyn slid his hand behind Julian's back, nudging him a little closer and looking into his eyes. Heat blossomed in Reg's chest. Davyn needed to be protected. Julian couldn't be allowed to play with his heart.

"And you heard about the investigation?"

Davyn looked at her uncertainly. "Julian said that everything had been straightened out. That you don't have anything to worry about."

So Julian had at least informed him that Reg had been the subject of his investigation.

"Yeah."

"I was glad to hear it. I wouldn't want a friend of mine to be in any trouble with Magical Investigations."

"Yeah. It could have been a lot worse," Reg hinted.

But Davyn just nodded casually. Reg looked at Julian. What was she supposed to do? Tell Davyn that Julian had only been using him? Break his heart? It really wasn't any of Reg's business at all, was it?

"So… I guess this is goodbye."

Julian gave a sweeping bow. "Yes, this is goodbye, Reg. It's been a pleasure getting to know you better." His eyes met her eyes, and she saw again his pride at knowing a siren. How excited he was that Reg had turned out to be something so rare and endangered, giving him cred with his department.

"We'll be keeping in touch," Davyn said, holding Julian's arm for a moment.

Of course they would. There was no chance that Julian would just return to his former obscurity so that she wouldn't have to hear about him or deal with him again. Now he was connected with her mentor. Who knew what kind of complications that was going to cause?

"Reg!"

Reg looked in the direction of the call and saw Damon in his security uniform. He approached gave her a light punch on the arm.

"So, how did you think it went? I was a little surprised by our unexpected guest. The thing about an event like this is that you have to be agile. You always have to be ready to change directions, handle an unexpected complication."

At least he appeared to have forgiven Reg for their failure to get Wilson to appear. Enough had happened that it was just a memory now, and it didn't seem to be one that was bothering him. Everyone was willing to forget what had happened in the Everglades.

Sarah nodded her agreement with Damon.

"Something always happens at the Games."

Did you enjoy this book? Reviews and recommendations are vital to making a book successful.

Please leave a review at your favorite book store or review site and share it with your friends.

Don't miss the following bonus material:
Sign up for mailing list to get a free ebook
Read a sneak preview chapter
Other books by P.D. Workman
Learn more about the author

STEP DEEPER INTO BLACK SANDS

Step deeper with Reg Rawlins into the mystical town of Black Sands

Reg Rawlins never thought she'd stay in Black Sands.
What started as a simple con turned into something else—strange cases, impossible choices, and a town where the usual rules don't apply.

If you want more, you can explore Reg's cases in a different way:

🔮 **Ask the Crystal Ball**
Find out which case you should read next

🃏 **Draw a Card**
Discover strange people, impossible situations, and dangerous choices

Get Exclusive Access
Special content, new releases, and reader-only extras

Welcome to Reg Rawlins's World

WITHOUT FORESIGHT

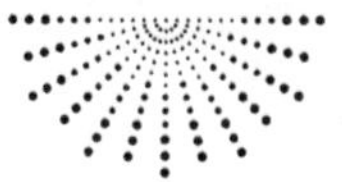

REG RAWLINS, PSYCHIC INVESTIGATOR #12

CHAPTER ONE

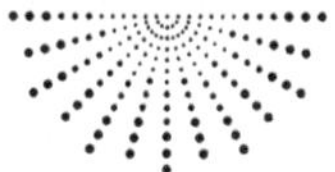

Reg looked with dismay at the broken eggshells and dried egg white and yolk that covered her door and doorstep. Who would egg her cottage? Teenagers? Someone who didn't like a psychic reading she had given them? Maybe it was a mistake, meant for one of her neighbors rather than her. It wasn't like she was involved in urban warfare with someone in the neighborhood; she couldn't imagine why she had been singled out for the honor.

Sarah returned from the big house with a bucket of soap and water and a scrub brush. She shook her head, lips pressed together grimly. "This is reprehensible," she said. "Vandalism. Who in Black Sands would do something like this?"

"I don't know. I can't understand it. Maybe it was a mistake," Reg floated the theory to see what Sarah thought of it.

Sarah scowled. "It was a mistake, all right. And you can bet that if I catch whoever did it, they're going to know how big a mistake it was."

"I meant… maybe it was meant for someone else. Not me."

"I don't know. I just know that it's here now, and it needs to be cleaned up."

"I'll do it." Reg tried to take the cleaning supplies from Sarah. "It's my door. You don't need to do that."

"It's your rental. It's my cottage. It's my responsibility as the property owner to keep it in good condition."

"Yes, but this isn't your fault."

"It isn't yours either." Sarah wet her scrub brush and started in on the door. Reg stood there, feeling helpless and guilty. She wished that Sarah would use magic to clean the egg off instead of manual labor. She didn't like the old woman having to do a job like that. Whatever Sarah said, Reg knew that the fault lay with her, and she should be the one to do the work to clean it up.

"Why don't you pick up the eggshells?" Sarah suggested.

"Okay. I can do that." Reg went back into the cottage to get a garbage bag. Starlight looked up from the patch of sunshine he was lounging in and made an inquiring sound.

"Someone threw eggs at the house," Reg told the tuxedo cat. "I can't believe it. I don't know why anyone would do that."

He cocked his head at an angle, looking puzzled. Reg tried to figure out how to explain it to him. Rather than using words, she opened her feelings to him. He sat up abruptly and looked toward the door. Reg nodded and sighed. She got the garbage bag and went back outside to help with the cleanup.

She painstakingly picked up all the eggshells she could find on the ground and doorstep. There was something on a large flat rock in the side garden, and she stopped to look at it.

"Sarah?"

Sarah put down her equipment and walked over to Reg, arching and rubbing her back. She looked down at the rock, where Reg had found several melted candles and markings, including a roughly painted figure that looked like a woman with a bird's body. Sarah picked up the candles one at a time and put them into Reg's garbage bag. She examined the markings and looked back at Reg.

"What does it mean?" Reg asked.

Sarah pointed to the bird woman. "It's a siren."

"A siren?" Reg puzzled over it. "But it's a bird. I thought that sirens were… more like mermaids."

"They are often represented in early art as birds." Sarah shrugged.

"Clearly, actual sirens cannot fly. It's metaphorical. Maybe because of their song. But they are not mermaids either. While they operate in the sea, they can't live and breathe underwater."

Reg stared down at the picture, trying to understand what it all meant. "So… does that mean that someone knows… about me? That my mother was part siren?" Reg couldn't bring herself to say that she herself was part siren or had siren instincts or powers. She was still trying to work that all out herself. But of course, that was what she meant.

Sarah nodded her agreement. "Someone knows about your heritage. And that is why you were targeted. These candles and that representation… and the other symbols… it is a spell of protection."

"Against me?"

"Against sirens. Yes. And the eggs… well, I guess their meaning is clear." Sarah shook her head. "Witches are peaceful. They live in harmony with nature and their communities." She looked back at Reg's door. "They don't engage in this kind of… hate."

But obviously, they had. They hadn't been satisfied with a spell to protect themselves from sirens; they had to take it further. They had to make a personal gesture against her too. To make sure Reg knew that they did not appreciate her presence in Black Sands.

"Should I… what should I do?"

Sarah raised her eyebrows in query.

"I mean… should I… is there something I can do? Should I just ignore it? Should I try to find out who did it and tell them to knock it off, or I'll turn them in to the cops or their coven? Should I… leave?"

"You can't leave," Sarah protested immediately. "No, that wouldn't be right. You can't let them force you out. Just ignore it; I'm sure that once people have vented their worry, it will die down. They'll see that nothing has changed, realize that you're not hunting here and not a danger to them."

Reg swallowed and nodded. She didn't like to think about how close she had come to doing harm due to her siren instincts being inadvertently triggered. The people in Black Sands were right to be worried. But she wasn't going to give in to those instincts. Corvin said that the more she resisted them, the easier it would become. And considering his own predatory nature, he probably had a pretty good idea what he was talking about.

CHAPTER TWO

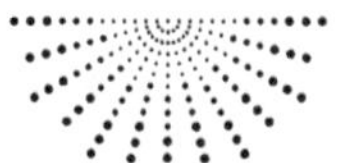

It took time to get everything cleaned up, and when Reg and Sarah finished and everything looked the way it should, Reg felt pride in their accomplishment. They had erased the mark against her name. She felt energized, as if the cleaning had been a catharsis. Getting rid of all the bad and starting fresh and clean. It felt good. Sarah too was smiling.

"There you go. All taken care of. That wasn't so bad after all, was it? Probably needed a good spring cleaning anyway."

Reg nodded. "Yeah. It feels… welcoming," she said, looking at the front door of her cottage.

"Yes, it does. Well, now we don't have to worry any more about that. How does your schedule look?"

Reg walked back into the cottage to look at her datebook on the kitchen island. Sarah probably had a better idea than she did how everything looked. She seemed to find more clients for Reg than she found for herself, and kept everything neatly organized.

She flipped through the next few days. "Pretty light. But that's okay. I could use a break. Things have been kind of crazy lately."

Sarah nodded. "Yes, things always seem to pick up around this time of year. May as well take your break while you can get it. And," she lowered her voice, even though there wasn't anyone else around to overhear them, "it isn't like you desperately need the money. You have what you need, even if you do go through a dry spell."

"It's not a dry spell. It's just… a break. I need it," Reg insisted.

"Okay. Yes, of course. Everyone needs time for rest and recovery."

Reg closed the book so that she wouldn't have to look at the mostly blank pages. Sarah was right. She was the only one who knew about the small chest of gems Reg had received from the fairies to compensate her for her services. It wouldn't do to tell other people about it and make herself a target. If she was the only one who knew about her wealth, she didn't have to worry about burglars breaking in to steal from her.

Even if she didn't have anyone else coming to her for readings or seances, she could live off of the gems.

"I'm just going to kick back and relax for a while," Reg told Sarah. She'd gotten up earlier than usual when Sarah had discovered the mess on the door. She would probably have a nap to catch up on the missed sleep. And to build up her strength after everything else that had happened recently.

"All right, dear. I'll see you later, then." Sarah bent down to pet Starlight, and then let herself out of the cottage.

* * *

Reg decided to go to The Crystal Bowl for supper. She didn't want the food Sarah had left in the fridge and she didn't want to order in. And she didn't cook much.

To be honest, she never cooked.

And she wasn't about to start. But The Crystal Bowl had been her go-to restaurant since that first day she had moved into Black Sands and had met Sarah there. Pleasant atmosphere, good food, plenty of other practitioners around who saw nothing strange about the psychic with her red hair in box braids and flamboyant fortune teller clothing. There were plenty of cloaks and capes and other odd fashions in evidence at The Crystal Bowl. Reg didn't stand out even with her eccentricities.

She sat down in a booth, not wanting to chat at the bar. She waved at Bill the barman and nodded to a few other people she knew casually.

Their reactions were a bit *off* from what they usually were. People looked puzzled by her wave instead of responding with a smile and wave of their own. They turned away from her and whispered together. Talking about Reg? She didn't like the feeling that everyone was watching her, waiting for her to do something.

A waiter approached Reg's table. He looked at her, then looked around for assistance from the other wait staff or his manager. No one stepped forward to help him or give him any instructions. It wasn't like he was new; he knew how to take an order. He frowned, then walked up to Reg's table.

"Uh… how are you today, Miss Rawlins?"

"Reg." She shrugged. "I'm fine. What's going on here? You look like you're waiting for a bomb to go off."

"Well…" He again looked around for help, and still no one else stepped forward to assist. "It's just that… we were wondering if you wouldn't be happier going somewhere else."

"Somewhere else?" Reg repeated blankly.

"Yes… maybe a different restaurant… or staying home tonight. Ordering in."

"No. I came here because this is where I want to eat." Reg looked at her hands, half expecting to see that she was changing color or into some other creature. What was wrong with Elliot? He'd never acted that way around her before. He was usually casual and pleasant, good-humored, exchanging jokes with her or telling her stories about everyone else's problems. "Why would I want to leave?"

"It's just… we don't serve your kind here."

"My kind? I've eaten here a hundred times before. What are you talking about? I'm a paying customer. You're not going to turn away paying customers!"

He looked increasingly uncomfortable. "That was before. When nobody knew about… you know."

"When nobody knew what?" Reg demanded. But, of course, she was already putting it together. The worried looks, the mention of "her kind." She'd been turned away from restaurants plenty of times in the past. Back then, "your kind" had meant a person they deemed homeless or unable to pay. But that wasn't the case in Black Sands.

"Miss Rawlins," he said in a low voice, ducking his head down and looking around as if he were afraid other people were going to hear her making a scene. She hadn't raised her voice. But she certainly could, if he were doing what she thought he was. "I'm sorry. It's nothing personal. The Crystal Bowl is for human practitioners of magic and the supernatural arts. We don't serve… other types here."

"You've always served me before and I've always paid my bill and never caused any trouble. So why is it a problem now? Nothing has changed. I'm still going to enjoy the meal and pay you afterward. If you're looking for a bigger tip…" She shrugged. "I'll do what I can. But I don't see why there should be any problem."

"I know… but it's policy. We can't have people in here… hunting. We can't take the chance of putting our other patrons at risk."

"That's crap. You let Corvin Hunter eat here, and you know he's a predator. You let Norma Jean eat here when she was in town, and her bloodline is more pure than mine. I've seen all kinds in here in the months that I've lived in Black Sands."

"I've been asked to pass the message on to you," Elliot said, raising his hands palms-out in a defensive gesture. "Don't shoot the messenger. I'm really sorry."

"You think I'm just going to start… attacking people? Really?"

"No." He looked down at his feet. "No, *I* know that…"

"You can go back and tell your manager that I'm not leaving. He or she can come out here and talk to my face. What are they doing sending a kid in here to try to get rid of me, anyway?"

Elliot looked relieved at this. He wasn't going to end up being Reg's next victim. "I'll go get you someone, Miss Rawlins."

He disappeared into the back hallway. Reg shook her head. He hadn't even served her a drink. If they were going to try to kick her out, couldn't they at least give her a drink first?

It was a few minutes before anyone came to see her. Obviously, they hadn't been hanging out in the back room just waiting for Elliot to fetch them.

Eventually, a woman came out. Reg had seen her around before, but didn't know her well. Mona, a petite, dark-haired woman with a crisp white shirt and little black tie. Usually, there was a man who was in charge. Similar in coloring to Mona, but tall and thin. Maybe her brother.

Did they send a woman out to take care of Reg because they were afraid she might attack a man? She hadn't attacked Elliot.

She hadn't ever attacked anyone in The Crystal Bowl. It was silly to think that she was going to start now.

Mona gave Reg a determined smile. "I'm sorry for the trouble, Miss Rawlins. But you must be able to see the position we are in. We are responsible for the safety of our patrons. And someone like you… who could possibly be a danger… well, we really can't risk it."

"I've never hurt anyone. I've eaten here a hundred times before. I've never caused you any trouble."

Though she did remember a series of glasses breaking. But that hadn't been her fault. It wasn't something she could control. She grimaced and thought it best not to mention that small point.

"I understand that," Mona agreed. "But then, we didn't know about your… nature. And now that it has been revealed, and you have been… hunting in Black Sands…" Mona shook her head. "You can see how it is, can't you?"

"I didn't *hunt* here," Reg indicated the interior of the restaurant. "And I've never hurt anyone. That's ridiculous. I'm not going to hurt anyone here. I'm obviously not here to hunt. Except maybe a fish burger!" Reg laughed, hoping that Mona would join in with an obliging chuckle.

But she didn't.

"Just take my order," Reg urged. "I'm not sitting close to anyone. I'm not having anyone over to join me. I'm just going to sit here by myself and enjoy a meal. I'm not trying to… lure anyone to their death."

Mona shook her head and cleared her throat. "The liability is too high. If something happened to someone here… if it became known that we knowingly let a predatory creature into the restaurant… insurance doesn't cover that kind of risk."

Creature insurance? Was there any kind of rider a person could buy for that? It seemed like they could protect themselves from any kind of risk lately. Though there had been Vivian. She hadn't been able to get any kind of insurance after all the accidents that had happened to her. She had been too high a risk.

"How about a drink and you get me something to go?" Reg suggested, trying to come up with a compromise. She didn't want to go home empty-handed. She didn't want to leave and try to find another restaurant that would accept her patronage. She was hungry and just wanted a meal. Like every other time she had come to The Crystal Bowl.

Mona paused, apparently considering the merits of this suggestion. It would get Reg out of her restaurant. But she would still be getting Reg's trade.

But evidently, Mona decided after due consideration that even just a drink was too big of a risk. She shook her head again. "I'm sorry, but you really are going to have to go."

"I'd like to talk to the owner," Reg blustered, hoping that Mona wasn't the owner of the restaurant and there was still another level to appeal to.

Mona shook her head. "The buck stops here, I'm afraid. Don't make me call the police to have you removed."

"Oh, come on! What are you going to tell the police? That you think I'm a predator who is going to eat your other customers?"

The police in Black Sands were of the non-magical sort. There were a few around, like Detective Marta Jessup, who knew about magic or came from magical families, or even had some minor powers themselves. But those who were "in" on the secrets of Black Sands did not bring it up. If Mona called in the police, she would have to come up with some much more mundane excuse for not wanting Reg there.

"I will tell them that you were making a disruption. Or that you've passed bad checks or counterfeit cash here before. There are lots of reasons I can give."

"But it's a lie. You don't have any evidence that I did any of those things."

"They don't ask for proof. There isn't any big investigation into why I want someone removed from the restaurant. They'll just take me at my word."

That didn't seem particularly fair. But Reg had been kicked out of enough shops and restaurants in the past to know that the police wouldn't be on her side. They would just escort her out. And if she gave them any trouble, they would arrest her and throw her in the tank for the night.

"You won't even give me a drink?" Reg wheedled again. "Does it look like I'm here hunting?"

She remembered when she and Corvin had seen a siren and a mermaid hunting down at the marina. It had been obvious what they had been up to. They had been ensorcelling a sailor. It had been clear. The same as when Norma Jean had been trying to lure Corvin. She got close to him, touched him, smiled, and flirted with him until he was utterly lost, with no way for him to return. Luckily, Norma Jean had not been able to close the deal or something had interrupted her from her plans. Corvin said the bloodlines were weak; a young or inexperienced siren might not have the instincts to take her prey down to the water or otherwise dispose of him. Like an animal raised in captivity that didn't know how to kill. Or if it could kill, didn't know what to do with its prey.

Mona looked pointedly at her watch. "I think we've wasted enough time on this. If you aren't out of here in five minutes, I will be calling the police. We are not serving you, even one drink, so please leave."

Reg stood up abruptly, her anger flaring. There were a couple of pops and the sound of falling glass as a couple of glasses exploded in the bar area. Mona stepped quickly back from Reg, her face pale. She pulled her phone out of her pocket and held it up for Reg to see. One last warning that she would call the cops.

And Reg didn't want any involvement with the police. Nothing that would raise her profile in their eyes or make them want to run background on her. There was too much to be found about what had happened in the past. She had no desire to go back to Tennessee or Maine or any of the other states where she had operated under various names.

She liked Florida, and Black Sands in particular.

Reg sighed in exasperation. "I'm not doing anything to hurt you," she snapped, irritated at Mona acting like she was a violent criminal. She couldn't do anything about the exploding glasses.

Reg headed to the door, struggling to control her breathing to convince herself that there was nothing to be angry about. So they didn't want her there at The Crystal Bowl. There were plenty of other restaurants that would accept her patronage.

As she reached the double front doors of The Crystal Bowl, she felt an unexpected rush of warmth and a magnetic pull toward them.

Reg knew what that meant.

* * *

Without Foresight, Book #12 of the *Reg Rawlins, Psychic Investigator* series by P.D. Workman can be purchased at pdworkman.com

* * *

ABOUT THE AUTHOR

P.D. Workman is a USA Today Bestselling author and multi-award winner, renowned for her prolific output of over 100 published works that span various genres. With a knack for crafting page-turners, Workman captivates readers with everything from cozy mysteries like the Auntie Clem's Bakery series to gripping young adult and suspense novels.

A prolific reader and writer since childhood, P.D. Workman crafts emotionally powerful stories that don't shy away from hard topics. Her books tackle mental illness, addiction, abuse, and trauma with raw honesty and compassion, giving voice to the often unheard. If you crave authentic, character-driven page-turners that hit deep and stay with you long after the final page, you're in the right place.

With each new release, fans eagerly anticipate another thrilling blend of thought-provoking storytelling and relatable characters that define P.D. Workman's brand as an author of unforgettable page-turners—gripping tales that leave a lasting impact long after the last page is turned.

> P. D. Workman, does not shy from probing the deep psychological scars of childhood trauma, mental illness, and addiction. Also characteristic of this author, these extremely sensitive issues are explored with extensive empathy, described with incredible clarity, and portrayed with profound insight.
>
> — —KIM, GOODREADS REVIEWER

Some of Workman's titles have been translated into Spanish, French, Portuguese, German, and Italian.

Workman began writing at an early age and is a prolific reader as well as writer. She is also passionate about teaching and learning, expresses her creativity through art and cooking, and loves exploring the Calgary parks and green spaces where the Parks Pat Mysteries are set. She was a legal assistant for many years and has done extensive charitable work.

Workman was born and raised in Alberta, Canada, and is married with one adult son.

Please visit P.D. Workman at pdworkman.com to see what else she is working on, to join her mailing list, and to link to her social networks.

If you enjoyed this book, please take the time to recommend it to other purchasers with a review or star rating and share it with your friends!

tiktok.com/@pdworkmanauthor
facebook.com/pdworkmanauthor
x.com/pdworkmanauthor
instagram.com/pdworkmanauthor
amazon.com/author/pdworkman
bookbub.com/authors/p-d-workman
goodreads.com/pdworkman
linkedin.com/in/pdworkman
pinterest.com/pdworkmanauthor
youtube.com/pdworkman

Find P.D. Workman's books at

PDWORKMAN.COM

Scan the QR code below

www.ingramcontent.com/pod-product-compliance
Lightning Source LLC
Chambersburg PA
CBHW070632310726
48982CB00001B/267

9781774680971